PRAISE FOR EMILY R. KING'S

THE HUNDREDTH QUEEN SERIES

THE HUNDREDTH QUEEN

*Winner of the 2017 Whitney and UTOPiA Awards
for Best Novel by a Debut Author*

"King's debut is built on a solid premise that draws on Sumerian mythology for inspiration . . . The tale maintains a consistent thread as King embarks on a deep examination of sisterhood, first between Kali and her best friend Jaya, and later when she must fight the rajah's other wives to keep her place within the palace."

—*Publishers Weekly*

"*The Hundredth Queen* plunges readers into a fantasy world full of love, betrayal, rebellion, and magic."

—*Deseret News*

"King writes multiple strong female characters, led by Kalinda, who has the loyalty and bravery of spirit to defend her friends even if that means facing death. Strong characterization, deep worldbuilding, page-turning action scenes and intrigue, as well as social commentary, make this book stand out. Readers will be eager to get their hands on the next installment."

—*Kirkus Reviews*

"This lush and lovely first novel brings a beautiful and brutal culture to life. The ending is left open for sequels, and readers will eagerly follow Kalinda and Deven on their future adventures."

—*Booklist*

"Filled with many action-packed sequences, forbidden romance, and unexpected surprises, this debut fantasy will appeal to teens who enjoy epic dramas with strong female characters."

—*School Library Journal*

"*The Hundredth Queen* is a culturally rich tale of both self-discovery and self-mastery. Emily R. King transports readers to a lush and fascinating world where our heroine, Kalinda, pitted against hardened and clever antagonists, embraces her weaknesses and follows her heart. King leaves you wondering, 'What happens next?'"

—Charlie N. Holmberg, *Wall Street Journal* bestselling author of
The Paper Magician Series

THE FIRE QUEEN

"King treats the readers to stunning descriptions of Kalinda and her sister warriors' characters, even giving villains redeeming traits and hints of sympathy. A descriptive action-packed fantasy in a vivid world . . ."

—*Kirkus Reviews*

"The most poignant and important parts of this novel are the relationships that blossom and grow. If you're a fan of *The Hundredth Queen*, rest assured that *The Fire Queen* is definitely its equal. It's just as fascinating, heartbreaking, and exciting . . ."

—Hypable

"A great follow-up to the series. King writes with such a vivid detail that the imagery of *The Fire Queen* is stunningly real. The world she created is both extremely dangerous and invitingly beautiful. You will be drawn into this world of fantasy with ease and it holds your attention till the very end."

—*Fresh Fiction*

THE ROGUE QUEEN

"King delivers a fiery fantasy-adventure in her fast-paced third installment to The Hundredth Queen Series. *The Rogue Queen* moves the series' main action from a tournament to a large-scale war, injecting a feeling of freshness and vitality to The Hundredth Queen books . . . Kalinda's crusade to save and unite her empire, regardless of the cost, will leave readers on the edge of their seats."

—*Booklist*

"*The Rogue Queen* exposes new angles on established ideas and stories that make it a really enjoyable novel. It has the perfect amount of action and strategic planning, as well as a healthy dose of female empowerment. Fans of the series certainly won't be disappointed with this new installment and, by the end of it, will be cheering 'Bring on *The Warrior Queen!*'"

—Hypable

"This book is all high-stakes action and magic. The characters come alive even more . . ."

—*Night Owl Reviews* (Top Pick)

BEFORE
THE
BROKEN
STAR

ALSO BY EMILY R. KING

The Evermore Chronicles

Before the Broken Star
Into the Hourglass (forthcoming)
Everafter Song (forthcoming)

The Hundredth Queen Series

The Hundredth Queen
The Fire Queen
The Rogue Queen
The Warrior Queen

BEFORE
THE
BROKEN
STAR

THE EVERMORE CHRONICLES

BOOK ONE

EMILY R. KING

SKYSCAPE

SKYSCAPE

Text copyright © 2019 by Emily R. King
All rights reserved.

No part of this book may be reproduced, or stored in a retrieval system, or transmitted in any form or by any means, electronic, mechanical, photocopying, recording, or otherwise, without express written permission of the publisher.

Published by Skyscape, New York

www.apub.com

Amazon, the Amazon logo, and Skyscape are trademarks of Amazon.com, Inc., or its affiliates.

ISBN-13: 9781542043786 (hardcover)
ISBN-10: 1542043786 (hardcover)
ISBN-13: 9781542043762 (paperback)
ISBN-10: 154204376X (paperback)

Cover design by Kirk DouPonce, DogEared Design

Printed in the United States of America

First edition

For Jason Kirk.
Onward!

Dead men don't bite.

—Robert Louis Stevenson, *Treasure Island*

Prologue

In the beginning, there was no time, and no man or beast walked the world. Where the ocean met the land, an ivory mare was born, her mane crafted from sea-foam and her body from barnacles. She was the Creator, goddess of all conception and supreme ruler of seven worlds.

The Creator planted the seed of life in her most precious world, and a mighty elderwood tree grew to hold up the sky and nourish life. The elderwood bore creatures of all kinds—including giants from her bark, elves from her leaves, and mankind from her acorns. This elite triad of brothers and sisters dwelled in harmony, but the Creator knew peace was temporary. Avarice, wrath, and pride would set her children against each other, so she appointed a lesser god as guardian over them and commanded that he give every living thing a time to be born and a time to die.

But this story isn't about death.

Not yet.

Chapter One

A cacophony of ticktocking resounds through the otherwise hushed clockmaker's shop. When I first came to live with Uncle Holden, the relentless ticking drove me mad. A decade later, the chant of time is now a comfort—his handcrafted timepieces echo the cadence of my wooden clockwork heart.

The bell on the front door jingles, and I look up from my book to see a blond gentleman step in from the foggy street. The man is a naval officer—a lieutenant, judging by his gray wool uniform and somber expression. He must be a noble. He's too young to have worked his way up through the ranks, and only noblemen may enlist in the queen's navy as officers.

The lieutenant admires the assortment of fine clocks, his eyes a startling blue. His high forehead is offset by a full mouth and a stern, square jaw. He fixates on the one clock in the shop decorated with delicate hand-painted daisies. Though his shoulders remain unerringly straight, he walks with a slight limp to the daisy clock and runs an admiring finger over the top.

My lips tense. "May I help you?"

The lieutenant's gaze shifts to me at the clerk's desk. "Good afternoon, miss. I'm here to pick up an order."

"Name?" I set aside the map I was studying and open the customer log.

"I'm Jamison Callahan, but the order is under Markham."

My fingers rattle against the paper. Before I allow my mind to spin away with unfounded conclusions, I remind myself that Markham is a common enough surname in the Realm of Wyeth. The lieutenant could be on an errand for someone else.

Another jingle as the front door opens and a second customer enters.

"Lieutenant Callahan," says the man, embracing the young sailor, "I didn't expect to meet you here. I thought the captain would be meeting me."

My neck hairs bristle as I glance from the corner of my eye at the older naval officer, middle-aged with a service sword sheathed at his waist. I could never forget that voice; its gut-shaking deepness is scored into my memory.

A ticking booms in my ears. My clockwork heart, a device like a pocket watch that functions in place of my real heart, trips into a sprint.

"The captain is overseeing the arrival of the first prisoners," the lieutenant explains. "He asked that you forgive his absence, sir."

"All is forgiven," says Governor Killian Markham. "I'm glad you're in my service again, Callahan. You'll be a tremendous addition to the first fleet. What changed your mind about going?"

Callahan's countenance turns rigid. "My father and I had a disagreement in which he disavowed me of my inheritance. He was within his bounds."

The governor pats the lieutenant's back. "My apologies for prying. You're an understanding son. In time, I'm certain you and your father will mend this."

Hidden under my clothes, the regulator for my clock heart chimes a warning to calm down. I cannot. Not as Lieutenant Callahan and Governor Markham continue their conversation. Not as the lieutenant turns his curious gaze to the ringing coming from my location. Not as the governor's gaze narrows on me. I clutch the neckline of my dress closed over my scar. *The monster has found me.*

Uncle Holden's footfalls echo at my back and then he rests a heavy hand on my shoulder. "Everley, I'll assist Governor Markham. You may go."

I usually attend to the storefront while my uncle tinkers in his workshop, unconcerned by our customers, but Markham is not a typical patron.

The governor crosses to the desk, a flintlock pistol as well as his rapier at his waist. His boots have been shined to a polish, by a servant no doubt, and his dress coat fits his trim chest and waist impeccably, his silk neckerchief matching his wolfish gray eyes. The noisy clocks in the shop drum louder. I wait for him to recognize me, to picture me as the raven-haired seven-year-old girl I was when we met a decade ago. Uncle Holden squeezes my shoulder, a command to flee. But Markham does not recognize me. Why would he? He thinks I'm dead.

I want to scream—*I am Everley Donovan, daughter of Brogan Donovan!* But terror arrests me, as real and raw as the night Markham came to my family's seaside manor under the guise of friendship. He was an admiral then, my father's expedition partner. By some fateful trick, he looks the same. From his trimmed beard to his chestnut hair tied at the nape of his neck to the overconfident tilt of his lips. I recall his smile as he held a sword to my mother's throat. He later battled my father with that same sword, its blade slick with my mother's blood.

I duck into the workshop out of view and press my back to the wall. The striking clocks of the showroom pursue me. I cannot break free from the clawing hours or the bleeding seconds. My heart regulator rings again, a backup alarm for the ticker. I cover the sound emitter, muting the warning blare, and peer around the doorway.

"Holden O'Shea," Governor Markham says, shaking my uncle's hand. "I've been told you make the finest clocks in all of Wyeth. Have you finished our order?"

"I have, sir." Onto the counter my uncle sets the marine chronometer, which uses longitude to guide ships by means of celestial navigation. The cords of my trust fray. My uncle did not mention who would receive his latest model of the portable time standard. According to him, Markham didn't associate with the O'Sheas. My father, the Baron McTigue, married my uncle's sister, a woman of lower standing.

"How does it function?" Markham asks.

I miss my uncle's reply because the governor's voice evokes a memory of Markham ordering his men to force my siblings and me at gunpoint out of the room, separating us from our mother and father.

Pain unfolds across my chest. I lean in from the doorway and press a clammy palm over my clockwork heart. I should rest. My ticker could seize if I push it too hard, but Markham has been gone from Wyeth for years. I cannot let this opportunity pass.

The governor counts out a fat stack of bills. "Here's your payment, Mr. O'Shea. Pardon my leave, I've other matters in need of my attention. I'll entrust the remainder of our business to Lieutenant Callahan. The queen thanks you for your service."

He picks up the chronometer to go. My sword is stashed beneath the desk, but Uncle Holden won't let me grab it in time. My gaze falls to the tools scattered across the workbench.

The bell on the entry door rings.

I swipe a chisel off the bench and round the corner into the storefront. Through the street window, I spot Governor Markham climbing into a horse-drawn carriage. Each strike of my heart punches through me—*no, no, no*—as the governor's buggy hastens away.

Chase him, my fury urges.

But he's already out of sight, and I won't be able to distinguish his black carriage from the countless others on the streets of Dorestand in time. I glance at my sword beneath the desk, which is worthless now, and shuffle backward, stepping in time with my ticker. *Gone, gone, gone.*

Callahan glances at the chisel in my fist. I glare into his wide eyes, pouring the full breadth of my anger on him. The lieutenant serves in the governor's fleet. No man under Markham's supervision deserves respect.

"Everley," Uncle Holden says quietly. His round eyes, the same cornflower blue as my mother's and mine, relay an apology.

Shoulders sinking, I set down the chisel. I lost Markham. The monster who murdered my family and stabbed me in the chest as a girl has gotten away.

Uncle Holden picks up the chisel and slips it into his pocket. He's worried I will demolish his shop in a fit of temper. He thinks I am reckless, unpredictable.

I have never been more focused.

Markham has returned to Dorestand—the man himself, not some ghoulish nightmare harassing my dreams—and I froze like a winter lake.

He left without even knowing my name.

My heart ticktocks louder than any clock in the shop, a shout in a symphony of murmurs. I should lie down, but I want to learn everything I can about Markham's return.

Callahan clears his throat and speaks to my uncle, casting wary glances in my direction. "The governor asked that I take the second marine chronometer to the captain of the *Lady Regina*. We're bound for Dagger Island with precious cargo."

Gooseflesh scuttles up my spine. Over a decade ago, Queen Aislinn commissioned my father and Markham to settle more land and expand her rule, which is, according to our ruler, the destiny of the Realm of Wyeth. As such, we are at the forefront of exploration and ahead of the other three realms in transportation. Our naval fleet is the greatest in the world. The second closest realm has but nineteen ships, and we have seventy.

With our fleet, the queen set out to claim uncharted lands. My father, a great explorer, rediscovered Dagger Island. He was the first person in centuries to set foot on the mystic isle known as the Kingdom of Amadara.

Every child has heard the tales of the Ruined Kingdom and the tragic separation of Princess Amadara and her lost prince. Legends of this bygone world discouraged many from claiming or charting the isle. After my father completed his exploration, he recommended that the queen not settle the wild, remote island. Queen Aislinn listened until recent years, when her need for land increased. Concerned about the danger of prison riots in her overcrowded jails, she commissioned a fleet of ships laden with male convicts and soldiers to sail to Dagger Island and leave the men to settle there, and then she promoted Markham to govern the outpost.

Uncle Holden lifts a second marine chronometer onto the desk. "Can you say what the precious cargo is, Lieutenant?"

"Female convicts." Callahan's gaze flattens to an unreadable wall, hiding his opinion on the matter. "Queen Aislinn is sentencing them to serve as wives of the settlers at the penal colony."

I dream of sailing and exploring like my father, but the isle is no place for people. Thousands of leagues away from Dagger Island here in Dorestand, we have heard the accounts of the settlers' starvation and sickness and, odder, rumblings of men disappearing in the island's dense forest. It is said the Ruined Kingdom, at the center of the isle, is protected by a curse. But the queen doesn't believe in sorcery.

"You're assigned to the outpost?" Uncle Holden asks. "I've been told the survival rate is one in four."

"My orders are to oversee the female convicts on their voyage," Callahan replies, shifting his weight from one leg to the other. "We embark day after tomorrow."

"And the governor?" I ask, ignoring my uncle's silencing look.

The lieutenant's attention sharpens on me. "Markham's ship departs at dawn."

Bloody bones. The governor has been stationed overseas on Dagger Island for years. Come morning, he will be out of my reach again.

"Governor Markham paid for both chronometers in full." Uncle Holden dusts his hands off on his breeches. "Will that be all, Lieutenant?"

"Actually, no." Callahan points behind him, his wavy hair brassy like the inner workings of a timepiece. "How much for that clock?"

"Which one?" Uncle Holden follows him between the shelves.

"This one here," says the lieutenant, touching the daisy clock.

That is my favorite timepiece, a twin to one my uncle gave my parents on their wedding day. The original burned to ash long ago. I generally keep the clock out of view from customers, but this morning when I dusted, I moved it to the front of the shelf and forgot to push it back.

"It isn't for sale," I say.

Both men swivel toward me. My uncle's graying mustache twitches over stern lips. A lady customer enters from the street, saving me from explaining.

Uncle Holden lifts the twin clock off the shelf and passes it to the lieutenant. "My apprentice is mistaken. She'll ring you up." He leaves Callahan in my care and greets the lady.

The lieutenant carries the daisy clock over and sets it on the desk. "I've been looking for a keepsake to bring on my voyage. The flowers remind me of the daisies outside the front gate of my family's estate."

I cannot begrudge him for wanting the clock as a reminder of home since I want it for similar reasons. My mother would read to us by our drawing-room hearth, with my sister, brothers, and I crowded around her skirt, and my father in his chair. The clock rested above us on the mantelpiece, a sentinel watching over us all, while mother told tales about fantastical creatures and worlds beyond our own.

"You seem fond of this clock," the lieutenant remarks, studying me.

The lieutenant is too perceptive, too conversational. My ticker is still struggling to recover from Markham's visit. It beats like a normal heart, though it looks and sounds like a clock. The inner workings—balance wheel, torsion spring, escapement, and gear train—are strained by emotional exertion more often than physical labor.

"I'm fine," I say. "It's just a clock."

My ticker stutters, triggering my regulator.

Ring!

Callahan's gaze drops to my waistline, where the small regulator for my ticker is hidden beneath my dress. "Do you have a bell in your pocket?"

"What an absurd question."

My regulator is a nuisance. The tiny noise box connected to my heart detects spikes in my pulse and rings three bells inside of it when I should rest. The outbursts are not unlike a tolling cuckoo clock, minus the wooden figures popping out. The alarm sounds when I'm nervous, overworked, or poorly telling a lie.

The lieutenant reads the price tag on the daisy clock and lays down his money. "Paid in full . . . Everley, isn't it? Have we met?"

"No." If I were lying, my ticker would tell me.

Callahan squints at me in doubt. I don't know why he thinks we are acquainted. He's a nobleman and I'm a shop clerk. Except at night when my uncle is fast asleep; then I become someone else. But the lieutenant would not know about my nocturnal escapades. Few do.

My fingertips tingle, a consequence of my offbeat pulse. I fumble to package the daisy clock with paper as my heart ticktocks erratically. While working faster, I drop the spool of twine.

"Let me help you," Callahan says, retrieving it from the floor.

"I can do it." I take the twine back and pain stabs my torso. I double over the desk. The gears of my ticker clunk and grind, the balance wheel swinging erratically.

The lieutenant's morning-sky eyes cloud with worry. "Are you all right?"

I wave him off.

Uncle Holden excuses himself from the lady customer and strides toward me. "Everley, go to the workbench and find my caliper."

He has fabricated an excuse to send me away.

I hold down my hitching chest and start to go. Two steps from the desk, my heart clunks to a halt as the balance wheel quits turning.

RIIIIIING . . .

My regulator emits a continuous, high-pitched warning. I stumble forward, agony punching out to my limbs. Big hands catch me, and Uncle Holden lifts me into his arms, sturdy from hauling stacks of lumber. Darkness edges into my vision and dims his troubled face.

"Sir?" Callahan asks. "How can I help?"

"You can show yourself out." Uncle Holden nods at the door where the lady customer has left, then carries me into his workshop and kicks the door shut.

Chapter Two

I cling to my uncle's sawdust-covered apron. Deadness spreads out from my chest, my grip fading and my muscles slackening.

Uncle Holden sweeps his cluttered worktable clean and lays me down. His shaky hands unbutton the top of my dress, revealing the scar above my shift. His most prized timepiece and invention has gone silent.

"Hold on, Everley." His tools ting as he searches for the right one.

RIIIIING!

The regulator's strident call strengthens. Gray eclipses my vision, and my breaths grow harder to draw, as though I am inhaling through a shrinking pipe.

Uncle Holden bends over me with his calibrator, his old face creased with twice as many lines. He detaches my regulator and the alarm stops. An unmarked beat of time resonates between us—and then he starts to crank.

I clamp my teeth down on a shriek as grinding gears rip through my chest. Each turn of my uncle's calibrator wrenches me in half, like hooks prying apart my rib cage. Black stars dive at me. Unconsciousness lies only a crank away, but pain straps me to the table. I would sob, I would beg, but I have no strength to instruct my tongue, no breath to push past my lips.

Uncle Holden winds the mechanism. Rewinding and recalibrating. Cranking, cranking, cranking . . . I wait for the rhythm of life. Tick of time. March of forever. I fear Father Time has come to take back the years I stole.

Let me stay. Spare me to live another day.

The nothingness opens its jaws—

Tick . . .

. . . tock.

My clock heart reanimates and I gasp on life's breath. Blood soars out from my chest, rushing to the far reaches of my extremities. Tiny stars fleck my vision, their brightness and glory swelling with the same steady crawl as the rising sun.

But dawn is frigid. Cold burrows into my bones, as though my insides are crystallizing with hoarfrost. Uncle Holden appears in my widening vision.

"Everley, can you hear me?"

I nod, my teeth chattering.

"I recalibrated the escapement and reset the torsion spring. I'll fetch a quilt."

He goes, and air skims across my breastbone where the top of my dress hangs open. Having my ticker exposed is unbearable. Though I am more decent than most ladies of fashion in their fancy low-cut gowns, I try to cover myself. My arms are heavier than blocks of ice. They stay at my sides as drowsiness plays with my focus. The last time I felt this cold . . .

I fight the pull to return there, but it is too strong.

Tavis struck the man blocking the bedroom doorway and urged me to run. I raced to the drawing room. Mother lay crumpled on the carpet in her birthday gown. Her eyes, open and blank, gazed into oblivion. Blood was pooling around her.

Gunshots blasted in the nearby bedchamber. One, two, three—Isleen, Carlin, Tavis. One boom for each of my siblings.

A masked soldier held Father at gunpoint. He shouted for me to run. I was his good girl, so I did what he said.

Markham was as quick as a snare; his iron arms locked around me. I thrashed to break free, kicking over the music stand. The sheet music Carlin had given Mother spilled to the floor. I bit Markham's hand.

He released me, yowling like an animal. I scurried away. Father lunged at Markham, and they grappled with the hilt of his sword. The masked soldier fired. Father's eyes stretched wide and he slumped to the floor beside Mother, drowning in her sea of scarlet.

Markham pulled a burning log from the fire and tossed it onto Mother's reading chair. A flash of sparks blinded me, and then flames snapped and snarled. The scorching bite of the fire spread to the daisy clock over the mantel and chewed up our home.

Markham lifted his sword between us.

Though I shut my eyes to retreat, the cold locks me in the past. Nothing can stall fate. Time advances at the same reliable beat, yet it can pass in intervals of horrifying slowness and dizzying fastness that will not pause for anyone. Eternity trapped in a second.

The governor's sword ripped through me. Skin, sinew— ribs. I hardly made a sound as he yanked out his blade, swift and clean.

The world collapsed around me. All I felt, all I thought of, was the bitter winter of pain.

I hang on an icy wire, suspended between the past and present. My sluggish body shivers, neither here nor there. Some days I long to fall, to drop into that gap in time and never return.

Uncle Holden piles our only two quilts on top of me. "You were lucky."

He asserted the same when I woke days after Markham stabbed me. He said I was lucky he was able to revive me. He then explained that he set a rare timepiece in my chest, and the clockwork heart had brought me back from death's door.

Luck did not save me. Uncle Holden's miraculous invention did, and he said it was Father Time's will that I live. How this clock heart revived me does not plague me as much as the question *why*. Why did Father Time spare me and not my family?

My clock heart is not without flaws. After its installation, Uncle Holden and I did not trust its limits. Every day I waited for time to stop, but like a dutiful clock, my ticker plodded on. Eventually we quit expecting it to malfunction and my uncle allowed me to apprentice him. Almost a year later, I asked him to stop tutoring me at home and let me attend school. Living day after day as a shut-in was wilting my spirit. I longed to play with other children and make friends, to twirl in the sunshine and run through the schoolyard. My appetite waned, and I lost interest in my studies. I was arguing with my uncle about whether I was well enough to attend school when my heart gave out. He recalibrated my ticker before the cold consumed me, but I shivered for days and sustained nerve damage to my hands. On freezing nights, my fingers still tingle. Uncle Holden shut himself in his workshop and reemerged with the regulator—a tiny wooden box that connects to my heart by copper filaments. The regulator rings the bells inside when the clock is overburdened. I have worn the device strapped around my waist ever since.

Quiet stretches, broken by my fervent pulse. I loathe that tick even as I rely on it for my next breath.

"I'm sorry, Everley." Uncle Holden stoops, his concerns weighing heavy. "Markham wasn't supposed to come to the store. I intended to deliver the chronometers to him."

His serving that monster at all galls me. Everyone believes my family perished in a house fire and that I died with them. Uncle Holden was riding to our estate on the northern seashore for my mother's birthday when Markham set the blaze. He dragged me from the flames, installed this miraculous clockwork heart, and hid me. He told his neighbors he had adopted a street urchin as his apprentice, and we have been unsociable with everyone since.

"My cartography lessons," I say, my voice shuddering from the inner cold. "I can still go."

My uncle tucks the blanket around me. "I'll ask your tutor to postpone, just for a month or so."

I clench down to quiet my chattering teeth. I waited a year for my uncle to concede that cartography lessons aren't a waste of time. The queen won't commission a female explorer, so I cannot sail for the realm like my father did, but I still want to learn. It was another year before my uncle found a tutor who would teach a girl, and another two months before we saved enough notes to pay for the lessons. Uncle Holden will use this recalibration as an excuse to keep me near, but he cannot hold me here forever. Roving is in my blood. As a child, I begged my father to take me with him on an expedition. I crawled into his lap and cried against his shoulder. He stroked my hair, and calling me by my nickname, Evie, he said that great wonders and adventures were coming and the stars would wait for me to grow into my fate.

I huddle into the blanket and battle another wave of shivers. A better moment waits for me on the horizon. Then another and another, until someday the moment will be mine.

Chapter Three

I spend the afternoon warming myself by the kitchen hearth. A spring rainstorm knocks at our door, cold winds rattling the hinges.

After I regain sensation in my fingers, I pick up my carving knife. My latest figurine is nearly finished. Uncle Holden prepares dinner while I complete the fluke of the whale and set it in the windowsill with the other figurines—a pixie, a sea hag, and a sleeping giant. These were tests of my skill, characters my uncle picked from common stories that would require all my tools. I still have much to learn about carving before he teaches me to build gearwork.

My uncle side-eyes my completed pieces. I wait for the master carver to remark on their simplicity, but he says nothing.

The potato-and-carrot soup finishes boiling. He utters a prayer to Mother Madrona, and we dine in silence. I sip down the hot soup one spoonful at a time. The liquid warmth unfurls from my center and flushes my face.

Uncle Holden clears his dish and brews tea, adding splashes of whisky. He hums an old sea chantey my father used to sing. I know the words by heart.

> Sea, land, stars. Great Creator, your home is ours.
> Animals, plants, trees. Madrona, we rest upon our
> knees.

Gathered beneath thy leaves. Brothers and sisters three.

My uncle sets a steaming cup of whisky tea before me. I draw my shawl closer and dust wood shavings off my skirt. In evenings past, he regaled me with stories of warrior giants sleeping in the northern hills and brave gnomes stealing precious treasure from a sorceress. Tales that enthralled me as a lass no longer do. Though I once wished they were true, sorcery and creatures from the Otherworlds only exist in storybooks.

My uncle sighs, the song of a weary man, and plods upstairs to his loft. I sip my tea, deepening the warmth in my belly until the creak of his thin mattress sneaks down the stairs. Then I tiptoe to the back door, open it a crack, and call into the alleyway.

"Tom?"

A mew answers, then a blur of fur shoots past my legs. I set my bowl on the floor before my friend. Tom, a black cat with a white spot on his chest, licks it clean as I wash the dinner dishes and mend my uncle's breeches. When I was a child, a cook prepared our meals, servers cleaned our dishes, and a maid mended our clothes. I was too young to appreciate those luxuries.

Tom rubs against me, purring. The alley cat is one of the few neighbors I socialize with. My uncle and I keep everyone else at a distance to discourage questions, a precaution that is as necessary as it is lonely. I pet the stray's back and he purrs louder. He often sleeps in my room, curled at the bottom of my bed.

"Not tonight," I say.

I scoop him up, set the cat outside, and take the lantern to my bedroom. A narrow path runs between a bed against the wall and a wardrobe. Covering the wall over my bed is a patchwork map of Dorestand. I drew it over a year's time by scouting and navigating the city myself, then charting the network of streets by memory. My memory wasn't always consistent, but my sense of direction was. Even as a child, I could find my way, and I rarely got lost. My father had the same gift.

My all-black clothes hang in my open wardrobe. I exchange my work dress for a man's tunic, breeches, and waistcoat. I try not to glimpse my reflection in the mirror by the door, but my scar—a slash below my collarbone—is impossible to overlook. I have another on my back where the sword exited.

And there, on my left side, buried between two ribs, beats my clock heart.

The pocket watch has a round glass face and a ticking brass meter, the remainder of the device hidden in the cavity of my chest. Uncle Holden insists Father Time instructed him to build it. I don't doubt my uncle was inspired or that Father Time must exist, because time does. Even so, I don't understand how this clock has assumed the function of my heart. All I understand is that my uncle's invention, in conjunction with Father Time's grace, sustains me.

I tuck my regulator in the nook of my spine and button up my waistcoat. My long hair is easy to pull back, twist in a knot, and cover with a tricorn hat. I rub my hands together until the tingling in my fingers abates and then tug on my mother's red wool gloves. My uncle purchased them for her last birthday, the day she died. They have fit me since I was fourteen.

After tying on my cloak and boots, I pause to listen. No movement or sound comes from above. I turn down the lantern and slip out of my room. Shadows have taken up residence in the kitchen, cherry embers burning in the hearth. I follow the tang of axle grease into the workshop and sift through drifts of sawdust to the storefront. The shop has been in the O'Shea family for three generations. My grandfather and great-grandfather were clockmakers. My uncle, Mother's only sibling, has done well to preserve their family legacy. Someday he will pass this place on to me. Shopkeeper is a respectable livelihood for a woman, particularly one like me who doesn't intend to marry, but I cannot picture this place without Uncle Holden.

Kneeling by the clerk's desk, I pull out my sheathed sword. A relic from my father's final expedition, this sword is the only possession that survived our house fire. At the time, Uncle Holden was replating it here at the shop.

I lift the lightweight steel. The gold grip, guard, and pommel are tinged green from neglect. A shop clerk in possession of a sword of this finery would draw too much attention, so I have not shined it. I strap the blade to my hip and enter the sea of beating timepieces. The shelf where the daisy clock sat is bare. My uncle insisted we set the mantel clock among the merchandise because we could not refuse the profit from the sale, and he promised me he would craft me another if it sold. I already miss its cheerfulness.

Ever so carefully, I remove the entry bell and open the front door. A stormy gust coils in and furls my cloak. The lampposts glow, casting streaks across the gloomy, wet streets. Rain dampens the stench of people and horses left over from the day. Far down the road, on the wharf over the River Tyne, sailors and locals assemble. The nightly gathering is an ideal interchange for gambling, weapons, and secrets.

Uncle Holden's footfalls sound behind me. "Everley," he says, "please don't go."

I halt halfway outside. "You made Markham a chronometer." I sling the accusation as I would a stone.

"I was commissioned by the queen's navy. I couldn't refuse without drawing suspicion." My uncle comes nearer. "Please stay."

"This is the final time." The last time I steal down to the docks. The last time I disobey my uncle. The last time I prowl the streets and seek refuge in the shadows.

"One more night could be your undoing. There are dangers you don't understand. Think of your parents."

I grip the hilt of my sword. "I am."

"They wouldn't want this. Your father respected the sacredness of creation power, and your mother taught you all life is divine."

"And now they're dead."

He flinches from my directness. My mother and father worshipped Mother Madrona, the ancient elderwood from which all life springs. Around the time of my parents' death, the Progressive Ministry, a church organized by the queen, spoke out against the Children of Madrona and stated their beliefs were sorcery. Instead of thanking Mother Madrona for each autumn harvest and celebrating her power each spring during planting season, Progressives believe devotion to her disrespects the Creator, the goddess of all the worlds. Our queen's councilmen support her assertion that she receives direction from the Creator through visions, and our magistrates determined that anyone caught worshiping Madrona will be punished, so Uncle Holden is careful to pray in private. My brothers, sister, and I were raised to honor the sanctification of Madrona *and* the Creator. Our parents esteemed all creation power, but whatever faith I had died with them. Father Time is another matter. He, of course, is inescapably relevant.

I step the rest of the way outside. Rain patters against my boots and lays a fine mist over my hair. Uncle Holden follows me, raindrops staining his ivory nightshirt.

"Seeking out Markham will not help you find justice," he says.

"I deserve answers." My throat tightens on a surge of anguish. *Be calm. Be machine. Be indifferent, like time.* My uncle and I never pieced together why Markham came that night. The governor interrogated my father and searched our manor. My parents had no jewels or gold, and our prized possessions were family heirlooms, razed in the fire.

"Everley, this hunger for vengeance will rot you. Could you do it? Could you become a monster to destroy one?"

He must think I haven't the nerve. I was unprepared for Markham's visit today, but he will not catch me unawares again. So long as he can insert himself into my life, I am not safe.

"The only way to be rid of rot is to cut it out," I say.

Uncle Holden's eyes dampen. "Your heart can only handle so much."

"My heart should have stopped long ago."

We thought my ticker would last maybe five years. I have nearly doubled that estimate. But eventually this miraculous clock will fail and Father Time will reclaim the years I stole.

"You mustn't go," Uncle Holden pleads. "You can take any lessons you want and I'll teach you to build gearwork. You're ready, Everley. The store, the workshop, our home—this will all be yours someday."

Maybe I am naive to have my own aspirations. Maybe my future is to inherit this shop. I love my uncle, my only true friend, and I am forever in his debt for taking me in and giving me his name and a new life. But I do not want to hide anymore. I've lived longer than either of us thought possible, and I cannot let this time go to waste.

"Thank you, Uncle," I say, raising my hood. "I'll return as soon as I have my answers."

Sweeping my cloak behind me, I dash into the cover of night.

Darkness whispers a velvet welcome against my cheek. I have come to thrive in the midnight hour, where the truth of daylight cannot reveal my secrets. Between the steel at my hip and the cloak shielding my face, no one approaches me. Here in shadow, I am formidable.

My nighttime strolls have become a pastime. I've memorized the route from the shop to the docks. Even without it or my keen sense of direction, I could easily seek out the lights along the river. Through training and practice, my ticker abides my physical demands. The emotional side of having a clock heart is far harder to control.

A cry from an alleyway stops me. I peer through steam seeping from the gutters at a man trapping a girl against a wall. My toes curl in my boots. Men of every class pay for the companionship of streetwalkers, but what may have started as a mutual meeting is no longer.

The sight of them calls to memory the night Markham came to my family home with his masked men. Before I ran to the drawing room, they knocked out Carlin and attacked Isleen while our older brother, Tavis, pressed my face to his chest. I was too young to comprehend what the soldiers were after. What they took from her. Time has a way of unraveling secrets, and with age, I came to understand the vileness done to my sister.

The girl pushes against her captor, so he shoves her harder against the wall. No one else is here, and no sign of the constable corps in their pompous scarlet jackets. The storm has washed everyone indoors. I could leave her to defend herself, but I cannot shake free from my sister's haunting cries.

My ticker beats faster.

Be still, I command it. The clock is machine. I—*I* am flesh. It evens to a submissive tap and I reach the alleyway. The lass, no more than fifteen years old, spots me.

"H-help," she says.

Her attacker lifts his gaze. "Go away," he grunts.

Sneering under the cover of my hood, I draw my sword. They both still, the lass blanching. The man has no weapon in sight, but his calloused knuckles belong to a fighter. I calculate the extension of his reach and stay out of swinging range.

"Fine," he says. "Wait your turn."

Fool. He thinks I'm a man seeking a piece of the girl.

I throw off my hood. He reads the imminence of his pain in my glare and wrestles his trousers up from his knees. I immobilize him with the whip of my steel beneath his chin.

Kill him, growls my rage. The yearning to steep my blade in blood startles me. I hold myself, on the verge of springing at him.

"Go home," I tell the girl. She straightens her dress and clips away through the puddles, vanishing into the fog.

The man gulps hard, his neck tendons bulging. "I didn't mean no harm."

He reeks of liquor, his bloodshot eyes wide and worried for himself. He won't give the girl another thought, except perhaps to regret not completing his intentions. As I pull back to strike, Isleen's final moments call out from the past.

After the men were done with her, and her screams died off, what followed was also difficult to hear—her whimpered pleas for our father.

My fist cramps on my sword poised to slay. Father could not save Isleen. Could not save Carlin or my mother. He could not save me or Tavis. Could not, in the end, even save himself. Someone should pay, yet the memory of Isleen calling for him restrains me. I must be known as Everley O'Shea, but I am Brogan Donovan's daughter. Retribution will not be attained by punishing just any man, only Markham.

I lower my sword, slicing the man's belt in two, and his trousers slip to his ankles. He waddles away, but I am far from satisfied. As I stalk out of the alley, escaping my near lapse in judgment, my uncle's admonishment pursues me.

Could you become a monster to destroy one?

Chapter Four

By the time I reach the waterfront, the rain has lessened. I stand at the shoreline, where the cobblestones end and the River Tyne slithers by. Patches of fog cling to the lamplit wharf that stretches over the river in the shape of a hammer. In the center of the channel that cleaves the city in two, several ships are anchored in a line. I eye the largest ship, Markham's vessel. The *Cadeyrn of the Seas*, a 180-foot first-rate barque, is the pride of the queen's navy. Though its stern lanterns glow, the cabin windows are dim. Markham and his crew will spend their last night at port ashore.

I start down the long dock toward the Hammer, my gloves and cloak shielding me from the cool air drifting up through the cracks. Farther out, moonlight scatters the fog. The riverbank opposite us has half as many lights as this side of the city. Last year, autumn rains flooded the area, yet miraculously there were no casualties. The night before the river breached the bank, Queen Aislinn had a vision from the Creator to evacuate that region. Once the rain stopped, attendance at the Progressive Ministry church swelled and the Children of Madrona receded further into the underground.

The crowd on the Hammer is bigger and rowdier than usual. Dozens of sailors assemble to gamble, glug yeasty ale, and watch the duels. The sailors serving aboard the *Cadeyrn of the Seas* are bound for

Dagger Island in the morning. With all the sobering stories of the penal colony, I would revel in my last night on land too.

In the trench—a circle enclosed by waist-high barrels—streetwalkers Claret and Laverick cross swords. Corsets pump up their bosoms, and petticoats flounce about their knees. Black-striped stockings emphasize their sleek legs and agile feet. Their violent dance engages the crowd in hollers. I push through the crush of bodies to the bettors' booth. Vevina stacks notes and coins into neat piles. Her curly hair, like waves of satin, spills around her ebony shoulders. Her shiny gaze floats over me.

"Everley, darling. What brings you out tonight? Come to join my crew?"

"Answer's still no, Vevina."

"A shame. Your face would fetch a wealth of interest. I could fill your pockets with gold, split it eighty-twenty."

"Still no."

"Seventy-thirty, and don't go telling my girls. They'll be in knots that I'm paying you more than them."

"That's a fine offer, Vevina, but I have to pass." Resting my hip against the table, I nod at the duelers in the trench. "Who's slotted to win?"

"Two to one Laverick." Vevina's rouged lips slide upward, emphasizing her petite chin and long neck. "If I were betting, I would put money on Claret going down at the end of this round."

I chuckle at her game. Although she's only five years older than me, Vevina is the most lucrative street mistress in Dorestand. She rose to the top through hard work, cunning—and cheating. Claret and Laverick are on her payroll; every streetwalker cruising the wharf works for Vevina. Street duels are a clever way of displaying her merchandise while dipping further into customers' pockets. Any man who fancies her fighters can pay for time alone with them. Some nights Laverick wins; other nights Claret wins. Every night Vevina rakes in more coin than she loses.

She adjusts the bodice of her wine-red gown and winks at a well-dressed sailor. He flushes, oblivious that from the second she set eyes on him, she started plotting how to swindle him out of all the coin in his pocket.

I watch the city lights glistening off the onyx river. "Have you seen Harlow? I have a question for her."

Vevina shifts closer to my side. "Maybe I can help."

"Thank you, but I need Harlow." No one hoards more secrets than her.

Roars erupt around the trench. Within the dueling circle, Laverick disarms Claret with a meticulous swirl of her sword and then unbalances her with a push. Claret lands on her bottom, and her going down ends the third round. The mediator blows his whistle and calls the win in Laverick's favor. The duel finishes just how the mistress predicted. Sailors swarm the bettors' booth to win back their losses.

"One at a time, gentlemen," Vevina says loudly.

Leaving the mistress to her work, I weave through the crowd, past a streetwalker and a sailor entangled on a heap of ropes. The giggling young woman seems to like his touch, and from the position of his hands, he's enjoying himself. This audience takes little interest in a woman dressed in men's attire, yet I leave my grip on my sword. Liquored-up sailors can be impetuous. I vault over the water barrels into the trench with Laverick and Claret. Bloodstains speckle the dock planks. I have bled enough of my own drops here to claim this as a second home.

"Here for a duel?" asks Laverick, wearing a feral grin. Laverick resembles a fox, with a long, straight nose, close brown eyes, and thick chestnut hair.

"I'm looking for Harlow," I say.

Laverick swaps a glance with her best friend, Claret, and asks, "What for?"

I shrug, feigning unimportance. The three of us are sociable, but I know as little about Laverick and Claret as they do about me. I haven't inquired about their pasts. I couldn't without offering them bits of my own.

"I saw Harlow earlier," Claret says. "She's here somewhere."

As much as Laverick resembles a fox, Claret has the features of a cat—slanted amber eyes, deep-tan skin, and a feline stride. She has a northern Wyeth accent, wherein she rolls her *r*'s almost like a purr. Vevina nicknamed this inseparable duo the Fox and the Cat for good reason.

Laverick leans over the water barrels and smiles at a merchant. While he is taken by her, Claret pinches a bag of hard taffy off his tray. She would strip him of his pistol, but she cannot reach it. Laverick blows the dazed merchant a kiss, and he moves on, unaware that he was robbed by two very pretty, very sneaky thieves. I learned long ago not to have anything of importance on my person around the Fox and the Cat. Before Vevina hired them, they were successful pickpockets and vandals. Claret specializes in pilfering, and Laverick has an affinity for powder explosives and artillery. They steal pistols and fence them, an interesting side business, since neither owns a firearm.

Claret offers me a candy. I decline and she pops it into her mouth. I glance at the swollen crowd of spectators. This many people may attract the constable corps. I need to find what I came for and get out.

"There she is," Laverick says, pointing across the trench.

Harlow sits on a barrel, swinging her legs back and forth, her rapier at her hip. Her golden hair and elegant features attract an audience. A sailor grabs her from behind and tries for a kiss. She fists the back of his shirt and throws him over her shoulder into the trench. While he's down on his back, she hops off the barrel and kicks him in the groin.

Onlookers applaud and chortle as the man rolls away groaning. He isn't the first, nor the last, to mistake Harlow's divine looks for a pleasing temperament.

Harlow takes a tobacco pipe from her pocket and lights it with her fire striker. She is our age, but she isn't one of Vevina's girls. Harlow works for herself selling high-value secrets. I draw my sword and point it at her, extending her a challenge. She grins, her pipe clamped between her teeth.

Duel on.

"You really want to do this, Everley?" Laverick asks.

"My rematch with Harlow has been a long time coming," I reply, adjusting my gloves.

Laverick pats my back and wishes me luck. She and Claret exit the trench, petticoats flouncing and heels clicking. Harlow sets aside her pipe and saunters toward me.

"Prepared to lose again?" she asks.

I have come a long way since our first duel long ago—the second time my ticker failed. At fourteen years of age, I came to the Hammer for the first time to learn how to fight with my father's sword. Assuming Harlow was a wide-eyed, wispy blond, I selected her as my opponent. I limped home an hour later, bleeding and dragging my sword behind me. My uncle reprimanded me for my foolishness. While I was arguing for my right to learn swordplay, my clock heart seized. He revived me, and as soon as I was well again, I returned to the Hammer to train in earnest. Professional swordplay lessons weren't an option, so I studied experienced street fighters and practiced against them.

The mediator stands atop a water barrel and hollers, "Next in the trench, Striker versus Marionette!"

Bystanders press in around the barrels and bettors flock to Vevina's table. Many girls have entered the trench in search of acclaim. The few of us who win often earned nicknames. Harlow is Striker, for her habit of setting off tempers. I crumble like a marionette with snipped strings when I go down, hence my title. The nickname began as unflattering, but after countless wins, it evolved into a show of respect.

The mediator places his whistle between his lips. He will enforce the only two rules: duelers must not leave the trench, and the first person knocked on their backend forfeits the round. Regardless of whether the duel is impromptu or premeditated, such as those between Vevina's girls, the mediator's task is to call each round, three in total, and serve as lookout. Though the Hammer has never been raided, a quadruple whistle blast from him would be the call to vacate. A couple of constables take bribes in exchange for ignoring us, but we keep our guard up.

Harlow rolls her shoulders to stretch. "You must want something terribly bad from me."

"If I win, you'll tell me where to find Governor Markham."

Her brows arch, confirming my intuition—she knows where he is. "When I win—"

"If."

"*When* I win, you'll explain to me what you want from Markham."

Her wager is high, but Harlow won't ever find out that I am the believed-dead daughter of the queen's former explorer, because I will win. "Deal."

I raise my sword and she mirrors my stance. Neither of us has formal training. Like every competitor in the trench, we taught ourselves to fight through experience. Harlow is taller than me by a finger length and quicker, or she was, so I ready myself.

The whistle sounds. Before the shrill call leaves my ears, she swings and steel jars against steel. We sidestep, in and out, forward and back, swords clashing between us like arcs of lightning. I breathe lightly, my heart a gentle drone.

I spin away from her thrust. "I'm stronger than I was."

She redirects her blade for my side and catches the hem of my cloak, slicing a strip of cloth free.

"You're still slow." Harlow kicks me in the kneecap. I drop to the planks. She grabs a fistful of my hair and wrenches. "You think you're better than the rest of us."

"I've never said that."

She yanks so hard my scalp burns. "You don't belong here, shop clerk." Fear acts as a pressure point in my throat. Harlow has figured out who I am during daylight hours. "Go home, Everley. You don't belong here."

I thrust my elbow into her side. She grunts and lets up on her grip. I twist from her hold and knock into her with the blunt hilt of my sword. She crashes onto her back. Sweeping my blade down, I halt shy of her middle.

"I don't think I'm better than you. In fact, I hardly think of you at all."

The mediator blasts his whistle to conclude round one. We have two more rounds, yet he blows his whistle three more times, four in total.

The warning to evacuate.

My gaze flickers over the audience to the waterfront. Dozens of torches wink along the shoreline, bobbing closer to the docks. *Bloody bones, a raid.*

Harlow flashes a smirk. "I guess we both lose."

Everyone around the trench stills. Then, as though someone snapped their fingers and woke them from a magical sleep, people bolt in a hundred directions. Streetwalkers clutch their skirts and sprint down the pier while sailors push to the longboats docked along the wharf. Claret and Laverick jump into the river and swim for the bank. Other streetwalkers follow the sailors rowing across the channel, swimming toward the other side or to their ship. Vevina scoops up her winnings and shoves them down her corset. I slam my sword into my sheath and tug on Harlow, but she's dead weight.

"What are you doing?" I demand. "Get up!"

"Go away, Everley."

"You'll be arrested!"

"So will you." Harlow folds her arms across her chest like a child.

All around us, boats row out into the river. My instincts shout at me to flee, but I cannot find Markham without her. "I'll tell you one secret right now if you come with me."

"You think you can bribe me?" She laughs, an apathetic sound. "You think too much of yourself."

I consider hitting her over the head and dragging her off, but her weight would slow me down.

Constables along the riverbank capture Claret and Laverick sloshing out of the water and then chase after other escapees swimming farther down shore. Dozens more constables spill onto the dock, a swarm of shadows headed our direction. The first line of corps seizes people fleeing. Another group of constables charge up the wharf toward us.

"Fine," I snap, releasing Harlow. "Find your own way out of here."

Harlow salutes me snidely. I sprint to the edge of the dock and scan the waterway. All the longboats are gone, and diving into the channel is not an option. My older brother Tavis taught me to swim, but my clock heart cannot go underwater. The mechanical workings would become waterlogged. Not even recalibration could save my ticker should it flood.

The constable corps thud closer. I duck behind water barrels and curl into the shadows. Muffling my regulator, I strive for calm.

Be still. Be a machine . . .

From between the barrels, I see Vevina scraping up the last of her winnings. The constables surround her. She brushes the lapel of a corpsman's jacket coyly with a stack of bills. He pushes her over, front down onto the table. Her lips form a surprised circle as he shackles her wrists. Vevina set aside a hefty sum in bribes to the corps so they would disregard her business practices. Someone with greater means and power must have initiated this raid.

Footfalls pound closer, vibrating the wharf beneath me. Harlow sits a few feet away, still out in the open. What is she doing?

A wave of corps hurdle into the trench and encircle her. My ticker does double time, triggering my regulator to ring. Despite my cloak smothering the box, the sound carries in the night and two constables pause. Their rounded hats are tipped low over their foreheads. One of them squints through the shadows at me.

"There!" he hollers.

Another constable leaps over the barrels and aims his pistol between my eyes. "Disarm yourself!" he says.

Across the trench, Harlow tosses aside her sword. I start to set down my own blade, and the constable whacks me over the head with his pistol. I fall forward, hissing in pain. Rough hands disarm me and slam me facedown. The constable wrenches my arms back and clamps on the heavy, tight manacles. I sag forward, my fingers uncurling to useless nubs.

Harlow watches me while she, too, is shackled. For some absurd reason, she's smiling.

Chapter Five

From street level, the lower entrance to Dorestand Prison is a non-descript stairwell leading to a dark hole. Prison guards haul Harlow and me out of the carriage into the cold of the night. The gallows in the courtyard outside the main gate of the jail are vacant. On execution days, hundreds attend the hangings, and even more come for the burnings.

Rain runoff bleeds leftover ashes from the stone pit in the courtyard. Accusations from the Progressives against old-world followers, heretics of Mother Madrona, have increased since the queen offered a considerable reward for their identification. What were once seasonal burnings for severe crimes like treason or murder have become daily celebrations of our queen's purging of the Children of Madrona.

Our guards prod us down steep stairs and open the thick wooden door. The stench of rot hits me as we are elbowed into the city's underground. Lanterns illuminate the narrow stone corridor. I slosh through puddles of muck that shine like oil slicks. Huge rats skitter about, the only willing patrons of this place where freedoms expire. The farther we tread, the faster my nerves quiver.

We are taken to a locked cell. Dirty faces peer out from behind the iron bars. At least twenty women of various ages huddle within, filling a cramped area no bigger than the back of the wagon that brought us here. How will Harlow and I fit?

A guard unlocks the door, and another removes my manacles. As I rub my chafed wrists, I am pushed inside, and Vevina catches me. I did not pick her out among the other solemn faces. Claret and Laverick sit together at the back of the cell, soaked and shivering. Harlow shoulders her way into the cell and searches for a gap on the stone floor.

"That's the last of 'em streetwalkers," one guard says to the other.

I pull from Vevina's grasp and step up to the door. "I'm not a streetwalker. I'm an apprentice to a clockmaker. Please send a message to my guardian, Mr. O'Shea. He'll confirm that I—"

He slams the door and locks it. "Save your sniveling for the magistrate."

The guards depart, and I shout after them. "Where's my sword? I want my sword!" Harlow scoffs at me, so I aim my glare at her. "Be quiet. You're stuck in here too."

"Difference is I'm not wallowing. I've got a roof over my head and a dry place to rest. You won't hear me complaining."

Harlow is entirely too calm. Dorestand Prison is a sarcophagus, better suited for the dead. Considering her relaxed pose, I would guess she had planned the raid, but she lacks the means and power. It is far more likely that Harlow knows who sent the corps upon us, though she would not tell me, not for anything less than a hefty ransom.

She sits against a wall and stretches out her legs, occupying more room than any other woman. Her reputation as a spy discourages protests from our cellmates. Harlow has been rumored to sell and gather secrets for the queen, a piece of gossip she may have started to inflate her own importance. It is hard to tell what is true about Harlow and what is a lie.

Vevina crosses the cell to Claret and Laverick. They do not invite me to sit with them. It wasn't my intent to insult their livelihood. I'm not a streetwalker—that's the truth—though I could have been less condemning of the guard's accusation.

I settle near the iron door, away from the other inmates. They are poorly dressed, unwashed, and infested with fleas. The closest woman eyes my red gloves. I wrap my cloak closer and scowl back at her until she stops.

Markham was so close. I should never have tried to make a bargain with Harlow. I should have tried to look for him myself. By now, I could have my answers and be on my way home.

"Don't fret, shop clerk," Harlow says, lowering her hood over her eyes. "We'll be out of here tomorrow."

The skinny window high in the corner reveals the midnight hour. Soon dawn will come, and Markham will embark for Dagger Island. I drop my forehead against my knees and fall into the hollow beat of my ticker.

Once again, time is my greatest adversary.

Daybreak comes and goes without fanfare. Markham has set sail for the island, gone away from Wyeth for months, if not years. The murdering blaggard is free to go and do as he pleases, while I'm trapped in this dank hole awaiting trial. Harlow's confidence about our quick release was ignorant optimism. I overheard an older woman tell another prisoner that she's been here a full month and hasn't had her trial in court.

Vevina sits cross-legged between the Fox and the Cat by the far wall. Claret pulls pieces of salted meat from her pocket and passes one to Laverick.

"I swiped these off a constable," she says.

Laverick rips into the food with her teeth. She doesn't seem to notice the famished stares from the other prisoners—or those of us who are repelled.

Children of Madrona don't consume meat or fish. They believe all life is sacred and ending another human's or animal's life causes bad luck. My parents told me stories of our ancestors slaughtering cattle for sustenance and the calamity that followed. Whole villages suffered lice outbreaks, great storms blew in from the sea, and locusts destroyed crops. Only after the people gave seeds to the land as penitence did Madrona withdraw her plagues. Progressives don't view the mythical elderwood as a deity. They think the Creator gave us animals to feed and clothe ourselves, and extreme penalties are permissible when employed by the law.

My nonmeat diet was taught by my parents and upheld by Uncle Holden. He isn't rigidly devout. He consumes meat in times of famine and wears leather as long as the slaughter of the animal is humane. I haven't felt persecuted by Madrona for sampling a bite of a boiled egg or sleeping on a down pillow instead of straw. Someone more superstitious could perceive my misfortunes as punishments, while others could say my trials are part of life. Neither the Progressives nor the Children of Madrona seem fully right or wrong. Any belief taken to the extreme is dangerous.

"How long 'til the guards return?" Laverick asks, licking salt from her fingers.

"Won't be long." Vevina's gaze drifts far away. "They have to adhere to the departure docket."

"I heard the ship's full," says Claret.

"They're almost done gathering their allotted prisoners. Not just any woman will do." Vevina regards our cellmates. Most of the women are in their later years. "The queen needs healthy stock, servants and breeders for her settlement. We can make it aboard with the others if we behave."

They must be referring to the *Lady Regina*, the second ship leaving for the penal colony that will be full of female convicts. I tilt my head to hear them better, my interest piqued.

Laverick scrapes her nail across her lower lip nervously. "I've heard soldiers would rather desert the navy than be assigned to Dagger Island."

"A transportation sentence is better than hanging for treason or rotting in here," Vevina replies. The Fox and the Cat nod solemnly. "The women on the ship will have clean clothes and beds, food every day, and fresh water. The queen won't tolerate anything less for the future mothers of her colony."

A transportation sentence might appeal to them, but the *Lady Regina* is a floating prison. The queen is sending convicts because no one else will go. The history of Dagger Island goes back further than the penal colony. Tragedy befell the isle's previous rulers, Princess Amadara and her lost prince. What remains of their fallen kingdom was justly forsaken. No good can come from invading a broken world.

A greasy-haired guard unlocks the door and points at Vevina. "You there. You and your lasses come with us."

Vevina leads the way across the cell, she, Claret, and Laverick stepping over the other prisoners. Out of spite, the inmates tug at their skirts and slap their ankles.

"'Tisn't fair!" one grouses. "They've been here one night!"

"What about us?" asks another.

"Shut it," replies the guard. He pushes the trio out beside a second guard, then points at Harlow and me. "You two come as well."

"Where are we going?" I ask.

He spits at me, the gob landing near my foot. "Just get up."

I rise and follow Harlow from the cell. The guards snap manacles around our wrists and then nudge us down the corridor and up a staircase. They throw open a door to blinding daylight. My vision clears to reveal a chamber lined with polished benches and clean windows. On the other side, by an interior door, stands a naval officer.

Lieutenant Callahan draws up in astonishment. Of all the arrogant blaggards in Wyeth, I didn't intend to come across him again.

He strides to me, his gait purposeful. He carries the authority given to him by his nobility and rank of command with ease, and his confidence compels every eye in the room. Claret and Laverick appraise him as though he's a sweet to swipe and stash in their pocket. His presence repels me. The lieutenant has on the same standard blue uniform Governor Markham wore the night he murdered my family.

"Miss Everley, why are you here?" Callahan asks, frowning deeply. "Are you feeling all right?"

My neck warms as I recall my condition when he left yesterday. "I'm much improved."

"Step back, sir," the greasy-haired guard advises. "She's dodgy."

"Her?" Lieutenant Callahan laughs. No one else makes light of the guard's warning, so the lieutenant sobers. "This must be a mistake. Miss Everley is a clockmaker's apprentice."

"No mistake, sir," replies the guard. "The corps rounded her up with these streetwalkers."

The lieutenant straightens, standing a hand taller than the guard. "Careful," he says, quiet yet direct. "You will treat Miss Everley with respect."

The guard withdraws on a harrumph. Vevina and the other women gape at the lieutenant. For all the stars in the sky, I cannot comprehend why I have his backing. He must assume I was a bystander swept up in the raid. Or perhaps he has another motive. Callahan would not be the first nobleman to place presumptions upon a woman of lesser standing.

"Why are we here, Lieutenant?" I ask.

Sympathy softens his stern brow. "For your trial."

I rock back on my heels. It's time for my trial already.

A court clerk opens the far door and beckons our group to come in. I cross my arms over my beating ticker and follow Callahan. The magistrates burn people for praying to Madrona. Discovery of my clock heart, which could be confused for a mechanism of sorcery, would surely lead to an execution sentence.

In the high-ceilinged courtroom, gentlemen and ladies occupy wooden pews before the lofty magistrate bench. The gallery is packed, and after a glimpse of our judges, I understand why.

The older, portly magistrate in a heavy white wig and plain robes sits beside Her Omnipotence, Queen Aislinn. Our gray-haired monarch has donned a fashionable buttercream brocade dress with an ivory lace bodice and three-quarter sleeves. Her air of deportment reveals no emotion beyond strict power.

During my father's service, the queen's unsmiling portrait hung in our home. Some say she hasn't smiled since she was fifteen. She woke in the middle of the night screaming that she had seen a vision of her father dying. Palace guards investigated and found the king had been disemboweled. Aislinn was sworn in as our queen a day after his wake.

The guards usher the streetwalkers inside the courtroom after us. We take turns bowing before Her Omnipotence and form a line in the dock. Callahan stands off to the side with two soldiers. Our guards leave, and the clerk directs our attention to the green-and-blue Wyeth flag over the magistrate's bench. It displays a symbol of the seven worlds, ours in the center and the six Otherworlds encircling it. The myth that our world is one of seven worlds in existence has survived the queen's purging of the old ways, as it exemplifies the Creator's greatness and supreme rulership.

"Hand over your heart," says the nasally clerk. "Repeat after me: 'I swear by our beloved queen, great seer of benevolence and omnipotence, that the evidence I provide shall be the unerring, uncompromised truth.'"

I recite the oath with the other women. Harlow has a glint in her eye and Vevina purrs as though promising her very soul. Laverick and Claret appear terrified, barely whispering.

At the finish, the magistrate adds, "Perjury is punishable by public execution. Her Omnipotence will know if you lie." He gestures for the first accused to come forward.

A soldier leads Harlow to the witness box before the high bench. A barrister, a bald, stout man with a pinched chin, works from a low table beside the box.

"State your name and age," says the magistrate.

"Harlow Glaspey. On my last birthday I was seventeen."

"Then you're seventeen years old?"

Her lips twitch. "That's what I said, my lord."

I wait for the queen to reprimand Harlow for her impertinence. She utters not a word, allowing the magistrate to run the proceedings. He frowns, his jowls hanging over his neckerchief.

"Charges?" he asks.

"A plethora," replies the barrister. "This isn't Miss Glaspey's first offense. She's evaded capture on multiple occasions for conning, fencing, and theft. She's widely known as Striker."

"Striker?" queries the magistrate.

"Her dueling name, sir. The Realm of Wyeth would recommend the gallows for her, but she may yet be of use to the throne."

The magistrate whispers to Queen Aislinn. The queen gives a weighty blink, and he voices their verdict. "Her Omnipotence foresees that Miss Harlow Glaspey will be an asset to the realm. She's sentenced to seven years' transportation and will embark on the *Lady Regina* tomorrow at dawn."

Harlow hops down from the witness box and strides out the opposite door, her head high, a soldier guiding her. Before I can process that she has been sent away for seven years, Claret is summoned to the witness box, and the barrister lists her offenses. After another short deliberation with the queen, they also deem Claret valuable to the realm and sentence her to seven years' transportation at the penal colony. My ticker sprints faster as Laverick is condemned to the same. The reason for the speedy trial and presence of the queen becomes apparent. She is handpicking the wives and mothers of her future colony. Her ambition to expand her power is at the root of these trials and, most likely, the raid on the wharf.

A soldier comes for Vevina. The gentlemen in the public gallery admire her swaying hips as she strides to the witness box. I press a palm over my cramping stomach, too anxious to concentrate. My turn on the stand is next.

Vevina charms her more severe charges down with a demure gaze and repentant tears. Her theatrics earn her the same sentence as the others. She curtsies to the queen and glides out.

"Next accused!"

Lieutenant Callahan appears at my side and escorts me to the witness box. The walk to the center of the courtroom feels eternal, each step heavier than the last.

"State your name and age," says the magistrate.

"Everley O'Shea," I reply, my voice scratchy. "Age seventeen."

The barrister sets my father's sword on his desk, evidence of my misdeeds. "The accused was arrested for participating in illegal gambling duels."

Queen Aislinn sits forward, her attention on my weapon. My tongue goes papery.

"My lord, if I may speak on the prisoner's behalf," Callahan says.

The barrister shoots him a quizzical look.

"State your name for the court," barks the magistrate.

"The Earl of Walsh." Callahan drops his shoulders and lifts his chin. "First Lieutenant Jamison Callahan. I'm here on official business for Governor Markham."

Attendees in the public gallery titter. Lieutenant Callahan is the Earl of Walsh? My uncle has sold clocks to his father, the marquess.

Yesterday, I overheard Callahan mention that he had been disinherited, which must account for the jeering from his peers.

My ticker thrums as the queen continues to stare at my sword.

"Ah, yes. Governor Markham told us he left his best man to round up prisoners," remarks the magistrate. "Do you know this woman, Lieutenant?"

"We have met. Miss Everley is an apprentice for a reputable clockmaker."

"Then why was she caught participating in a bettors' fight?" asks the magistrate.

"She was on an errand for me," a voice calls from the rear of the courtroom. Uncle Holden rushes forward, flushed and out of breath. I close my eyes briefly at the sight of him, relief and shame swamping me. He tugs off his hat and bows.

"Who are you?" demands the magistrate.

"Holden O'Shea, the girl's guardian, my lord." He kneads his hat. "Everley is my apprentice. She's a good lass."

"So we've heard," the magistrate drawls, "yet Miss O'Shea was found dueling in the trench among other characters of ill repute, disrupting the peace of our city."

"Everley exercised poor judgment," Uncle Holden says. "She won't do it again."

I would, if it meant confronting Markham.

Although I am ashamed of where I am and what this has come to, the thought centers me. Getting arrested was a mistake, yes, but it could also be an opportunity. This could be the moment I have been waiting for.

Queen Aislinn clears her throat, and every soul in her company stills. "What say you, Miss O'Shea?" she asks, her voice as soft as powdery snow.

My regulator will surely ring if I lie, which would be loud in this silence, so I answer honestly. "This wasn't my first time in the trench. I often participate in street duels."

The witnesses in the gallery murmur again, and Callahan's eyes broaden.

"Are you one of Mistress Vevina's streetwalkers?" the queen asks, ever gentle.

"You're under oath," reminds the magistrate.

Uncle Holden shakes his head. Pleading guilty to streetwalking, a higher crime than disrupting the peace, will surely upgrade my punishment from prison time to the same sentencing as the other women. Transportation to the penal colony is a one-way voyage. I will be confined to Dagger Island, halfway around the world in an abandoned land of legend. Regardless of what I plead to or what punishment I receive, I have disgraced my uncle's name and harmed the reputation of his shop. I doubt the nobles in attendance will purchase his clocks now.

"Miss O'Shea?" the magistrate presses.

My heart has never felt more fragile. The wrong decision could mean no answers, no silence, no resolution. My choices knock against each other. Stay here in prison or travel to the isle?

Markham is only at one of those places.

But Dagger Island is a terrifying possibility. I cried when my father left to explore it, afraid he would never return. Would he tell me not to go? Or would he understand that I'm like him? That I want to follow the stars and see where time takes me?

I press my elbow over my regulator. My ticker drives me forward, a metronome of loss, a beat of resilience I haven't yet earned.

Father would be brave, so I will be brave too.

"Your Omnipotence," I say, my tone level, "I am a dueler. In the trench, I'm known as Marionette. I'm also employed by Mistress Vevina."

My regulator rings. *Liar,* it says. No one appears to hear it over the nobles' haughty rumblings. The magistrate calls for order, and the soldiers move into the gallery to intimidate the attendees into silence.

Callahan leans closer. "What are you doing?"

"Answering their questions." My open stare challenges him to contradict me. He thinks I'm a shop clerk prone to fainting spells. He knows nothing about me.

While the magistrate confers with the queen, my banging pulse sends shocks to my toes.

Ring!

Callahan's attention zips to my waistline. "What was that?"

"What was what?"

My regulator rings again, a quiet snitch. Callahan cleans his ear out with his fingertip.

"We've reached a verdict," the magistrate announces. The courtroom shushes under the queen's scrutiny. The moment slows, both sluggish and swift. "Her Omnipotence foresaw this young woman's unseemly habits and praises her honesty. Nevertheless, on account of the accused's testimony, we have increased the severity of her punishment. Miss O'Shea is hereby sentenced to seven years' transportation at the penal colony. I surrender her and the other women condemned today to Lieutenant Callahan's custody so he may prepare for departure."

My uncle stumbles sideways against the wall as though he is suddenly faint. I harden my jaw and accept my sentence as I would a well-executed blow. Callahan grabs my arm, his grip firm, and guides me from the witness box. I exit on rickety legs. As we pass my father's sword on the desk, I lunge for my weapon, but the lieutenant restrains me.

"You won't outrun their pistols," he says of the soldiers.

"What do you care what I do?"

"I don't like innocent people paying for crimes they did not commit."

His grumbled reply hushes me. I search out Uncle Holden to send a silent plea for him to secure my father's sword. Convicts' possessions often become property of the realm, so my sword could disappear forever. Unfortunately, the place where my uncle stood is empty. He has left, probably run off by my public humiliation.

Queen Aislinn watches me approach the exit, her eyes glinting. I have no time to contemplate her self-satisfaction as I am dragged out.

Uncle Holden waits in the foyer. He tries to come forward, but soldiers block him. He rises onto his toes and speaks over their heads. "Lieutenant, I beg a moment with my apprentice."

"My apologies," Callahan replies. "I must take her to the ship."

"Please." My uncle kneads his hat in his fists. "She's my niece."

Callahan releases a short breath. He wavers while my uncle mangles his only hat and then waves aside the soldiers. "You have one minute. We'll be right here."

Uncle Holden crushes me against him, my bound hands between us. "When I heard the corps raided the docks, I went straight to the prison and a guard told me you were here. What were you thinking, Everley?"

"I was only on the docks to duel for information. I wanted to find out where Markham was staying. I don't work for Vevina. Never have."

"I know you don't. The queen didn't foresee that you're a street-walker. What utter rubbish."

I shush him before the guards overhear us and lock him up too.

"I'll appeal your sentence," says my uncle. "I'll visit the magistrate and tell him you misspoke—"

"You can't. I'll hang for perjury."

"Everley," Uncle Holden says, equal parts furious and exasperated, "there are things about that island . . . Your father . . . It's not what it seems." He shakes his head at himself, as though he cannot find the proper words to explain. "I warned you of this. I warned you to let go of the past."

I lay his palm over my ticker and force him to feel the cold, heartless drumming. "I can't let go. Markham broke me."

"Oh, Everley." My uncle runs his thumb across my cheek. "You underestimate yourself." His warm blue eyes—so like my mother's—brim with tears. "I haven't been as attentive as your parents. I shouldn't have let you go to the docks."

"This isn't your fault. You couldn't have stopped me."

"Mister O'Shea," the lieutenant cuts in, "time's up."

Uncle Holden removes a pouch from his breast pocket, the tool kit he carries with him for work, and passes it to Callahan. "I neglected to include this in your purchase. It's for repairs."

The lieutenant peeks inside at the silver tools, tools that are needed to adjust my clock heart and maintain my regulator. Tears fuzzy my vision. Uncle Holden gave the kit to Callahan, but he intends it for me.

"Lieutenant," my uncle says, tugging on his wrinkled cap, "protect my niece."

"I will, sir." Callahan grasps my bindings and tugs me away.

I call over my shoulder to my uncle, "Secure my sword."

"I'll do my best. Be careful, Everley."

"You too." If the guards weren't here, I would beg him not to hum chanteys about Madrona anymore or vocalize another prayer.

"Love you, lass."

A hot lump rises in my throat. I have cared for him all my life, since before I had a clock heart. "I love you too."

I hold his grief-stricken gaze until I exit the building. A throng is gathering in the courtyard in front of the courthouse and prison. Soldiers stack wood around a stake, building a pyre. Someone is scheduled to burn today. Did Queen Aislinn predict that person's guiltiness too?

Lieutenant Callahan helps me into the rear of a wagon. Vevina, the Fox and the Cat, and Harlow steal curious glances at me. None of them inquire after what turn of events brought me into the navy's custody, though I'm certain they will interrogate me later. I sit away from them so they cannot hear my heart's soft ticking. Callahan shuts the door and the horse team sets off.

With each turn of the wagon wheels, the permanence of what I have done scores deeper. I may never see my city or my uncle again.

Hot tears burn behind my nose. I will them away by concentrating on the forward march of my ticker. This separation from my life and my home won't be for naught. My day is coming. Before I am finished, Markham will know my name.

Chapter Six

We row across the river, the lights of the city dimming in the evening fog. The other prisoners and I were released from our shackles for the jaunt to the anchored ship. Gulls circle above our longboat as I grip the bench and eye the murky water. One errant wave and the boat will capsize.

The bowsprit of the *Lady Regina* and her figurehead, the bust of a siren queen, materialize in the mist. The soldiers row us to the starboard side. The ship has several decks, including a gun deck, which is marked by cannon ports. Lieutenant Callahan ties off our boat, securing us to pulleys bolted to the main deck. An abrupt jerk throws my chest to my knees, and then we are hoisted. Fog masks the rolling waves below. I cannot see how high we are, and for that, I am grateful.

The groaning pulleys reel us to the top. Lieutenant Callahan lifts Laverick and Claret to the deck one after the other. Claret slips her hand into his jacket pocket and pulls out nothing. It must be empty. He assists the other two next. Vevina kisses him on the cheek before letting go, and Harlow digs her elbow into his side. The lieutenant weathers their antics with an amused expression. I clutch him tightly as he assists me over the gap between the boat and the deck and onto the vessel.

"Afraid of heights?" he asks.

"No," I reply, scooting away from the rail. My proximity to the water, however . . .

The *Lady Regina*'s sails are secured against its three masts, the shrouds bare. On each side of the main deck, a double stairway spans to the upper deck and the unattended helm. The soldiers climb back into the longboat for their return to land, and a crewman passes the lieutenant a glowing lamp. Callahan directs us across the main deck, through the hatch, and down a steep, creaky ladder into the lower decks.

Fresh winds diminish to cloying dampness and the stink of unwashed skin. Young women, numbering in the dozens, huddle in groups across the closed-in cargo hold. Each one is manacled and then tied together by long iron chains. The convicts hush upon our entrance.

"Clean clothes and beds, eh?" Harlow drawls.

Vevina raises her chin, veiling her disappointment. Our accommodations are as I assumed. The *Lady Regina* is an improvement over the underground cell, but the vessel is still a floating prison.

Callahan leads us to the outer wall. "Sit here."

I lower to the floor beside a girl eleven or twelve years of age. She's dressed as a boy and her hair is a mass of knots. She cries into the crook of her elbow. The prisoners are crushed in close, closer than I generally allow others in proximity to me. Fortunately, the creaking ship, clinking chains, and crying convicts drown out the faint ticktock of my heart.

The lieutenant shackles my wrists and weaves a long metal chain fastened to bolts in the floor through my manacles. He continues down the line, fettering us new arrivals together. My spine breaks out in a cold sweat. Should we sink, we will go down chained to the ship.

Vevina leans forward, giving the lieutenant an unobstructed view down her low neckline. She is not trying to be provocative. The style of her dress, of most of the women's attire around us, reveals more up top than I ever could. "Will we be locked up the entire voyage?" she asks.

He contemplates her question before he replies, "Once we're out to sea, the captain may consider unbinding you. In the meantime, a crewman will take you to the head when needed. Simply raise your hand and they will assist you. Meals will be served here in the hold."

Callahan crouches in front of the crying girl. Her muddy-brown hair hangs in ropy tangles. Grime stains her fingernails. "Would you like a drink of water?"

She shrinks from him, her face buried in her arms. I press my spine against the hard wall, shifting away from the lieutenant. In his blue naval uniform, he reminds me too much of Markham.

"Leave her alone," Claret says, glowering. "She shouldn't be here. She's too young to go to the penal colony."

"The lass will serve as a maid to the governor," the lieutenant replies. "She won't be given as a wife yet."

"That fixes everything," Claret retorts dryly.

Lieutenant Callahan's focus shifts to me, as if seeking my support or backing. I stare elsewhere and do not acknowledge him. Though I doubt he played a part in the girl's prison sentencing, I will not defend the detainment of a child.

On a heavy sigh, Lieutenant Callahan straightens. He treads down the line, assessing the needs of the other prisoners, and then disappears back up the ladder. Laverick speaks lowly to Claret, but the Cat twists away from her friend.

"Is Claret all right?" I ask.

"She will be," Vevina answers, barely above a whisper. "Years ago, when Claret was about the same age as the lass, she worked as a pickpocket for a brute of a man with a gold tooth. She was thin as a reed when I first met her. Her handler starved his underperforming workers, and she was struggling. When I made a bet that paid out handsomely, I offered him my earnings. He wanted twice as much for her, so he sent me away. Claret found me the next evening, her handler's gold tooth in hand, and asked to join my ranks."

I side-eye the beautiful and often unpredictable Claret. "Did she kill him?"

"Oh, no. She stole a bottle of his favorite whisky for him. After he was as drunk as a sow, she pulled out his tooth." One side of Vevina's mouth lifts in approval. "We traded that tooth for a big bottle of wine and a box of biscuits. We ate and drank all night long."

I can easily picture them passing a bottle back and forth and cackling over the brute's comeuppance. "How did Claret come to work for the handler?"

Vevina waves the question away. "Same way everyone comes to call the streets home—a string of bad luck."

A group of sailors pass out blankets. I take one for myself and spread another over the weeping girl. Evening speedily descends upon the ship's hold. Shadows commandeer the gaps between the lantern lights, dropping a grayish blur over the women. Many abandon the day and fall asleep. Claret and Laverick settle against each other to rest, and the crying lass finally quiets.

Vevina shifts forward into my line of sight. "I thought the queen would go lenient on you."

"She needs women for the settlement," I say, shrugging. "How many prisoners do you think are down here?"

"Around two hundred." Vevina observes our fellow inmates with troubled eyes. "Every woman here has a story not unlike Claret's. They've hardly lived. They aren't fit to become the wife of a hardened criminal or lonely soldier."

I tuck my knees to my chest. "Neither am I."

Vevina sweeps a curl of hair off her shoulder. "Neither of us would make a good wife. I'm not the doting sort, and you . . . darling, you're as frosty as a blizzard."

Maybe it's good that she thinks so. Perhaps I can increase my unfriendliness to put off interest from the men at the colony. Anything to evade getting married.

Vevina looks up without lifting her chin, as though she can view the crew on the main deck. "It'll be a long voyage to the isle, Everley. A woman's fortune can change in that time."

Time. I went from having not enough to more than plenty manacled aboard this vessel. Time pretends it's constant, but it stretches and snaps at will.

Vevina yawns and curls up beside the Fox and the Cat. I press my palm over my heart, seeking solace in its sturdy beat. We won't reach Dagger Island for a long while, yet the possibility of being given in marriage to someone still disquiets me. No one told me I wouldn't ever marry. My uncle and I didn't speak of it. I arrived at that decision on my own, though it was not a particularly insightful conclusion. I could ask anyone their opinion, and I am certain they would agree. Girls with clock hearts aren't made for falling in love.

We do not have portholes to view the passing shoreline, and our departure from the river into the sea is marked by wider, faster sways. I cling to my iron chains to prevent myself from sliding. Uncle Holden's jumbled warning about Dagger Island stirs inside me, an eddy of worry that will not drain. I cannot puzzle out what could be more dangerous about the isle than what I already know.

The other prisoners are fittingly distressed about the long passage ahead, many of them weeping about leaving their home behind. Their hearts are fixated on what they lost and miss. None of their discomfort or homesickness clarifies my uncle's warning for what waits ahead.

Sailors bring cooked oats for breakfast. Cold and mushy, the oats are flavorless without butter or spices. I choke mine down to fill my hollowness. The guards return to collect our bowls and pass out slop buckets to those with seasickness. None of the women I came with are ill, though Claret's color has paled.

The crying lass will not be consoled. I rested little last night while she whimpered in her sleep. I did not know it was possible to shed so many tears without dissolving away. Guards deliver the midday meal—more oats. The lass mewls into her untouched bowl like a lost kitten. Vevina, Claret, Laverick, and even Harlow take turns soothing her. By late afternoon, the guards send for the ship's surgeon to check that the lass isn't suffering from an ailment beyond a timid spirit.

The surgeon arrives with his wooden medical chest. He looks thirty years old or so, approximately how old my eldest brother would be had he lived.

"Quinn, I'm Dr. Huxley. Are you in pain?" Quinn—that must be the lass's name—hides her face. The surgeon transfers his attention to me. "How long has she been this way?"

"Since I came aboard."

Dr. Huxley removes a flat medical instrument from his medical chest. Quinn curls into a ball, her limbs tucked close. He takes a bundle from his pocket and unties the twine to reveal a small yellow cake.

"I brought this from home. Would you like to smell it?" I expect Quinn to refuse, but she leans forward and sniffs. "Smells good, doesn't it? Would you like to share it with me? You have to stay very still while you have some."

Quinn nods and wipes her soggy nose across her sleeve. While she eats the cake, Dr. Huxley examines her scalp, parting her hair with the wooden tool. Then he places a hand on her back to feel her breathing. He has a pleasant, expressive face and adept hands. His thick brown hair and mustache are trimmed short, his gray-blue eyes as stormy as the sea. His gentle manner reminds me of Tavis. My eldest brother was bigger and stronger, but he never hurt me.

Dr. Huxley sits back. "Quinn, you show no signs of illness. I'll petition the captain to allow everyone up on deck soon. These manacles don't help anyone's constitution." His smile warms on me. "Thank you . . . ?"

"Everley O'Shea."

"A pleasure, Miss O'Shea. Lieutenant Callahan mentioned you may need an examination. He said you had a spell recently?"

"The lieutenant was mistaken," I say, muffling my regulator. "I'm perfectly well."

Dr. Huxley stares at me so long that heat creeps up my neck. "May I ask what brought you to the *Lady Regina*?" he asks.

"Streetwalking."

The women near us quiet. So much for keeping my trial proceedings private.

Dr. Huxley offers me a sympathetic smile and then stands. "I must see to my other patients. Should you or the lass need care, don't hesitate to send for me."

As soon as he's out of earshot, Vevina laughs. "Everley, do you think anyone believes you're a streetwalker?"

"The queen did. She foresaw my admission of guilt."

Vevina chortles harder. "I don't know what you're after, but Creator help you once you get it. You're bound for the penal colony now."

"I know," I snap. Quinn flinches at my raised voice, and I glance at her in apology. "The surgeon was only being kind."

"You were born with airs, Everley O'Shea." Vevina aims a finger at Dr. Huxley, who is treating a woman with seasickness down the row. "Right away, he sensed you're of his class."

"I'm a shop clerk."

Vevina clucks her tongue. "I con people for a living, study them and unmask their secrets. You weren't born a clerk, darling."

I have nothing to say. My highborn inheritance is no more. After my father died, along with my brothers, without male descendants to succeed him, my father had his title, Baron McTigue, dismantled by the queen.

"You were a shop clerk?" a small voice asks. Quinn wipes cake crumbs from her lips, her eyes sad. "Have you ever caught a thief?"

"I worked in a clock shop. We didn't draw much interest from thieves." From the corner of my eye, Harlow catalogues my every word. "Is that why you're here, Quinn? Did you steal something?"

Her head droops. "A frock."

"That's all?" With all her bawling, I presumed she had maimed someone.

"The frock belonged to a noblewoman's daughter," the lass explains. "She was having the hem altered. I pinched it from a dress shop."

"Ah." Thievery of a higher born is a severe offense. Quinn's tears bloom anew, so I pat her knee. "No sense weeping over a dress."

"Ma couldn't afford one. I'd outgrown mine."

I push up Quinn's chin and fix her with a stare. "You don't have to justify yourself. Not to us." The unfairness of her sentencing worms through me. She should have served a brief time in prison and been released. Now she may never see her mother again.

Quinn rests her head against my shoulder. Her shudders lessen and her breaths become even. To her credit, she does not shed another tear.

Three days later, hammocks for the prisoners are hung in the hold. The women swing in their hammocks in pairs, their chains hanging from their arms and dangling between their feet. We are still confined belowdecks, but Quinn is no longer crying, and Dr. Huxley treated the seasick women with crystalized ginger, nursing most of them to wellness.

After a midday meal of mushy oats, Lieutenant Callahan enters the hold. He wears neutral-colored work clothes and carries an iron anvil. I have not seen him since he brought us aboard. He crosses to the closest prisoners.

"Wrists out," he says, his tone official.

The prisoner in front of him obeys. The lieutenant swings the anvil down and pounds out the manacle pegs, releasing her from her confines. One by one, he goes down the line, the clang of iron against iron coming closer to us. He arrives at Quinn sitting in our hammock; I stayed on the floor to avoid her overhearing the beat of my ticker. The girl cowers from Callahan, and he has the audacity to appear wounded. She has every right to be wary of him, yet it would feel very good to have these blasted bindings removed.

I sit up onto my knees and put out my wrists. "Do mine first."

He scrutinizes me, plainly displeased that I, a prisoner, am ordering him about. But for the benefit of the lass, he strikes the anvil against my irons, popping out the peg. I remove the metal bands and rub my chafed skin.

"See?" I show Quinn. "It doesn't hurt."

She extends her wrists and scrunches her eyes. The lieutenant swings the anvil down and frees her.

"Better?" he asks, and Quinn nods quickly. "I have a gift for you." He slips her a wooden hair comb, a rare item among the inmates. "My younger sister's hair was light brown like yours."

Quinn gawks at the fine lady's comb, then startles us both by throwing her arms around the lieutenant's waist. "Thank you," she says.

Callahan pats her head and extracts himself from her grip. As he continues onward with the anvil, Quinn inspects the detailed carvings of flowering vines along the top of the wooden comb. I don't want Quinn to fear him or any man, but she should be slow to trust our captors. No matter how handsome or generous he may be, Callahan still serves Governor Markham.

Upon unchaining the last prisoner, the lieutenant calls out, "Everyone on deck!"

I join the line of women scaling the ladder. Quinn stays close behind me and climbs slowly, her new comb in hand. At the top steps, briny winds barrel over us, tugging at our clothes and hair. My father smelled of sea air when he returned home from expeditions. My brother Carlin called it the scent of adventure. Squinting into the glaring daylight, I step into a forest of rigging. Quinn grips a line to offset the rolling ship. Above us, the canvas sails are puffed like clouds.

My first sight of the glistening sea captivates me. Father said people have two responses to sailing: all-consuming loneliness or an abiding well of serenity.

I am far from lonely.

"Miss O'Shea," Dr. Huxley says, stationed beside the hatch. "Grand to see you."

"We must have you to thank for our emancipation," I reply.

"I had help. Lieutenant Callahan had it in his mind to let you ladies roam about and wouldn't relent until the captain complied."

Callahan emerges from belowdecks helping a seasick woman ascend the ladder. His jaw juts at the sight of the surgeon close to Quinn and me.

"Everyone go to middeck," he says. "The captain will begin announcements momentarily."

While Callahan assists the sick woman, Quinn and I gather with the other prisoners and Dr. Huxley stands with the crew. Three dozen or so sailors encircle us. Their hefty builds range from broad chested and long legged to stout and scrappy. Each man is armed with both a sword and a flintlock pistol.

Lieutenant Callahan escorts the ill prisoner to sit on a barrel and then joins the sailors. The captain oversees us from the upper deck. His seaman uniform of tan slacks and a cream button-down shirt is made formal with a long black jacket and bronze cuff links and toggles. In the sunshine, his trimmed beard and eyebrows are so blond they are nearly white.

"Welcome aboard the *Lady Regina*," he says. His voice has a discourteous snappishness, like a canine's defensive bark. "I'm Captain Bow Dabney. We have a three-month voyage to our destination, sooner in fair winds. All women are banned from the gun room, gun deck, stores, galley, and afterhold. Stay out of the crew's cabins—unless invited." A handful of sailors chuckle. Their laughter leaves a sour aftertaste. "As for my men, Governor Markham has offered a boon for your service. While at sea, any bachelor aboard may take a female prisoner to wife."

My gut rolls with the next dip of the ship. The women break into discussion and the crewmen mumble to one another. Both groups seem equally surprised.

Captain Dabney shouts over the swelling voices. "Sailors who take a convict to wife will be reassigned to serve on the penal colony. They will work there while their wife completes her sentence. The queen will gift each couple with a parcel of land on the isle for their inheritance."

This is a masterful incentive to build up the colony. Lower-ranking sailors, the majority of those aboard, do not earn enough wages to buy and maintain their own land. Wedding one of us will secure a piece of the isle for them to put down roots.

"Crewmen who take advantage of the queen's generosity will make their selection for a wife on the morrow during a matrimonial ceremony," explains the captain.

The sun beats down on my back. *So soon.*

Vevina raises her hand. "Are *you* taking a wife, Captain?"

"I've no intentions, ma'am."

Vevina toys with a strand of her silky hair. "I hope to keep you company, sir."

The captain's fair cheeks burn rosy.

A large crewman with lank hair and shaggy sideburns raises his hand. Captain Dabney calls on the oily sailor. "What is it, Cuthbert?"

The sailor hobbles to the front of the crowd on one foot, his other a pegged leg. "What if more than one man takes an interest in the same lass?"

"The higher-ranking officer will secure her hand in marriage," replies the captain.

Cuthbert regards Harlow from her crown to her toes. "I'd put my hat in for you."

She sticks out her tongue at him. Much to my surprise, I side with Harlow.

"What if we refuse?" I ask loudly.

Men and women twist in my direction. Quinn presses closer to my side and grips my hand.

"Who spoke?" the captain demands. He follows a collection of gazes to my location. "Refuse what, miss?"

"Marriage."

Captain Dabney arches his spine, puffing out his chest. He clasps his hands behind his back and descends the stairway to the main deck. The crowd parts for him, his boots banging against the planks. Quinn tucks behind me, and the snapping sails mask the ticktock of my heart. I hold my stance as the captain stops before me. Head high, I coax my ticker not to react to his posturing. I have never missed the security of my sword more.

The captain rakes his gaze down the length of me, rancid with disrespect. "Is marrying one of my men not up to your standards? If you prefer, I can arrange for them to pay you for your services."

My lip curls, my nerves crackling. "No, sir."

"You're a prisoner of the realm, property of the queen, and under Governor Markham's rule. Don't forget your place." Captain Dabney releases me from his scathing glare and addresses the crowd. "Dismissed!"

The women appraise the crew like ladies waiting for a gentleman's notice at a ball. Marrying a crewman could immediately improve a woman's standing on the ship, but there are more sailors than prisoners, so they will have to compete for a sailor's favor. The women can have them.

Quinn withdraws her hand from mine. Only then do I notice my fingers are trembling. "Everley, let's explore the ship," she says.

My heart thuds raucously. I need a quiet moment away from this audience of men to settle down. "All right. You lead the way."

Dr. Huxley meanders up with his hands in his pockets. "Would you like to take a turn about the deck with me, Miss O'Shea?"

I would rather jump overboard.

Ring!

I tuck my elbow against my hip, muffling my regulator. Neither Quinn nor the surgeon appears to have heard the alarm. "I promised Quinn we would walk together," I say.

"Oh." Dr. Huxley waits for an invitation to come with us. After an excruciatingly long moment, he summons a flat smile. "Another time, then."

I tug Quinn away. In my haste, I do not notice we are traveling toward Lieutenant Callahan until we are nearly upon him.

"Can Callahan come too?" Quinn asks, her big eyes earnest. I find myself incapable of denying her request.

"If he must," I say.

Quinn gives a little hop in place and waves at Callahan. As he strides to her, I take the stairs to the upper deck, pass the helm, and go to the farthest place at the stern.

Deep-blue waves roll to the horizon, the vastness of the remote sea and persistent winds drowning out all else. I strangle the rail in my grasp, tears welling in my eyes. Marriage is another prison sentence, one that lasts a lifetime. The captain insists we prisoners have no choice. I always have a choice. I have to find a way to evade marriage and hold on to the final shred of my freedom. I just don't know how.

Uncle Holden would know what to do. While other young women my age were courting and seeking out husbands, he taught me to occupy my mind through work, and reading, and dreams. He knew how dangerous it was to let others near my ticking heart.

I should have never left home, never gone after Markham, never tried to find answers.

Callahan and Quinn catch up, their footfalls preceding their arrival. She runs to the far corner of the stern, and the lieutenant leans against the rail beside me. Gusts ruffle his golden-oak hair, swirling strands about his face, which is tan from working in the sun. I scrape my nail into the wooden rail, longing for the familiarity of my uncle's workshop, the scent of pine shavings and the rhythmic beat of his hammering and chiseling.

Quinn runs to us to share an observation with Callahan about the sea and then darts off again. He smiles to himself.

"You shouldn't dote on her," I say. "She needs to prepare for the hardships to come."

"Let her be a child."

"*I* didn't sentence her to the penal colony."

Callahan winces. "I had a younger sibling, Tarah. She would have been about the same age as Quinn."

I tilt back to glance at him. "Would have?"

He stares off into the horizon, his gaze pained. "She was in an accident. I should have been there, but I wasn't."

"It's better you weren't," I mutter, my thoughts swinging to my own siblings. Isleen, a talented seamstress, was kind to everyone, and Carlin was brilliant at games and music. My favorite sibling was Tavis. Ten years my senior, he let me ride on his shoulders and hide under his bed during thunderstorms. Tavis was a handsome dresser with a taste for finery. He never raised his voice to me and was swift to dispel disagreements between us younger siblings. I have missed him every day since he passed.

Callahan props his elbows against the rail. "I overheard something that I think you should know. Dr. Huxley has mentioned he admires you. You should be prepared for him to petition for your hand in marriage. His rank as surgeon places him above all the crew except the captain and myself. Should he ask for you, his request will be granted."

I dig my nails into the wood so hard my fingertips ache. "I've no interest in marriage. Not now, nor on the island."

Callahan tips his head forward in acknowledgment—perhaps agreement?—and returns his focus out to sea.

I peel my fingers off the rail and call for Quinn. She scampers back to me and waves goodbye to the lieutenant.

"Jamison is pleasant company," she says, skipping alongside my rapid strides.

"Jamison?" I ask.

"The lieutenant calls me by my given name, so he said I could do the same to him."

Callahan is more charming than I accounted for. I carve on a smile. "You must be thirsty. Let's find something to drink."

Quinn and I maneuver across the deck, circumventing flirting couples and lewd-eyed sailors. I climb down the hatch, my determination building with each rung of the ladder. I have given up everything to pursue Markham. Any man who interferes will be sorry.

Chapter Seven

The music starts at sundown. A tin whistle player, drummer, and violinist perform a jaunty tune that drifts down the hatch. I overheard two women discussing their intentions to kiss some crewmen, so I insisted Quinn stay in the hold with me. We swing opposite each other in our own hammocks, backward and forward in unison, while everyone else is up on deck.

Quinn falls asleep despite the noise. I shift positions in my hammock, unable to get comfortable. Tomorrow's matrimonial ceremony nags at me. To preoccupy myself, I mentally map the layout of the vessel. Quinn was impatient to visit every level of the ship, and I was grateful to keep busy. The *Lady Regina* has three belowdecks. We were able to sneak down to the others. The crewmen sleep in a bunkroom on our level, the gun deck is below us, and under that is the lower hold. The galley is near the stern, and the surgeon's cabin and the captain's and lieutenant's quarters are off the main deck. Mapping my surroundings quells my anxiety. I start to drift off when a shadow looms over me.

I open an eye and groan. "What is it, Harlow? I was almost asleep."

"I overheard Dr. Huxley say that he plans to wed you," she replies. I groan again, irritated that she woke me to tell me something I already know. "You should marry him so you can live in his cabin."

"I won't get married to improve my lodging."

"You'll have to marry him whether you want to or not. You should benefit from the arrangement somehow." Harlow peers down at Quinn, who is still fast asleep. "Cuthbert asked the captain if any of the crewmen can take her to wife."

I push forward in my hammock. "She's a child!"

"Don't spin off into another world," Harlow says, all surliness. "Lieutenant Callahan got mad and Captain Dabney took his side. Quinn won't be given into marriage."

I silently thank Callahan, even as I begrudge him the leadership he serves.

"About the lieutenant . . ." Harlow says too nonchalantly. I recognize her snide expression from when she is about to needle me. "Do you know he's a disgraced earl? A man with a torrid past might settle for a woman of lower standing. Laverick and Claret are vying for his attention. They think winning his fancy will discourage other crewmen from taking an interest in them. Vevina is attempting the same tactic with the captain. You should see the display they're putting on. The Fox and the Cat are draped all over the lieutenant."

"Why would I care?"

"You wouldn't." Harlow shoves my hammock, sending me swinging, and saunters off.

Good sin, she could annoy the wings off a butterfly. I shut my eyes and try to rest, but more worries about the matrimonial ceremony slither in. Avoiding Dr. Huxley and hoping he will change his mind doesn't seem to be working. I need another approach.

Rolling out of the hammock, I sneak past Quinn and up the ladder. The western sky is awash with purples and pinks, the eastern horizon a depthless blue deepening by the second. Sailors and prisoners are scattered everywhere, their faces lit by the hanging lamps swinging in the wind. Lieutenant Callahan strums a violin alongside a drummer and a whistle player. His fingers fly across the strings as he moves the bow up and down the neck of the instrument. I haven't a trained ear for fine music, but his showmanship is mesmerizing.

"Miss O'Shea," Dr. Huxley says, coming to stand alongside me. "I thought you wouldn't come."

"I was keeping Quinn company."

"It's kind of you to look after the lass." His praise itches, as though his compliment was to establish his own complimentary nature. "Would you like to take a turn about the deck?"

"I would. Thank you, Doctor."

"Please, call me Alick." We walk side by side toward the starboard rail, close enough for me to suffocate on his amber cologne. "I recognized the moment we met that you're of a higher class than your fellow inmates."

Rudeness seems like an advantageous approach since he presumes I'm a lady of manners. "You're overexaggerating my station. I come from generations of humble clockmakers." I allow myself this truth, guessing he will not interrogate me about my parentage.

Dr. Huxley sidesteps a little, giving me room. "I meant no offense, Everley. I thought you might appreciate having an ally on board."

"An ally I can tolerate. I've no need for a husband."

"Someone disclosed my intentions. I hoped to tell you myself." He speaks as though I should be delighted. "You and I can assist one another. I can offer you comfort and better accommodations in exchange for your company and care."

I would rather be stabbed again than depend on him for my welfare.

"You're willing to live on Dagger Island?" I ask.

"The rumors don't frighten me. I've already agreed to stay and assist their current medic." He reaches for my hand. "Life on the isle will be lonely."

"I've no interest in marriage," I say, jerking away from him. "Not now or ever."

"Pardon my frankness, but you cannot make that decision." Dr. Huxley must hear how officious he sounds, because his manner gentles as though he's tending to a patient. "What difference does it make if you wed now or at the settlement? I would treat you better than a convict."

"*I* am a convict, Dr. Huxley." Stepping nearer to him, I speak as if I'm pointing a blade at his gullet. "My dueling name is Marionette. My competitors will tell you that I am heartless. Any man who compels me into wedlock will shorten his life significantly."

Dr. Huxley gulps, the whites of his eyes spreading.

Lieutenant Callahan comes around the mast with Claret and Laverick on each arm. He walks stiffly, his limbs close, as though he tried to pull himself from their hold and failed.

"We're sorry to interrupt," Laverick says, eyes gleaming.

"Would you two like to be alone?" Claret adds archly.

Callahan studies me with the same expression of worry as he did when my heart seized. My ticker winds up, beating faster and faster.

"I was just leaving." I push past them and hustle away into the dark.

The shadows offer me promises of privacy and solitude. I slide into their clutches and sit near the gangway overlooking the sea, still vexed by my conversation with Dr. Huxley. I was direct, unflinching, as callous as a mariner's thumb. My only regret is that I didn't deter him sooner.

Late afternoon the next day, the crew distributes new dresses to the prisoners. The casual frocks in various colors are a gift from Governor Markham to lift our spirits. The timing is questionable. Markham wants us to look our best for the matrimonial ceremony. He cares nothing for our morale.

All day, the women have been speculating about the ceremony. The noise of their prattling peaks as they slip into their new attire. Quinn selects a yellow frock in the smallest size, and though Vevina prefers to wear wine red, she settles for a brighter ruby-colored dress. She and Quinn change and then go to the main deck to comb their hair in the natural light.

Claret holds up a blue frock. "Everley, this one matches your eyes."

"So?" I pose, swinging in my hammock.

"Don't you want to change out of those men's clothes and wear something clean?" she asks, her r's rolling heavily.

"I don't care what I look like." A change of attire would be refreshing, but I won't accept anything from Markham.

"Marionette is putting on airs again," Claret mutters to Laverick.

While they dress in similar sea-green frocks, the Fox and the Cat whisper to each other. I am almost certain they are gossiping about me.

"How am I putting on airs?" I ask.

The Cat pounces with a swift response. "You keep a distance from everyone. No man in the seven worlds is good enough for you."

Though I have slightly bluer blood than them, I am trapped in the same hold, sentenced for the same offenses, and like them, I am nervous about what's to come. "I don't think you're beneath me. Is that really what you think?"

"I think you push people away," Laverick answers gently. My lips draw down, and she explains. "My father built cannons for the realm. When I heard Papa was dead, killed in a black powder explosion, I couldn't shed a tear. He would whip my two older brothers and me over the slightest disobedience. My brothers were worse to me. They would wait until I was asleep and then whack the bottoms of my feet with cannon fuses. Sometimes they hit me so hard they left cuts. I had no shoes, so I had to walk about barefoot. When I was nine, they tore up the bottoms of my feet so badly I bled for days. After that, I waited until Papa was away, then while my brothers were in the barn, I tied the door shut and ran."

My siblings were nothing like Laverick's. They were good and gentle, and yes, they often annoyed me, but I annoyed them just the same. "Where did you go?" I ask.

"I lived on the streets of Dorestand. The first thing I stole was a pair of shoes."

"Then we met," says Claret, nudging the Fox. "She and I tried to swipe the same coin pouch off a gentleman. I let Laverick have it and invited her to meet Vevina."

"No one had ever been that kind to me," Laverick says. "It took me a while, but I came to trust them. Claret and I have been partners since."

Claret slides her arm through Laverick's. Standing side by side in their identical sea-green dresses, their friendship seems invincible. I envy their closeness, even though it is precisely the type of relationship I must avoid.

"Everley!" Quinn scurries down the ladder. "It's time!"

She swirls in her dress while I reluctantly get out of the hammock.

Everyone congregates on the main deck, the women separate from the men. The evening air is mild, the winds patiently pushing the sails while the sun lies down in the west. I dare not look in that direction, for there Dr. Huxley is standing.

Lieutenant Callahan enters my side vision. He has exchanged his work clothes for his officer's uniform, the navy coat and slacks that remind me of Markham. The lieutenant gives his attention to Captain Dabney on the upper deck.

"Tonight we will unite four couples in matrimony," says the captain.

Four. Only four crewmen accepted the governor's boon. Sailors are a superstitious lot. Fears of Dagger Island must have discouraged them.

The captain reads from a parchment. "The first match is between crewman Cuthbert and prisoner Glaspey."

He invites the couple to the upper deck to a round of applause. It takes some prodding from the women around her, but eventually

Harlow goes. At the top of the stairs, Cuthbert tugs her against him for a kiss. She kicks his pegged leg, and he stumbles backward. Captain Dabney threatens to lock her in chains and then calls the next couple, a lower-ranking sailor and a round-faced young woman. He announces the third pair, more names I don't recognize. My unease plateaus as the chance that I will be called lessens. Claret, Laverick, and Vevina smirk at each other. Their strategy of spending time with the lieutenant and captain to discourage the lower-ranking sailors appears to have worked.

"One couple remains," says the captain. "Prisoner O'Shea was requested by Dr. Huxley . . . and Lieutenant Callahan." Before his words breach my shock, he goes on. "As Callahan is the higher-ranking officer, I grant the lieutenant's entreaty."

Quinn is the first to clap, awash with glee. Others join in, but the ringing of the lass's initial ovation drills into my bones. The lieutenant strides to the stairway and pauses for me. He can wait there until he dies. I hate his uniform, hate that he works for Markham, hate that I sympathized with him over the loss of his sister.

"Go on," Quinn says, pushing me forward.

My knees bend and my legs move even though I am wholly numb. My gait starts off sluggish and picks up speed. I storm over to Callahan and hiss in his face, his expression undaunted. "What are you doing?"

"I promised your uncle I would protect you."

"I don't want your protection."

Dr. Huxley stomps up and bumps his chest against Callahan's arm aggressively. "How could you do this, Lieutenant? You know I requested her first."

Callahan lays his palm on the surgeon's front, and in one controlled movement, pushes him back. "I met Everley before we embarked from Dorestand. You should see how beautiful she looks when she smiles."

When have I smiled at Callahan? I cannot recall, so he must be exaggerating.

Great Creator, save me from arrogant men.

Dr. Huxley flushes and marches to his sleeping quarters, slamming the door behind him.

"Lieutenant Callahan and Prisoner O'Shea," the captain says, "join us."

The lieutenant climbs the stairs ahead of me. A thousand emotions, the foremost fury, seethe in my veins. How dare Callahan usurp my future. I cannot pledge my life to another and set aside my hunt for Markham, or my ticker will haunt me and drive me into madness. That is if Father Time doesn't collect on my debt first.

I smooth down Quinn's hair, buying a moment to compose myself, and start up the stairs. Callahan watches me approach, my glare wielding the full blaze of the sun.

"Miss O'Shea," he says, bowing.

I slap him.

He takes the hit without a wince of pain. "Is this how you show appreciation?"

"Don't expect my gratitude in any form."

Callahan grabs my waist and pulls me forward, his cheek against mine and his lips near my ear. "They must think I desire you or I'll be plagued with questions."

My face burns. He must establish why he, the Earl of Walsh, wishes to wed a convicted streetwalker, so he will let his crewmates assume he's blind with lust. I should slap him again, but that would entail touching him, and he repulses me.

"Let them think what they wish," I reply, pushing free. "I don't care."

RING!

Liar, my regulator says. Lieutenant Callahan hears it and frowns.

"The nuptials will now commence," Captain Dabney proclaims. "We will begin with Lieutenant Callahan and Prisoner O'Shea."

I'm Everley Donovan, my mind screams. It may be cowardly to beg, but I toss aside my pride. "I won't wed him. Please don't compel me."

"You're property of the queen," replies the captain. "As sovereign of this ship, I may marry you to any man I wish. Be grateful it's the lieutenant. He's an honorable sailor."

Honorable? I told him I didn't want to marry, and he reduced me from the queen's property to his. He and the captain should be pitched overboard and left to the sharks.

Two of the other chosen wives don't appear to mind that they are exchanging one prison sentence for another. Harlow, however, could tear off Cuthbert's peg leg and beat him with it. After her speech last night, I could gloat at her predicament, but our mutual reaction reminds me of her advice: *You should benefit from the arrangement somehow.*

A calm thought pierces my panic.

This could be an advantage.

Markham and Callahan are comrades. The lieutenant's association with Markham could further my hunt.

The captain's low voice rumbles. "You'll not ruin these fine couples' wedding day or I'll have you manacled and gagged."

I balk at the audacity of him lecturing me about thoughtlessness when *he's* marrying me against my will.

He speaks over my sputtering. "This will be prompt. Lieutenant Jamison Callahan and Miss Everley O'Shea, by the authority of our majesty Queen Aislinn and by the rights as the captain of this royal vessel, I pronounce you husband and wife, united across the seven worlds, bound together from this day forward and until the end of time."

Good sin, the end of time could be any second. I am afraid to move, breathe, or accept this is happening for fear that my clock heart will freeze. My elbow covers my regulator, smothering the alarm.

Lieutenant Callahan clasps my hand. "Everley O'Shea, I promise to honor and protect you forevermore."

"You don't even know me." I pry my fingers from his. "Don't touch me again."

"If that's what you wish, you have my word."

His unruffled vow silences me. Why would he consign himself to living on the isle? Why would an earl wed a convict? Either his sense of duty and honor is greater than I can comprehend or he desires our union for other reasons.

Callahan leads me down the stairs into applause. Each step feels like gliding into a strange world where I am no longer alone.

Quinn throws her arms around us. Callahan hugs her and waves politely in acceptance of the crowd's cheers.

Above all the happiness, my heart beats a vacant ticktock.

Chapter Eight

The other wedding nuptials are prompt. At the conclusion of each one, the groom kisses his bride. Harlow accepts a peck on the cheek from Cuthbert, luring him in with a docile smile and then kneeing him in the groin. The Fox and the Cat snigger, but Vevina chortles loudest. She has effectively dodged marriage.

Captain Dabney allows his men to open bottles of spirits for the festivities. The musicians strike up a tune on the tin whistle and drum. I stand off to the side while Callahan and Quinn dance under the lanterns. He spins her, one hand in hers and the other on a glass of whisky. She is a braver version now than the girl who came aboard. Her resilience is a relief. She will need a strong constitution to endure Dagger Island.

Claret and Laverick twirl over to me.

"Dance with us," the Fox beckons.

"I didn't celebrate when I was thrown in prison. Why would I now?" I leave them and march up to Callahan on the dance floor. "I'm ready to go."

He sips his whisky. "I haven't finished my drink."

I snatch his cup, down the last of the spirits, and shove it back at him.

"Ladies don't drink," he says, giving his empty cup a double take.

"I'm not a lady."

Years back, Uncle Holden traded a grandfather clock for several cases of whisky from a distiller in the highlands. Every night before bed, he drinks a cup of whisky tea. When I turned twelve, he began making me one too.

Lieutenant Callahan passes his cup off to another sailor. "Quinn, go dance with Laverick and Claret. My wife needs to rest."

"Don't call me that," I snap.

He winks at Quinn. "My wife is testy."

Quinn giggles and scampers over to the Fox and the Cat. Callahan loops his arm through mine and leads me off the dance floor, his footsteps weaving.

"You're drunk," I say.

"Pleasantly numb. You should try it, melt some of that iciness. Or is it wood, since you're Marionette? Why *do* they call you that? Is it your red gloves?"

"I have no idea."

Ring!

"There's that noise again," he says.

"What noise?"

"The bell I hear when you're around."

He's too observant for his own good. Fortunately, he is also drunk and may not recall hearing my regulator in the morning. On our way to his cabin, we pass a group of sailors who make suggestive comments about our wedding night. I keep my attention forward until we enter his quarters.

Built-in shelves line one wall, stacked with hardbound volumes. A violin case is propped between the bed and the narrow wardrobe. His desk is tidy, and the room smells of clean linen. His collection of possessions is scant but expensive and well cared for. A book rests on the bed—the tale of the Creator and her seven worlds.

"You like mythology?" I ask.

"It's a family memento." He picks up the book and shelves it. "My ancestors were believers in the Otherworlds. Two generations back my great-grandfather on my mother's side transcribed the oral tales into a text for posterity."

Stories about the Otherworlds—the notion that ours is one of seven—are common. They speak of secret passages to far-off lands and magical creatures beyond our sight.

"My mother told us stories about the Otherworlds," I say.

"Most children would say the same."

I don't miss his tone of sadness. "Except you?"

"My mother passed away when I was young. I hardly remember her. This book is one of the few possessions I have of hers."

A fishbowl is secured to the writing desk near the door. I peer through the glass at a goldfish swimming in its dome.

"That's Cleon," the lieutenant says. "Tarah scooped him out of a neighbor's pond. I took over care of him after she passed."

I spot a map of Dagger Island pinned to the wall, a grayscale print of the original that hangs in the queen's palace. I touch the signature at the bottom right-hand corner.

My father's name.

"Brogan Donovan was the greatest explorer of his time," Callahan says. "I would have liked to meet him."

Hot tears swell behind my eyes. I have tried to find a reproduction of this map as a memento, but they are scarce in number. "Where did you get this?"

"Governor Markham gave me a copy when I served as his personal clerk."

A mix of disgust and validation swamp me. He *is* close to Markham. "How long did you work for him?"

"My first post was aboard his ship. Killian was an admiral then. I was transferred to the *Lady Regina* after he was promoted to governor."

Callahan walks past me and draws my attention to a lower shelf. "I thought you'd like to see this."

"My uncle's clock," I breathe. I touch the painted daisies on the timepiece. My heart beats in rhythm with it, as though recognizing they were crafted by the same master.

"It's our clock now," says Callahan.

I swivel toward him. "You shouldn't have married me."

"Most women would be grateful, even flattered."

"You highborn blowhard. I told you I didn't want to get married, and what did you do? You assumed I would be so taken by you that I would forget my senses and bow in gratitude to you for sacrificing what's left of your reputation and forcing me into wedlock?"

He cranks his jaw left and right.

"Why did you do this? Don't say out of obligation or for my protection. No one can fully protect another person. One will always fail the other."

Callahan trails his fingertips down the spine of his mother's book. "I didn't act out of arrogance, though I admit it may appear so. I have my reasons."

"Creator forbid you tell me."

"I will if you quit shrieking."

"You think this is shrieking?" I say, my voice pitching higher. He arches a brow, indicating my response should serve as my answer.

He deserves my outrage. He also deserves having a pillow thrown at his head, but I restrain myself.

"My parents were a love match," he says. "My mother was my father's whole world. Her death destroyed him. I swore I wouldn't give another person that much influence over me." Callahan searches for my understanding, his expression earnest. "You said you're averse to marriage. This civil arrangement will suit us both. You won't have to play wife to Dr. Huxley, and it doesn't conflict with my views. I'll care for you as a husband, and in return, I require only your honesty."

Only my honesty. He must be joking. Absolute sincerity is a greater demand than I am willing to meet, and why would I? It's still unclear what he aims to gain from this union.

Callahan sits on the corner of the bed and removes his jacket. As he rolls up his sleeve, he reveals a rope burn across his forearm. "I caught it in a line this morning. Bring the bottle of whisky from the drawer there, please."

I locate the bottle in his desk and pass it to him. "You need a surgeon."

"I doubt Dr. Huxley will attend to my wounds anytime soon." Callahan uncorks the bottle with his teeth and splashes some of the liquor on the cut. He hisses a breath, then takes a long pull from the bottle and offers it to me.

I wave in refusal. "Stop trying to garner my sympathy. You think I'll feel sorry for you and patch you up and nurse you back to health, but I won't."

"You don't have much compassion, do you?"

"Compassion is a waste of heart."

"If that were true, you would be spending the night with Dr. Huxley." Callahan gulps another glug of whisky, his hair falling in his tired eyes.

I take the bottle and recork it. "Do you have bandages?"

He looks up, surprised, and then points to the bottom drawer. I find the bandages and hand them over. Callahan wraps his wound and kicks off his boots. Lying back, he makes room for me on the other half of the bed.

I can think of no circumstance in which sleeping beside him is acceptable. *I should have had that drink.*

"Lie down, Everley. I won't touch you. I keep my promises."

His every other word is slurred. After the lantern is turned down, his drunken self may change his mind and attempt to exercise his husbandly rights. He would be wise not to try that unless he wants the bottle of whisky smashed over his head.

Though I'm inexperienced, I know love isn't essential for coupling. The people I have observed paying for streetwalkers seek purely physical relations. I will never experience that intimacy. No amount of curiosity or loneliness justifies the risk of someone discovering my clock heart.

I set the second pillow on the floor and fetch the spare quilt hanging over the desk chair.

Callahan rises beside me. "Why are you here?" he asks, his blue eyes vivid in the muted light. "I know you lied in court. You aren't a streetwalker."

I've no hope of lying without triggering my regulator, so I repeat, "Marrying me was a mistake."

"I have many thoughts about the past twenty-four hours, but that is not one of them." He takes the pillow and blanket from me. "The bed is yours."

Callahan settles on the floor in the narrow gap between the bed and wall. I turn down the lamp and lie on the bed, my back to him. The bedsheets smell of the lieutenant, clean and warm. I hug a section of the blanket to my chest to muffle my ticker and wait for him to fall asleep. He has made several promises and reassurances tonight. Maybe I will eventually believe them.

About half an hour later, my mind lets go of the strain of the day. As I doze off, a whisper fills the dark.

"Good night, Lady Callahan."

The sound of a door shutting wakes me. I go from lying down to sitting up in half a second. Callahan's temporary bed has been cleared off the floor. He stands by the cabin door, dressed for the day in plain work clothes and carrying a steaming pail of water.

"This is for you." He sets down the pail, his gaze averted. The neckline of my shirt shifted during sleep. I rearrange the cloth; thankfully, my ticker and scar were covered. "I've laid out clothes like the ones you're wearing now, or should you prefer, a dress. Trousers your size are difficult to find at sea, and these have no bells in the pockets."

"Bells?"

He makes a ringing noise, imitating my regulator.

I maintain a neutral expression and turn my attention to the garments. The men's clothes are folded in a pile on the desk, and the blue dress is draped across the foot of the bed. Much to my dismay, I cannot wear most gowns of fashion. The low, square necklines show my scar. In addition, this dress likely came from the crate of garments provided by Markham. I would rather invite a spider down my bodice than put it on.

"I'll wear the men's clothes," I say.

"That's what I assumed, so I left a section of rope for a belt. There's soap and a washcloth, and you may borrow my comb." Callahan puts on his tricorn hat and ducks out.

After he is well and gone, I climb out of bed and prop the desk chair behind the door to stop anyone from walking in. Washing with a pail of water is my normal routine. The last time I soaked in a tub, I was a child. I bathe quickly, scrubbing hard with the washcloth and dunking my hair in the warm water. The soap lathers well and smells of palm oil, and soon, I do too.

I dry off and dress, securing the breeches with the section of rope, and then pull on my red wool gloves and remove the chair from the doorway. As I comb my hair, I peek inside the desk drawers for papers or notes with information about Markham or my father. Finding nothing of interest, I open the wardrobe cabinet. The lieutenant hung up his dastardly blue uniform.

He reenters the cabin behind me. I shut the wardrobe cabinet and spin around. He sets down a food tray filled with a bowl of dried beans, a side of hardtack, and a cup of water.

"Here's your breakfast. Midday meal and dinner will be brought to you by another crewman, or you may dine in the hold with the other women." He puts away the soap and comb and then hangs the dress I declined to wear in his wardrobe cabinet. "Our cabin is small, so keep it tidy."

"Is that a rule, my lord?"

"A request." He straightens a couple of books on the shelf that I moved and then picks up the dirty pail of water. "Is there anything else you need?"

"Actually, there is one thing. May I have a portion of wood and a carving knife?"

Callahan startles, as though he expected me to have a more ladylike pastime. "I'll see what I can arrange." He opens the door, and a chilly wind sneaks in.

"Don't go out of your way for me," I say. "I can take care of myself, Lieutenant."

A ghost of a smile lifts his lips. "Call me Jamison."

He goes, shutting the door behind him, and the frigid air he let in settles in the cabin. I help myself to the bottle of whisky and huddle under the bedcovers with his mother's book of tales. After living belowdecks with all the prisoners, this quiet is divine.

A sailor brings me the midday meal. Also on the tray are several blocks of wood and a rope knife. I spend the rest of the day carving while the wind raps at the door.

Jamison returns an hour or so after nightfall and kicks off his boots. I lie facing the door, pretending to be fast asleep. He inspects the figurine on his desk that I carved of a cat, and then spreads out his bedding on the floor and turns down the lantern. It is a long while before sleep visits me.

Life at sea falls into a predictable pattern of mundaneness. Each day varies little. Jamison is always gone when I wake. His blankets are folded and set aside, and I have no memory of hearing him leave.

As the weather warms, Quinn visits our cabin often. She has taken it upon herself to feed Cleon a pinch of fruit flies from a jar that Jamison keeps for feeding the fish. Some afternoons I visit the women in the hold, while other times I invite Laverick, Claret, and Quinn to our cabin to keep me company while I carve. On warmer days, we sit on deck and snack on crackers that the Fox and the Cat pilfer from the galley. The sailors made us a rope swing that I push Quinn on when Harlow isn't occupying it. Two or three evenings a week, Vevina organizes side bets between the sailors over which of them can scale to the crow's nest the fastest.

Jamison spends his days meeting with the captain, delivering assignments and schedules to the crew, overseeing the health and care of the prisoners, and settling disagreements. He returns to our cabin after dark and falls into his bed on the floor.

I searched our cabin again for information about the governor and came up empty. My father's map and my uncle's daisy clock repeatedly bring back to mind why I am on this voyage. I often dream at night about what I will say and do when I confront Markham. Each nightmare ends in bloodshed, either his or mine.

It will be his.

Chapter Nine

Seventy-five days after Jamison and I wed, the weather warms to the point where, so long as I stay in the sunshine, I can go outside without my cloak. Nonetheless, I pull on my red gloves and venture out for a walk with Quinn.

The lass races ahead while I indulge in the briny air and deep-blue waves. Meandering the web of rigging and sails, Quinn and I come upon Dr. Huxley. He draws up short and quickly leaves in the opposite direction. We have not spoken, and I see no reason to break our silence now.

Vevina stands at the helm alongside Captain Dabney. He has been instructing her how to navigate the charts, discern the stars, and operate the marine chronometer. She clutches his arm and he speaks privately in her ear. Vevina has begun to reside in his private quarters, spending most of her time at his side. Since she rarely gives her full attention to one man for long, I suspect she's up to something, though I cannot begin to know what.

I let them alone and follow Quinn to the stern. We come here often to watch the ship's wakes grow farther apart until they are absorbed into the horizon. Quinn brought the wooden figurines I made for her—a cat and a girl. She lies on her front and plays with them.

Cuthbert dallies near the mizzenmast. I don't like how he stares at her, so I shift between them, blocking his view. In another few minutes, he wanders off.

The day is warmer than yesterday. I emerge from my cabin at the same time Vevina leaves the captain's quarters wearing a new gown. This is her third since we left Dorestand, gifts from the captain, I'm sure. We cross the deck together, passing Jamison and two other men arming a cannon with a spear.

"You're going to work that man to death," Vevina remarks.

"I haven't done anything to him."

"The lieutenant is distracting himself. Trying to forget he's married to you may cripple him."

Jamison's limp is more pronounced than usual. He hasn't explained how he got it, and I have not asked. Perhaps he damaged his leg from overworking.

"What are they doing?" I ask.

"Assembling the harpoon. A whale was spotted off our stern this morning. The crew think the Terrible Dorcha is trailing us, so the captain is taking precautions."

The Terrible Dorcha is a monstrous whale notorious for bashing apart ships and swallowing men whole. He's distinguished by his harpoon scars along his back. Seafarers believe that Dorcha hails from the Otherworlds, namely the Land Under the Wave, an entire realm born of water. The Land Under the Wave is said to have pearls as large as a man's head and endless beaches of gold sand. Sea tales, my mother would say, yet my father never dismissed the mariners' stories as lore.

I keep a weather eye on the horizon. According to superstition, Dorcha is sighted the most during tempests. It is said the whale ushers in storms that act as portals to the Land Under the Wave, and he travels the stormy doorways from our world to his. People have attached foolish fears to the whale. Even so, I am glad the sky is cloudless.

Vevina and I join the other women lounging in patches of sunshine. Harlow smokes a pipe she must have stolen from her husband while

Laverick and Claret comfort Quinn, who is crying against the Cat's shoulder.

"What happened?" I ask, sitting beside them.

"Harlow told her about Dorcha," Claret explains.

Vevina tsks at Harlow.

Quinn releases the Cat and clings to me. "I don't want to be at sea. I don't want to go to the Ruined Kingdom. I want to go home."

The women around us hush. I stroke Quinn's hair to distract her from the alarm she has drawn out in the others. "My mother would read *The Legend of Princess Amadara* aloud when I was young. It's not a frightening tale."

Quinn rolls her eyes upward. "Will you tell it to me?"

"I don't think—"

"I'd like to hear it too," Claret says. She shrugs at Laverick's slant-wise glance. "I haven't heard it told from beginning to end in a long while."

"For mercy's sake, it's just a child's tale," says Harlow.

"It's more than that now," replies Vevina.

Several women nod. Everything we know about our future home stems from legend. Many versions of the tale circulate, though none are as comprehensive as the one my mother told. She read the legend from a storybook the queen gave my father from her royal library as a gift for sailing on her behalf. The book was a casualty of the fire that destroyed our home.

The remnants of tears shine in Quinn's eyes. "Please, Everley."

"It's been years since I've heard the story or told it," I hedge.

"Oh, just tell the story," Harlow says. "Anything's better than listening to her cry."

All the women wait for my reply.

"All right," I concede. The tale of the Ruined Kingdom was a nightly favorite in our home. Mother would read from her chair, her corn-silk hair soft around her slim face, her eyes as enchanting as starlight. I think of her engaging voice as I begin. "This is *The Legend of Princess Amadara,* Majesty of the Trees, who felled a kingdom and tore time."

Laverick and Claret lean forward to hear better. Harlow inspects her nails, but her tensed posture gives away her interest. Vevina watches me with her full attention, as do Quinn and the many women around us. I swallow a barb of nerves and tell the story.

"Within the borders of a peaceful kingdom lay a gate to the Everwoods. In this walled grove, the seasons did not change. Princess Amadara, heir to the throne, looked out from her castle balcony at the Everwoods's leafy canopy. The trees towered higher than the tallest castle spire, and it was commonly believed that their crowns of leaves held up the sky."

"Do trees really hold up the sky?" Quinn asks.

"How else do you think the sky stays above us, if not for the trees?" replies Laverick.

Harlow scoffs. I expected her derision, so I push on before she can spoil the story. "One spring day, when the princess was your age"—I tap Quinn's head—"she snuck out of the castle and found a tunnel into the forest. Mortals were forbidden in the Everwoods. Father Time, the forest's guardian, patrolled the grounds for trespassers with his ancient sword, given to him by the Creator herself. He came upon the princess skipping through the ferny undergrowth but did not approach her. The trees welcomed the princess, dropping their branches so she could brush their leaves with her fingertips. Sprites braided her hair, pixies sang her ballads, and gnomes laid flowers at her feet. Father Time watched Amadara until dusk when she returned to the castle."

"Did she get into trouble for leaving home?" Quinn asks.

"The legend doesn't say," I reply. "Though she mustn't have, because thereafter the princess returned to the forest. Before long, her greatest friends were within its locked gates. Amadara was adored by the flowers, whose beauty matched her own, and taught by the wisest trees in the world, the elderwoods. Majesty of Trees, Father Time named the princess, for she spent every spare daylight hour under the forest canopy."

"Sounds wonderful." Claret sighs, and Quinn nods.

"Over the years," I say, "the princess grew from a spirited child to a fair young woman who Father Time fell in love with. He left sweet-scented flowers by her hand and watched as she napped, cradled in the elderwood's great roots."

Claret releases a dreamy exhale. Laverick rests her head against her friend, the two of them propped like bookends.

I used to sit with Isleen the same way back to back, sister to sister.

"Upon waking from a nap one afternoon, the princess blinked up into Father Time's ageless face. Amadara did not fear him or the sword in his possession. She had felt his presence and knew him through the steady beat of her heart. For time was always with her."

"If I woke up to a strange man staring at me, he'd meet the force of my fists," says Harlow.

"Fortunately for us, you aren't telling the story," Vevina answers.

Harlow grumbles something indecipherable but unmistakably spiteful. I talk over her.

"Princess Amadara and Father Time became dear friends. Theirs was a bond as strong and deep as the twisting roots that tied the elderwoods to the land. At the end of each day, when the trees could no longer bear the burden of the sun, the princess lamented over leaving her friends. She wished to always dwell in the Everwoods. She feared the world, and in the forest, with Father Time as her guardian, she felt safe. He told her that could not be. Amadara would leave him someday and not return. She was so dismayed that she resolved to prove him wrong. The princess lingered in the forest after sundown and did not leave the view of the stars that night, nor the next or the next."

"She must have been missed," Quinn says, relaxing against me. "Did anyone search for her?"

"They tried," Laverick answers. "The forest wouldn't let them in and she wouldn't go to them."

"Several decades passed," I say, "and Amadara did not set foot outside the forest. She whittled away the days with Father Time, crafting crowns of daisies and sleeping in the treetops. The princess became so much a part of the woods that she learned its secrets. For hidden in the heart of the ancient elderwood trees beat creation power—*life* power, or the power to breathe life into existence—which nourished the forest, brightened the leaves, suspended the sky, and fed the foliage and fauna. This life-giving magic preserved the princess's youth. Though the days rolled on outside the woodland garden, time was not upon her. Amadara remained as lovely as when she'd last entered the Everwoods."

"Wouldn't that be grand," Vevina drawls. "Immortality *and* beauty."

A few of the women snigger.

"Then one day," I say, "a prince burrowed beneath the forest hedge. He'd heard a princess lived there. The elderwoods left him alone, for he carried a watch that beat time. He didn't go far before he came upon Princess Amadara sitting on a mossy log. The prince gazed upon her and fell in love."

I anticipate Harlow or Vevina will make a jest about love at first sight, but neither speaks.

"Princess Amadara marveled at the prince. She hadn't seen a mortal in ages and had forgotten the warmth of flesh and blood. The prince told Amadara that her family was long dead. She'd been in the forest for a century. In her absence, the prince's father had assumed the throne. Shortly thereafter, the king had passed on, leaving the prince as ruler. Amadara thought she had been gone a short while and desired to see the lapse of time herself. She searched for Father Time but found only his sword. She took it, for she still feared the outside world, and returned to her kingdom with the prince."

"She left without saying goodbye?" Laverick asks.

Vevina winds a curl of her own hair around her finger. "Can't say I blame her. She hadn't seen a man in a century, and the prince must have been handsome."

Laverick crosses her arms over her chest. "What about Father Time?"

"He knew she was going to leave." Harlow waves a hand to dismiss our collective surprise at her contribution. "What? You aren't the only ones listening."

"Harlow's correct," I say. "Father Time foretold that the princess would leave him, so he left the hidden passage from her kingdom to the Everwoods open should she wish to return."

"What happened next?" Quinn asks.

"The prince and princess wed."

"Shouldn't they be king and queen since they're married?" Claret asks.

I sigh, wondering if this is how my mother felt when I interrupted her storytelling. "For the sake of clarity, we'll refer to them as the prince and princess. They were happy together for some time, and then a far-off nation threatened to invade their kingdom. Conflict mounted to a declaration of war. On the eve of battle, the soldiers prepared to meet their enemy. The princess and prince spent a final evening together. The prince promised his return, but in truth, he was afraid of perishing in battle. To comfort him, Amadara confided in the prince that eternal life was hidden in the heart of the ancient elderwoods. She said a messenger would send word if the prince was wounded, and she would ask Father Time for access to this life-saving power."

Harlow sniffs loudly. "Why didn't the princess ask Father Time for help before the prince went to war?"

"Amadara didn't want to pillage the forest unless she had to," Claret replies.

"Both of you shh," Laverick says. "This is the best part."

Harlow and Claret swap glares, and I push on.

"The prince still feared he would die in battle, so he crept from bed while Amadara slept, took up Father Time's sword, and went through the passageway into the Everwoods. He wandered deep into the forest, kneeled before one of the oldest and tallest elderwoods, and drew the sword. The prince did not know the weapon was a holy blade forged from a star. He held the sword of Avelyn, the very weapon the Creator wielded to cut the seven worlds from the heavens. With the hallowed sword, the prince hacked into the elderwood to harvest its heartwood. As the blade pierced the bark, Amadara woke in her bed. Her own chest bled as though her heart was carved from her. She had spent so long in the forest, preserved by its powers, her spirit had entwined with the trees. Father Time heard Princess Amadara's cries and went to her. He drew her into his arms and foresaw that should the elderwood die, so would she. Upon returning to find the princess dead, the prince would fall into despair and their enemy would overcome them."

Quinn holds her breath. The whole of the area is silent except for the wind in the sails.

"As the princess lay dying, Father Time pressed a piece of time into her hand. As gossamer as butterfly wings and as pure as crystal water, he gifted her with the power to halt time and cease her suffering. Princess Amadara understood that she could not change the past, but she could save her prince. In the Everwoods, he was free from time and would remain safe."

Tears drip down Claret's and Laverick's faces. Quinn's eyes fill with sadness.

"When the prince was nearly finished sawing the heartwood from the elderwood, the princess tore the delicate fabric, breaking time in her world. From the protection of the Everwoods, the prince felt the shift into the eternities and looked to his frozen castle."

Quinn covers a soundless gasp, hanging on every word.

"Father Time appeared to the prince and told him of Amadara's fate. The prince raged at him for not coming sooner and lamented the loss of his princess. Father Time said he sprinkled a treasured elderwood seed upon Amadara's head just before she tore time. The seed would grow into a tree and preserve her. Then Father Time banished the prince into a lonely world far away from his kingdom."

"Wait!" says Harlow. "Father Time cast out the prince to another world?"

Vevina beats me to a reply. "The princess was locked in one world and the prince was banished to another."

"Amadara's entire world is frozen?" Quinn asks, dumbstruck. "I thought only her kingdom was trapped in time?"

"It depends on the storyteller," I answer swiftly to dispel confusion. "The version I was told teaches that Amadara's kingdom was in one world and the prince was banished to another. The Everwoods is the bridge that links the Otherworlds together."

Vevina bows her head in accord. Before they can ask more questions, I return to the tale.

"Branches swept the prince from the Everwoods and locked him out. Then, so he could not find the gate, Father Time cursed the island where the prince was deserted. Trees sprouted noxious thorns that impaled his arms, and terrible vines wrapped around his throat. He dropped the sword of Avelyn, which he was holding when he was banished, and lost it in the dire forest. The prince barely escaped, and when he looked back, a labyrinth of thorns stood between him and the gate to the Everwoods." My voice lowers and softens. "The princess remains locked in time, preserved by a sacred elderwood tree, and the lost prince still wanders, striving to find a way back to his bride."

Quinn sniffles, Claret and Laverick dry their tears, and Harlow keeps her head down.

"That's a deplorable ending," Vevina says, unmoved. "The prince betrayed the princess."

"He loved her," Laverick counters. "He didn't mean to hurt her. He didn't know she was connected to the elderwoods."

"Do you think the lost prince is still looking for a way back to Amadara?" Quinn asks.

Harlow's chin snaps up. "If he is, he's wasting his time. They had their chance, and it ended in tragedy."

"That's because he nearly killed her," Claret says, as if Harlow is dense.

"He was punished for his mistake," Harlow argues. "He lost everything, while the princess sleeps away—"

"Sleeps?" Claret says. "She's entombed in a tree!"

"Which is her fault," Harlow counters. "If Amadara loved the prince, she would have protected him."

"Father Time is the true hero," Vevina declares. "He loved the princess even after he foresaw that she would leave him. He loved Amadara despite her marrying another. Even after she betrayed the forests' secrets, he stopped her death."

They are all correct. The princess and prince both erred, and Father Time's solution made everything worse. If the legend is to be believed, Amadara is locked in her eternal sacrifice, waiting for her prince to find a way back to their world and wake her, which will restart time. The ending is unfinished, so it spurs much debate.

Quinn settles her head on my lap. "If Dagger Island is the cursed isle in the story, then what's to become of us and the queen's colony?"

In those simple words, fact and fiction collide. I do not doubt the far-off island is untamed, but not for the reasons the tale would have us believe. Dagger Island is not hiding a gate to an enchanted forest that serves as a bridge to the Otherworlds. A princess was not entombed by a magical tree and left for a prince to save her. We are voyaging to a penal colony ruled by Governor Markham, where we will toil tirelessly to build a settlement and expand the queen's rulership.

"We won't disturb the secrets of the island," I say, feigning a smile. "And when our sentences are complete, we will return home."

"I like that ending the very best," Quinn says, nuzzling her head against my lap, her lips lifted dreamily.

Chapter Ten

I wake before dawn and tiptoe out of the cabin. The wind has grown fangs, a biting chill that rakes across my skin. I tug on my gloves and hunker into my cloak. A tender red sky stains the eastern horizon. The deck is clear and the hatch open. I climb below, passing the women slumbering in their hammocks, and enter the galley. A cook prepares breakfast at the fire hearth. The huge iron stove is lit, smoke traveling up a chimney to the weather deck.

"May I have hot water for washing, please?" I ask. The cook grunts and pours boiling water into a pail. "When may I return for breakfast?"

"Half hour," he says, stirring the wet oats.

Hefting the pail, I retrace my steps up the ladder and onto the main deck. Cuthbert blocks my path. I stop short, catching the pail before it spills.

"Where are you going, lass?" He taps closer to me on his pegged leg. "Has the lieutenant made a woman out of you yet?"

I try to go around him, but he blocks me. I raise the pail of scalding water between us. "Come any closer and I'll toss this on you."

"You ain't worth the hassle," Cuthbert answers. "Too old for my taste."

"Go near Quinn and I'll cut you wide open." The threat slips off my tongue, as fervent as a prayer.

"With what? You ain't got a blade."

"I didn't say I'd use something sharp."

A sailor descends from the aftercastle from serving as lookout and lands on deck not two strides away. "It's your shift now, Cuthbert," he says.

I march around them and return to my cabin. The abrupt loss of light momentarily dazes me. I set the pail down and hit Jamison's boots sitting by the door. Water sloshes over the rim and onto my trousers.

"Creator's bones," I curse.

Jamison bolts upright from his bed on the floor. "What's wrong?" He lights the lantern and sees the water spilled down my front. Humor brightens his eyes. "People generally bathe in the nude."

"The wash water is for you." I blot the wet stains with my cloak while he stares at me incredulously. "Well? Are you going to get up and wash or sit there?"

He sits in the chair near the pail. I toss him a washcloth and a bar of soap. His feet are bare and his breeches have ridden up to his knees. Above the hem of his pants, his right knee is mangled, as though the kneecap was twisted off and put back on crooked. I glance away, thinking of my own hidden scars.

"Take your time," I say. "I'll return with breakfast."

"Everley, why . . . ?"

I loathe our marriage, but he need not work himself to death to avoid me. Jamison is not the man I wish to see suffer. "Don't misconstrue my meaning. This is a peace offering. Nothing more."

He nods slowly and then strips off his shirt. Flushed by the sight of his bare chest, I hurry out.

On the morning of the following day, we make port in a cove off a craggy coastline. Jamison, Captain Dabney, and several crewmen prepare to row to shore for supplies.

As their skiff lowers into the water, I grip the rail, my gloves warming my hands. Quinn plays with her figurines behind me. The port town in Galway, an ally realm to Wyeth, is smaller than Dorestand, yet the sight of civilization after months of water in every direction is heartening.

Most of the sailors remain aboard to oversee the prisoners, though it's not in anyone's mind to jump overboard and swim for land. While the anchor was lowered, several crewmen pointed out sharks prowling in the depths below.

Another creature surfaces near the hull. A dolphin, its silver back shiny in the sun.

"Quinn, come see," I say.

She is no longer behind me. Where in the seven worlds did she go? I climb to Vevina sunning herself on the gangway. "Have you seen Quinn?"

Vevina squints into the sun. "Not recently. Ask Claret and Laverick."

The Fox and Cat are playing cards against Harlow on the lee side of the ship. Between them are piles of hardtack they snuck from the galley. Come to think of it, they must have stolen the cards as well. Quinn isn't with them.

An unsettling feeling presses upon me. I cannot remember all the crewmembers who went to shore. I rush into the circle of card players, crushing hardtack underfoot.

"Watch it," Harlow says. "That's my betting pile."

"Where's Cuthbert?" I ask.

"Why should I care?"

"Did he row ashore?" I crouch over Harlow. "Answer me!"

"Everley, what's wrong?" Claret asks.

"I can't find Quinn."

"Check belowdecks," Harlow answers, "and get out of our way."

"Look on the gun deck," Claret adds. "Sometimes she goes down to pet the animals."

I descend the ladder, hopping down the last two rungs. Everywhere I search, crewmen scowl at me. No one has seen Quinn, so I sneak down another ladder to the gun deck. A long row of cannons occupies both sides of the ship. Crates of ducks and doves are stacked in the center of the deck near the pens for the livestock. Sheep bleat at me, and a few goats turn their heads to view their intruder. I am the only person here.

Quicker now, I return to the main deck and check the bow, Quinn's and my favorite place to watch the sea, and search between the masts.

As I approach the forecastle, Cuthbert's wide back comes into view. He has pinned someone against the rail. By comparison, Quinn is so small I almost miss seeing her.

My heart clock stalls a second in fear, sending a burst of pain to my fingers. *Be machine,* I tell myself. I grip down on my courage and charge.

Cuthbert hears my footfalls and spins. I slam my elbow into his face. He stumbles sideways, grabbing his bloody nose.

"Run, Quinn!" I shout.

She scoots past him and darts away.

"You shifty wretch," Cuthbert snarls.

His pistol is tucked in the waist of his trousers and his cutlass is sheathed. I try to run, but he swings out with his fist and hammers me in the middle. I fall on my side, wheezing. Cuthbert throws me on my back. My ears ring a high-pitched whine. He straddles my waist, crushing my regulator, and bends over me. He halts and gapes at my front.

"What in the stars?" he asks.

My shirt and waistcoat shifted, exposing my ticker. I grab his pistol from his waist and swing up, whacking him under the chin. Cuthbert's jaw emits a sickening crunch and he slants over. I roll out from under him and rise, straightening my shirt and waistcoat.

He saw my ticker, my mind screams.

Stay calm. He doesn't know what he saw.

Cuthbert clambers to his feet and draws his cutlass. Horror vibrates from his tensed muscles. "What—what are you?"

I aim the pistol at him. I have never shot a firearm, but the process seems self-explanatory.

Cuthbert smirks. "You have to cock the hammer."

I have no idea how to do that, so I hurl the pistol at him. Cuthbert ducks and the pistol spins overboard. I move inside his striking range and bash his arm against the rail at a painful angle. He drops his cutlass and I pick it up. My fingertips tingle on the cutlass hilt and my clock heart swings further off beat. No warning rings from my regulator.

"I told you to leave Quinn alone," I say.

Blood flows from his nose down over his sneer. "When I tell the captain about that thing in your chest, he'll hang you from the boom."

Claret, Laverick, and Quinn charge up beside us. While I'm distracted by them, Cuthbert lunges for his blade in my hand. His peg leg stumbles over a lip between two planks and he trips forward into me. He jerks to a halt. I stare down at the cutlass embedded in his soft belly. Blood seeps around the hilt, bright-red spots dripping onto the deck.

Laverick pulls Quinn against her to cover her face. I yank out the blade and the light in Cuthbert's eyes fades. He teeters backward, bumps into the rail, and topples over the edge. A splash sounds, washing sense over me. I drop the cutlass on the deck and wipe my bloody gloves across my waistcoat.

Two crewmen bound up to find us prisoners gaping at the rail. A sailor peers over the edge. He blanches and turns on me, the only one smeared in blood.

"Restrain her," he says.

Rough hands haul me across the deck. I hang my head and pretend not to notice the stares of the other inmates. A sailor manacles my wrists in front of me and shoves me inside my cabin. I stumble to the floor, landing on my knees, and he slams the door.

Too weak to get up, I lean my back against the wall. Cuthbert's blood has stained my mother's gloves. The red spots are drying and darkening to dingy brown. The smell of it, of him, ferments inside me. I vomit into the closest vessel—Jamison's dress boots by the door. He intended to wear them to shore with his uniform but changed his mind. I retch into them until I am empty, then curl up on my side.

Cuthbert tripped into the blade. The moment was unavoidable, as though we were shoved together by fate. Some people will deem his death bad luck, while others will blame me. Accident or not, Cuthbert was slain by my hand. No one knows he saw my clock heart, and I'm not sorry he won't get the chance to expose me. I'm not sorry he won't terrorize Quinn again. I'm not sorry his time living is finished.

But I am very sorry that I will always carry the mark of his death on my soul.

I wait hours for someone to release me. The supply party must have returned from the mainland, because I felt the ship turn out to sea a while ago. Captain Dabney and Jamison must be discussing my punishment. Every time I shut my eyes, I imagine myself strung up from a boom.

I was wrong to get close to Quinn. My fondness for her divided my attention between her best interest and my own. I cannot tether myself to her or anyone else. Finding Markham will require the entirety of my commitment. No strings can tie me down.

The door latch jiggles. Jamison enters, his footfalls heavy and slow. He's wearing his blue uniform, the one I hate. His gaze roams to his vomit-heavy boots and then me, ending on my bloodstained waistcoat.

"Did he hurt you?"

"No." My bruises will heal. I cannot say the same for my regulator. My bindings have prevented me from inspecting the damage. "How's Quinn?"

"Shaken. Claret and Laverick are with her."

"And Cuthbert?" I ask more quietly.

"The current carried his body out to sea."

Jamison trudges to his boots. No flicker of disgust or anger passes over him. He picks them up and sets them outside the door, and then returns to unlock my manacles. I pull at my wool gloves, but the blood soaked through the seams and stuck to my hands. I tug harder, nauseated all over again. Jamison covers my hands with his and removes my gloves finger by finger. Dried blood crusts the grooves of my skin. He wets the cuff of his sleeve with the water from the fishbowl.

"Cleon won't mind," he says and washes the blood away.

"I'm sorry about your boots."

"Don't give them another thought." His voice takes on a more serious tone. "Quinn, Laverick, and Claret told the captain that Cuthbert tripped into the blade."

I peel my dry tongue off the roof of my mouth. "He cornered Quinn. I couldn't let him hurt her."

"Even before the witnesses explained, I assumed it was an accident. You should have reported Cuthbert to the crew and let them handle him."

"I know that now."

Jamison washes my last dirty finger. "Three eyewitnesses are difficult to disregard. The captain and I agree that without a magistrate to try you in court, your transportation sentence stands. The captain has ordered that you remain in our cabin for the duration of the voyage and receive no visitors. You're too precious to the future of the queen's colony to execute."

"Lucky me," I mutter. "I'm of childbearing age."

I wait for his condemnation, but he's finished. Maybe he really does believe I was justified in my self-defense. Then why do I feel so filthy? As though I am stained with more than blood?

The moment Cuthbert's spirit fled his body, a light went out of him. The same light disappeared from my mother and father. One second they were full of verve, warm and animated, eternal stars. The next they were empty and lackluster, light shattered.

My uncle's warning returns to me stronger. *Could you become a monster to destroy one?* He was not asking whether I had the gumption to end Markham. He was warning me about the cost of violating Madrona's will by taking a life.

"Everley," Jamison says, and I blink myself back into focus. "I have something for you."

He kneels and roots around under the bed. After some time, he withdraws a long, skinny object wrapped in cloth. Resting it on the mattress, he opens the package.

"My sword," I breathe.

He lifts the weapon and inspects the wide, thin blade. "After your outburst in court, I had it brought on board." He lays my sword across my lap. "I asked for your honesty and gave you no safe place to heed my request. My company doesn't bring you comfort, but this might."

I hesitate to pick up my sword. Its return feels counterintuitive, a strange reward for stabbing a man.

"You aren't a villain," Jamison says softly. "I've watched you these many weeks. You have a good heart."

He should work on his judge of character, yet his trust in me is too great a gift to deny. I grasp the hilt and raise the blade. "Thank you." I anchor my gaze on his to drill in my sincerity.

"I'm merely returning what's yours, though I would appreciate your discretion. The captain may not take kindly to my arming a prisoner, even if she is my wife."

Jamison leans in and I arch away. He stills and then more cautiously reaches for my stained gloves. "I'll see what I can do about these."

He departs in the same manner in which he came, his footsteps weighted. I wait for the door to latch, then strip off my waistcoat and lift my shirt. The copper filaments of my regulator are still attached to my ticker, but the box is cracked and smashed at the corners. The bells move around loosely. I tip it sideways and they fall in my lap.

Damn you, Cuthbert.

I remove the broken regulator and detach the filaments from my heart. As I pocket the bells, the second hand of my clock booms, tick, then tock. The push and pull of time shoves me onward regardless of what I want, what I need.

This was not a day for forward progress. Some days push us ahead into better times, while others pull us back so far nothing can reverse the damage. Those are the days that redefine our future for the worst. Those are the days where I despise time the most.

Chapter Eleven

A sharp tilt draws my focus from the book. I've been lying across the bed and reading for an hour. While confined to the cabin, I fill my time carving wooden figures, studying my father's map of the island, shining the blade of my sword, and reading Jamison's collection of texts. Anything to occupy my mind and avoid idle time.

Cleon's water sloshes over the brim of his fishbowl. As I place a book over the top to stop more from spilling, a larger sway throws me into the shelves and tips over the daisy clock. I push it farther back on the shelf and block it in with books. The rowdy rocking mounted suddenly. In less than an hour, the sea has morphed from a gentle hand to a crushing fist. I teeter across the cabin to open the door.

I'm knocked this way and that by screaming winds, and heavy rain pelts me. Damp and breathless, I lean into the door and close it. The swells knock books off the shelves and open and shut drawers. I stumble to the bed and grab my sword, as though I could battle the wailing storm. For most of our voyage, I have avoided thinking about being surrounded by water. Now, a day's journey from our destination, the sea underscores my fragility.

Jamison throws open the door and enters with a visitor. Quinn peeks out from under a quilt draped over her. She runs to me and leaps onto the bed. I let her in, wet feet and all, and Jamison shoves against the door, shutting out the storm. His coat and hat drip salt water, and his damp hair is plastered to his forehead. His eyes stand out against his pale complexion.

"She was afraid, so I said she could stay with you," he explains. "I'll return when I can."

"You're going back out there?" I ask.

"The storm is driving us off course. We're too close to a reef and could run aground. You'll be safe here."

He wrings out his hat and reenters the tempest. The sea pitches the vessel sideways, and Quinn and I press our backs against the wall. She is close, but the noise of the storm drowns out my ticker. The lass fingers the hilt of my sword, her eyes round.

"It was my father's," I explain. "He found it while he was on a walk one day."

A crash of thunder rattles the ship. Quinn burrows in the blankets.

My sword isn't the distraction I hoped for, so I pull the blankets back. "How about a story?"

I pick up the book I was reading before the storm hit, the family heirloom Jamison inherited from his mother. As I resettle beside Quinn, my mind drifts again to my own mother. She had a special chair in our hearth room. Tavis and I would sit across from her on the settee, and Isleen occupied the stool near the fire so she could see her needlepoint work. Carlin knelt at Mother's feet and she stroked his hair. He was a pest for affection.

"Have you heard the *Creation Story*?" I ask.

"Mama said we could get into trouble for speaking about Madrona."

"You should always listen to your mama, but this is a short, happy tale. I'm certain you'll enjoy it."

Madrona has been on my mind since Cuthbert's death, and I wonder whether I will be cursed with bad luck for his accidental demise. I've read this story so many times, I almost have it memorized. I open the book to the marked page and start to read. "In the beginning, Eiocha the Creator, the goddess of conception and ruler of the eternities, crafted a world unlike any other. Volcanoes of lava, fallow deserts, and undefined valleys covered the whole of the newborn world. The Creator called it the Land of the Living, the birthplace of all life."

"Is our world the Land of the Living?" Quinn asks.

"It is," I reply, pleased that she's listening despite the heaving ship. "The Land of the Living is one of the seven worlds. The others are: the Land of Youth, the Land of Promise, the Other Land, the Silver-Clouded Plain, the Land Under the Wave, and the Plain of Delight."

"I like ours best."

"Me too." I lift the book between us and continue. "Into the quiet oblivion, Eiocha sent a trickle of water from the heavens. The stream flowed into a torrent that flooded the arid lands. Within a patch of the suckled soil, Eiocha planted a seed, and from the land a sapling grew. The Creator called her Madrona, Mother of All, and charged Father Time to oversee the seedling. Eiocha gave him a blade forged from a star to guard Madrona, for within the sapling's heartwood beat creation power."

Quinn stares at the page, but does not follow along, most likely because she cannot read. Nevertheless, she is involved, the tempest a far-off worry.

"Madrona grew into a mighty elderwood, Eiocha's strongest, most powerful creation. The tree shed acorns that sprouted into a forest of seedlings. Soon she was surrounded by a conclave of elderwoods that brought forth other plant life and creatures. Eiocha called her garden the Everwoods and set it apart from the Land of the Living, consecrating the hallowed ground as the bridge between the seven worlds. The Everwoods flourished, and from creation power, all mortal life was fostered. Though mankind may not enter the Everwoods, Madrona's face can be seen in the sunrise and her voice can be heard in a newborn's cry. It is said that if one holds an acorn to their ear, they can hear the call of life, as vibrant and joyful as a rainbow."

"What does the call of life sound like?" Quinn asks.

"My mother said it is anything that makes us grateful we are alive. It's a feeling in one's heart when we see or hear or taste something wondrous and breathtaking."

"Like when a cloud passes on a breeze?"

"Or waves tugging at the shoreline, or a full moon on a summer's night." My voice trails off, my insides aching fiercely.

Quinn stares at the page, her forehead creased. "The priest from the Progressive Ministry said we're only to worship Eiocha. He cast the spirit of Madrona out of us by washing our heads with lily water."

"Beliefs make us strong and give us purpose, regardless of what they are."

"What do you believe?"

"I believe you should rest," I say, tucking her in. I cannot offer Quinn assurances about the welfare of her spirit while the fate of my own is uncertain.

Our silence amplifies the tempest's howls and the savage pitching of the ship. We hang on to each other as the storm rampages. Exhaustion eventually wears Quinn down and she slackens into sleep. After tucking pillows around her to stop the swaying ship from throwing her off the bed, I sit at the edge and wait for the storm to stomp away or for Jamison to return.

The door barrels open, and a drenched sailor lets in cold gusts. "Sorry to disturb you, Lady Callahan. The mainsail has broken away from the ropes. We need all hands on deck to tie it down before we blow off course."

"I'm coming."

I tie on my cloak so my front is layered several times and slip into my boots. Quinn is still asleep as I step out.

Rainy gales lash at me, soaking my back and head in seconds. The thick wool at my front protects my clock heart. I follow the crewman through rushing waves that flow out again, emptying through the scuttles. We grip anything we can for security. The chill of the driving tempest numbs my bare fingers. I long for my gloves.

Shadows slide across the ship from the lanterns swinging wildly. Captain Dabney mans the helm on the quarterdeck, navigating our path through the starless night. Without my uncle's chronometer, we would surely be lost.

Ahead, men and women are tugging at a snared sail. Orders are shouted from above, half-eaten by the wind. I peer up the main mast into the deluge. Dangling in the lines, high above near the yardarm, Jamison works to tie down the mainsail.

The canvas snaps and strikes the workers. I grab a rope slithering about and hang on. The blasting cold winds are blistering. Crewmen untangle the mass of ropes, wary of the swinging boom. We each stretch out the rigging shrouds to prevent further knots.

Jamison loses his grasp and slips down the mast. He grabs the yard-arm and pulls himself back up to the high corner of the mainsail. He ties it down, his progress slow. The abrasive rope drags through my palms. At last, when the rope has nearly burned from my grasp, he finishes.

"Release!" he yells.

We all let go. The rigging snaps straight, locking the sail in place. Though my hands and feet are numb, my clock heart beats on task. Soaked from the knees down, I stumble across the slick deck for the cabin. A wave surges over the rail, catching my legs and sweeping me sideways. Someone grabs me before I hit the gunwale.

Jamison has hold of my forearm. We skid across the planking, steadying each other. Passengers flee the racing waves to the decks below.

"Dorcha!" the captain shouts from the helm.

Jamison and I halt near the rail. A great gray hump has risen in the choppy sea—swimming right for us. We brace against each other as the whale collides with our hull. The ship creaks and howls as the monstrous whale rams us again.

Sailors clamber to arm the harpoon cannon with a dry powder sack, an almost impossible task in the storm. Water drips down my front as the ship pitches portside. Jamison holds on to a line. I slip from his grasp and ride the downslope, hitting the end of the deck and hugging the rail. The mega whale thrashes beneath me. Dorcha is almost as long as the ship and half as wide. Except for his ugly white scars from harpoon wounds, he is as gray as the sea.

A series of sweeping waves rights the ship. I find my footing while Jamison and others fire their flintlock pistols at the monster. The Terrible Dorcha swipes its tail, sending a monumental splash over the sailors and throwing them down. The cannon crew aims the harpoon at our assailant. They stock the cannon barrel with a spear, light the fuse—and fire.

I cover my ears to the blast. The spear impales the whale's side, a shallow strike. Dorcha groans and rolls free of the harpoon. The cannon crew reloads, but Dorcha dives and disappears under the waves.

Jamison lurches across the deck to me. I duck behind him as a wall of water crashes over us. My front comes away damp, my back drenched. The cannon crew finish reloading the harpoon and watch for Dorcha's return.

Even more speedily than the tempest came, the gales and swells level. The captain faithfully guides his battered ship to safety. We climb out of the storm, and the clouds part to a glittering midnight reigned by a pearl moon.

If I were superstitious, I might blame Dorcha for the vicious squall.

Everyone but the cannon crew and captain clear the deck. Jamison and I shut ourselves inside our cabin. I lean against the wall, winded and shivering. He strips off my cloak. He lost his hat, his hair strewn wildly about his cross face.

"Of all the asinine things," he says.

"You needed help."

"Help be damned. You were nearly swept away!"

"Shh." I cast a glance at Quinn sleeping.

He took the only layer that he could off me without risking my modesty, so he proceeds to undress himself. Closing my eyes, I listen to my heart ticking sharply inside my skull. I reopen them and discover he's shirtless.

"Is Dorcha gone?" I ask, teeth chattering.

"For now. Good sin, you're frozen." Jamison drapes a quilt over my shoulders and rubs my arms briskly. I cover my chest with my arms, protecting my heart, and lean into his warmth. I stay against him as my shivers decline and the numbness relents. Though he touches me little, his warmth awakens the sensation of his nearness.

"You aren't like him."

Jamison's fingers tense. I assumed he was like Markham, but Jamison is not a monster.

"I don't know who hurt you, but you don't have to relive it." He bends down, compelling me to heed his gaze. "After my mother passed away, my father drank night and day. The whisky helped him forget his sorrow, but it also loosened his temper. The last time he beat me, he tore through my knee with a riding crop. I tolerated his anger for the good of Tarah, but after he damaged my knee, I couldn't stay. I enlisted in the navy as soon as I was recovered enough to walk out. Sometimes when my knee aches, the memories of that time return, so I think of something else."

"What do you think of?"

"Daisies. My mother picked them and put them in vases around our home." Jamison strokes my arms. "What do you think of when you want to forget?"

He expects that I will peel away another layer of distance between us, but I have already given him more of myself than I can bear.

"I don't think of anything," I say, breaking the chain of his arms.

He watches me in confusion as I shift away and then extends his gentle voice to me. "Who hurt you, Everley?"

He waits for my answer, my *honest* answer. I could regale him with the story of my past and deepen his sympathy, unload my secrets and let myself be seen. Even though I sense he sincerely wants to know, I won't tell him. He may not be a monster, but he still works for one.

"Good night, Jamison."

He mashes his lips together. As I turn down the lantern and slip into bed beside Quinn, Jamison does not move. A long moment later, he releases a profound sigh and lies down on the floor. I tunnel in the blankets and stare at the ceiling, my mind ripe for nightmares.

On the morrow, we will set foot on Dagger Island.

Chapter Twelve

Fog floats like a ghost over the placid sea. After last night's storm, I do not trust the eerie quiet. We are sailing headlong into a forsaken world.

Not long ago, around midday, a sailor knocked on my door to say the captain permitted me to come out. I hurried into the fog for a glimpse of the island.

The women line the prow, Quinn pressed between Claret and Laverick. I stay back near Harlow. I would apologize for her husband's death, but she abhorred the man and any admission of guilt would encourage her to nettle me more.

Captain Dabney guides the ship through the ominous haze. Silence grips every person aboard as the *Lady Regina* cuts through the mist. The first view of Dagger Island materializes, a slice of green amid a canvas of gray. The island has three distinct sides much like the tip of a blade. That was, in fact, what inspired my father to name the isle after a dagger. The pointy northern shore is stony and lacks vegetation. The rocky terrain gives way to a midland of dense forests and two mountain ranges that run parallel to each other. On the western leeward corner, a large cove is notched into the coastline. We cruise into the clear-watered bay under a cloud-washed sky, and in the center of the crescent beach, pillars of smoke rise from the settlement. A flag of the realm flies, visible from offshore. Snatches of the western mountains peek through the low-moving clouds, their hundreds of ridges like the spine of a sleeping sea monster.

The *Cadeyrn of the Seas*, the flagship vessel of the queen's first fleet, is anchored in the inlet. I step forward for a better view of Markham's ship, and Vevina spots me. She smiles in greeting. Quinn told me before she left the cabin this morning that the women agree Cuthbert's death was an accident. Still, as far as I am aware, I am the only prisoner aboard who has taken a life.

The crew hustles to lower the sails and drop anchor. Their shouts outrival the cawing seagulls overhead. Settlers ashore run out of their tents and wave. We are too far away to spot Markham among them.

Jamison descends from the upper deck in his gray uniform. He oiled his wavy hair and tied it at the nape of his neck. His clean-shaven jawline is accentuated by short whiskers below his ears, sideburns that add a refined polish to his straight carriage. Should he always look this dapper, it would be impossible to forget he's an earl, not just a lieutenant.

"Someone vandalized my blue jacket," he says. "I put it on this morning and the buttons were missing. I found this in my breast pocket." He holds up the bell from my broken regulator.

"I wonder how that got there."

The corners of his mouth twitch. "If you prefer that I not wear the blue jacket, you need only say so."

"Wear what you like, Lieutenant."

He tips his head back dubiously. "The captain will stay to direct the offloading. I'm rowing ashore to greet the commander. You and Quinn will come with me."

Crewmen carry the longboats to the starboard side and suspend them over the bay. Jamison climbs in first and then assists Quinn and me. A dozen members of the crew get in, and then we are lowered into the water. Jamison sits at the prow while four sailors man the oars and row us to land. I grip the bench, blisters building along my palms. The summertime water is vivid aqua, so clear I spot fish in the shallows.

Crouched up to the pebble beach dabbed with sand, tents and log cabins compose the settlement. Between the tents and forest are crop fields for tobacco, wheat, flax, corn, and more. Jamison jumps into the shallows and pulls the boat to the shoreline. While he lifts Quinn out, I jump into the low surf, cold water up to my shins.

"I would have carried you," he says.

"I have legs too." I disliked my uncle coddling my clock heart. Jamison might feel the same way about his bad knee, but he really shouldn't be hefting me around.

We slosh to shore. More longboats full of people row from the ship across the cove. The second my feet meet dry land, my heart gives a kick. I press down on my sternum until the pulsation abates. Markham is not among the soldiers and convicts in our greeting party. The shaggy-haired prisoners wear plain work clothes versus the soldiers' uniforms, guns, and swords. Their gazes rake over me. I feel sectioned apart, like an apple sliced up for consumption.

Jamison shakes hands with an officer. "Commander Flynn, this is my wife, Lady Callahan."

"A pleasure," he says. The young commander, perhaps in his mid-twenties, wears a bushy beard. "I was concerned the storm would drive you off course. We were hit hard by the winds. Half our livestock were set free from their pens. Governor Markham took a crew inland to find them."

A knot between my shoulders unwinds. Markham isn't in camp. I'm both grateful for the time to assess my surroundings and irritated that I must wait to see him.

I wipe away perspiration along my brow. The summer day swelters, the air thick and sticky. Misshapen tents keel partway over, and broken branches litter the beach. Even before the storm, I cannot imagine this settlement was an accomplishment. Less than a handful of the shelters are cabins, and of those, only the largest appears habitable. The outpost lacks signs of intended permanency. Even by minimal parameters, after ten years under the rule of Wyeth and two years under occupancy, it's a threadbare conquest.

"Do the convicts roam free?" Jamison asks.

"The Thornwoods are the only place to run to, and no one is that daft or desperate," says Commander Flynn. "We reserved your lodging near the women's end of camp. What of the lass, Lieutenant?"

"She's to serve as the governor's maid," Jamison replies, motioning at Quinn drawing in the sand. "For the time being, she'll stay with my wife and me."

The commander guides us into camp, pointing out the latrine, the cookery, and the dining tent. Sheep, goats, and pigs are penned near a grassy opening in the woods while chickens mill about pecking at sand fleas. Pails for collecting drinking water are set out along a stream that flows from the forest and empties into the inlet. We enter the main encampment, and the stench of unwashed flesh nearly sends me back to the beach. At the far end of the tents, trees have been sheared down and the logs chopped into woodpiles. The standing evergreens are tall, taller than my uncle's two-story shop. Nothing has been built in the clearing, nor are tents pitched.

"Why haven't you occupied the cleared land?" I ask.

"We don't linger near to the Thornwoods." Commander Flynn stops at the last canvas tent before the clearing. The interior has a carpeted floor, two cots, and a small vestibule. "This is yours. Dinner will be served soon."

Quinn goes inside to test the comfort of the cots. The commander pulls Jamison aside and they speak in low voices. Jamison nods grimly and they part ways.

"What did he say?" I ask.

"Men have been going missing. Strange beasts have been sighted in the trees, otherworldly creatures." Jamison shakes his head, dismissing the report as outrageous. My fingers twitch at my hip where my sword should be. Unexplained sightings or not, I want my weapon. "Neither you nor Quinn should go near the forest until I know more. I need to return to the ship for our belongings."

Quinn runs out of the tent. "Everley, may we look around?"

"You should stay here until I come back," says Jamison.

"We'll be careful," I reply. After the incident with Cuthbert, I promised myself I would keep my distance from Quinn, but our walk is the excuse I need to scout out the camp.

We wind through the women convicts who have arrived and are settling into their tents. Several of them squabble over who will bunk with whom. Vevina has secured a tent for her, the Fox, and the Cat. She twiddles her fingers at Quinn and ducks inside.

Quinn and I go around camp to the beach. From there, I can see directly into a large tent. Dr. Huxley is inside tending to men lying on mats. That must be the infirmary. I spot a shirtless man with gore wounds in his back and I pull Quinn along. Something else could have caused his wounds, not necessarily an animal, yet I am more on guard about our whereabouts. The male convicts give us a wide berth, and any attention they do give us is immediately discouraged by one of several armed soldiers on guard.

We toss rocks into the sea and then stroll on toward a solitary cabin flying our homeland flag. As it is the finest lodging here, I have no doubt it is Governor Markham's residence.

A meal bell rings near the center of the settlement.

"That's dinner," Quinn says, pulling me back toward the dining tent. When the wind blows our direction, I smell vegetable mash.

As we return to the main encampment, we pass a cemetery marked off by driftwood. The rock headstones are numbered by the dozen. My father warned the queen that settling Dagger Island would have a cost, yet she still sent these people and delegated Markham as their protector.

The queen was wrong, but what she knows of the isle came from Markham. These people's deaths, and any more to come, are on him.

Shouts of the governor's arrival spread across camp and find us at the dining tent. Soldiers abandon their plates of food and leave to meet the party of men exiting the trees. The extra men help to herd the recovered livestock back into their pens.

I swallow my final bite of the bland vegetable mash. Even from afar, I can identify Markham. His overconfident gait and pompous smile are unforgettable.

Jamison has returned from the ship and finished moving our belongings to our tent. He redirects himself from joining Quinn and me for dinner to greet the governor. They shake hands, and then Jamison draws Markham's attention to us at the dining tent.

I push aside my plate. "Let's go meet the governor, Quinn."

She grabs her crust of bread and scurries after me. I set my shoulders and fortify my heart as I do when approaching an opponent in the trench. My ticker obeys, thrumming excitedly. Finally, it is time to meet our monster. We stride right up to the men.

"Sir," says Jamison, "this is Lady Callahan."

I don a smile, my heart thudding a battle march.

Markham bows. He looks the same as a decade ago. *How has he not aged?* "Lady Callahan, you've a fine husband."

Sweet words from poisonous lips.

I double the width of my smile. Markham reveals no sign of recognition. The conceited bastard must not remember me from the clock shop. Oh, but I will be of importance soon.

"Lieutenant, did we run out of frocks for the women?" Markham asks, studying my masculine attire.

Jamison glances from me to the governor, stumbling for an excuse that does not label me as overly particular. "She, ah . . . we—"

"None of the dresses were to my taste," I say.

Governor Markham answers with a "hmm" and bends over Quinn. I squelch the urge to disarm Jamison of his pistol and knock Markham over the head with it. "Is this the lass you told me about?"

Quinn stares up at him, her little chin out.

"This is your serving girl," Jamison explains. "As I said before, Cuthbert didn't harm her, thanks to my wife." He's generous to defend me, but if he calls me his "wife" one more time, I may boot him.

Markham nicks Quinn's chin with a friendly scrape of his knuckles. "You're stronger for it, aren't you?" He bestows her with a dazzling smile, and a blush blossoms in her cheeks. "You and I will get along well, lass."

His closeness to her person unnerves me. "Please excuse us, sir, I must put Quinn to bed." Without waiting for permission, I take her by the hand and lead her away.

"The governor is fetching, isn't he?" Quinn asks.

"He's not to my taste."

That did not go as I hoped. I wanted to radiate flinty detachment. Instead, I hardly managed not to scream. I glance over my shoulder at them. Markham and Jamison have gone on to the dining tent. It's infuriating that Markham has no recollection of me, but this could give me an advantage. No one anticipates the danger they do not see.

Back inside our tent, Jamison left clothes for us and stashed my sword under a cot. While I help Quinn change into her nightgown and slide into bed, she asks me to recount the origin story of the sword of Avelyn. I've no tolerance for storytelling right now, but it's a short tale, so I appease her.

"Before the worlds came into existence, the heavens were dominated by thousands of stars. Two of the biggest and brightest stars wanted to prove they were the greatest light in all the heavens, so they agreed to race each other. Whichever could fly the farthest would own the sky. The stars took off, streaming as fast as they could. They were so fixated on how far they had flown, they weren't paying attention to their direction and the stars collided. Upon impact, one of them splintered into a million pieces. The second star broke apart, shedding its tines until only the sharpest, strongest prong remained. Eiocha plucked that new blade from the sky and, with it, cut the seven worlds from the cloth of the eternities."

"Eiocha was brave to touch a star," Quinn says, yawning.

"As the Creator, she was made to wield them. Now it's time to go to sleep."

I tuck Quinn in and leave her to sit on the opposite cot. As the sun dips behind the treetops, exhaustion overcomes her. I sit and listen to the animal noises in the forest, insects buzzing and owls hooting. None of them sound otherworldly.

Jamison enters and sinks down beside me on the cot. He stretches out his sore leg and undoes the top button of his collar.

"You're back soon," I remark.

"The governor and I have a meeting tomorrow morning." He bends forward to rub his knee, and a folded paper sticks out of his jacket pocket.

"What's that?"

"A list of the settlers." He tucks the paper away and peeks at Quinn sleeping. "I need to see Commander Flynn. The bed is yours. I'll be back soon." Jamison retrieves my sword from under the cot.

I straighten in alarm. "You're taking my sword?"

"I'm returning it to you," he answers slowly. He passes me the weapon, his grip on it lingering. "I've given you my trust, Everley. Don't exploit it."

"I won't." Fortunately, my regulator is broken and the bell is no longer attached to my ticker to expose my lie.

Jamison releases the sword, tugs the blanket higher over Quinn's sleeping form, and ducks out. I wait one hundred ticks of my heart, then tie on my cloak for cover and go outside.

The most sheltered path from our tent to the cabin is along the Thornwoods. I dart across the clearing to the tree line and pad down the trail. The shadows whisper hello. Bugs flit past my nose and crickets chirp from the thorny branches. My destination is not far, and soon, the cabin comes into view. Lamplight glows from the windows. I dash across clumps of grass to the rear of the cabin and squat below one. In the stillness that follows, voices sound from inside.

"I need you to organize the matrimonial ceremony," says Markham. "The queen has tasked us with establishing the colony's first families. We cannot disappoint her."

"How would you like me to match the convicts, sir?"

The second man sounds faintly familiar. I peer inside the window at Markham's profile. The other man stands with his back to me, his head covered by a cap.

"Let the men choose their mates," replies the governor. "Encourage them to decide in the next few days. We'll give the first five couples double plots of land as a reward for their decisiveness. We'll speak again in the morning. You're dismissed."

I crouch lower as footsteps thunk across the wood floor and the door creaks open. I creep to the corner and look around it. The governor's clerk exits the front door and then treads toward the rear of the cabin. I draw my hood down and press against the wall. The man does not notice me masked in the shadows as he passes by, but I see him.

Thousands of memories crash down on me. The moment my family died, I was cast off from the world I loved, anchorless and adrift. Until this moment, I thought a homecoming was impossible, yet my soul runs aground, scraping along the bottom of astonishment.

My eldest brother is alive.

Chapter Thirteen

Sharp prickles pour out from my ticker. I breathe through the pain, willing it not to seize. Tavis is older than I remember. His chestnut hair is longer and his clothes coarser. He is supposed to be dead, killed by the man he just took a meeting with. I remember nothing that links him to Markham, yet betrayal is the only conclusion for what I witnessed.

Tavis travels near the tree line. I prowl after him, not bothering to hide my approach. I should return to my tent, think now and react later.

I draw my sword.

Tavis whirls around. I shove him into the woods, far from the moonlight, and slam him into a tree. He winces as the thorns on the trunk burrow into his coat. I throw back my hood. "Remember me, Brother?"

His eyes broaden. "Evie?"

"Traitor." I press my blade to his gullet.

Fear fills his green eyes, the same shape and color as our father's. He's a younger version of him, from his hooked nose straight down to his pronounced throat knob. "I had no choice. Markham would have killed me."

"You should have let him. Isleen, Carlin, Mother—" My voice cracks and then returns on a snarl. "Did you know he was coming that night? Did you know what he would do?"

"I didn't know, I swear. Father betrayed him."

"Markham betrayed *Father*."

Tears simmer in my brother's gaze. "Evie, you're alive. Praise Madrona, I'm not alone."

His words should be a joyous sentiment, yet they blister my soul. I lower my sword and step back, disgusted by his weeping. "You're a coward."

"You were a little girl. You didn't hear the conversations between Mother and Father. You didn't see his relationship with Markham. Father wasn't blameless. He hid relics that didn't belong to him. He had no right—"

"*You* have no right!" Stabbing sensations spread out from my rib cage, little shocks jolting down my arms. "How could you, Tavis? Do Isleen's screams haunt you? Do you hear her cries at night?"

He draws into himself, his gaze flat. "Those men were punished."

"You should be punished too." I raise my blade again. My ticker swings off tempo, each labored beat a burst of agony.

"Father's sword," he says, gaping.

"*My* sword." I press the tip to his cheek, my fingers tingling.

"Meet me here tomorrow at noon and I will answer your questions. It isn't safe near the woods at night. The trees have ears, and the beasts of the Thornwoods are always hungry."

I hear a noise then, coming from farther within the Thornwoods—breathing. A chill ripples along my bare skin.

"There are things you don't know, little sister."

"Tomorrow." My arm gives out, dropping to my side. "Don't tell anyone you spoke with me or that I'm your blood, or I will gut you."

I stomp away, my firm paces swiftly giving way to rickety steps. Markham's cabin falls from view. The forest tilts as my knees wobble, but I stay upright, my sword dragging beside me. The tree line leads me to the white tents. There, my legs fail me, and I crumple to the ground. I turn onto my front and drag myself through the underbrush toward the grass. Through an opening in the woods, a man appears by the tents.

"Jamison!" I call. He stills, then comes toward me. I beckon him again and again, my voice fainter and fainter until he parts the ferns.

"Everley, what—?"

"Do you have the clock repair kit?" I wheeze.

"I think it's still in my bag in the tent. Why?"

"Bring it, and hurry."

He runs into camp. I drag myself onto my elbows and rest my head against a stump. The cold circles in, gnawing away the feeling in my nerves and devouring my vision. My heart kicks my insides, its irregular beats reverberating to my bones.

Jamison tromps through the ferns and kneels beside me. "I brought the tool kit."

"I need your help," I rasp. "Any second now I'll black out."

"What do you need me to do?"

"Open my shirt."

He hesitates half a breath, then undoes the top four buttons of my tunic. His fingers halt and his voice pitches higher. "What is that?"

"A clock. I need you to reset the balance wheel and torsion spring. Remove the glass facing, then use the silver instrument with the flat head to reach the gears."

Jamison pries off the glass front and finds the correct tool. My sight goes fuzzy, winter's grasp tightening its hold.

"The big cog in the center," I mumble. "It's slowing."

The balance wheel stops and my limbs wilt. Jamison says my name, a distant and garbled sound. I try to answer, but my words have no life. A curtain lowers over my vision, as bleak as a frozen fog.

Cranking sears through my chest, boring into every bone, muscle, organ. In the absence of life, silence ensnares me.

Tick . . .

. . . tock.

My heart recalibrates, the cogs and windup gears reanimating. The beautiful, burdensome tapping awes me once more, but the aftershocks of pain alternating with numbness are hard-pressed to retreat. I borrow Jamison's haven and imagine daisies bobbing in a clarion breeze, and the snarled aches and pangs gradually uncoil.

Jamison strokes my forehead, pushing back strands of hair stuck to my lips. "I knew we'd met before the clock shop. Years ago, you and your uncle delivered a timepiece to Clayborn Manor. You were the saddest girl I'd ever seen."

I clutch my shirt shut and will myself not to cry. Uncle Holden brought me along to the west end of Dorestand amid the manors with gleaming windows, fragrant gardens, and picket fences. While he unloaded the wagon, he told me to be polite, a marquess lived there. A butler answered, followed by a boy and girl come to gawk at my uncle's timepiece. Jamison had no limp and his little sister held on to a well-loved doll. I stood in the entry of their manor, so similar to my family's home, and cried. Jamison saw me, so I fled back to the wagon.

His attention falls to my ticker. "How is this possible?"

"I don't know how it works. It just does." I sit up and struggle to refasten my shirt buttons with my tingling fingers.

"Let me." Jamison closes my top, pausing over my scar.

Shivers shoot out from his touch, so I shift back. "I didn't want you to see this."

"On my sister's grave, your secret is safe. Does this have to do with why you've come to Dagger Island? Why you were out in the woods alone?"

My brother's reappearance returns to my mind, bringing with it the increased desire to weep. I stamp down that urge and speak quietly to stop my voice from quaking. "I can stand now."

Jamison assists me up, his warm hands splayed across my back. The tick of my heart is a clap of thunder, exacerbated now that he has seen the source of my secrets. "Who hurt you?" he asks. "Your scar—"

"It's an old wound." Once more, I think of my brother. Whatever he has to say will not change what Markham has done.

"Everley, I want to help you." Jamison's grasp on my lower back tautens. His lips are slightly parted, like an open door. The truth builds upon my tongue. I want to tell him, but my success depends on my silence. Secrets only hold power when they are locked away.

"You can help by forgetting this happened."

Slipping from his hold, I stride for camp.

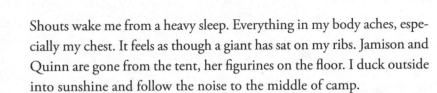

Shouts wake me from a heavy sleep. Everything in my body aches, especially my chest. It feels as though a giant has sat on my ribs. Jamison and Quinn are gone from the tent, her figurines on the floor. I duck outside into sunshine and follow the noise to the middle of camp.

Vevina has set up a gambling table near a hollering crowd of men. Quinn watches off to the side, chewing her cuticles. Two cats, one much larger than the other, are trapped inside a wire circle. A bald soldier takes turns poking them to provoke a fight while Vevina takes bets on which cat will win. The bigger cat, a tabby, pounces at the other, claws flying. The smaller feline, a black-and-white one that reminds me of Tom, swipes at its larger opponent.

"Everley," Quinn says, "can't you do something?"

Intervening won't gain me any favors, but I cannot allow this cruelty. I push through the crowd to the enclosure and high-step over the wire into the circle. The black-and-white cat is bleeding from a slash across its nose. I scoop it up and the spectators boo.

"What are you doing?" asks the bald soldier. "Put him down."

"You're done harassing these creatures. Let the big one go too or camp will be overrun with vermin. I doubt the governor would be pleased to find mice in his cabin."

Mention of the governor quiets them. The bald man opens the holding pen and the cat runs off.

I pass the runt to Quinn. "Careful, he's hurt."

"Oh, precious one," she says, cradling him.

The spectators amble away, some of them complaining about having their merriment ruined. I glare at them until they leave us be.

Vevina swaggers over, her fist full of coins. "Thanks to you, I've taken a loss."

She has never pitted animals against each other for earnings. Either the island is addling her brain or she was worn down by her empty pockets. "Put the Fox and the Cat in the pen next time. The men will appreciate the show."

"That's what I'm trying to avoid," says Vevina. "They shouldn't be parceled off for marriage. Captain Dabney said he would request the three of us for the right price, but I need more coin to make it appealing to him."

"The captain can take you all as wives?"

"Scullery maids for him and his officers. The governor may not allow it, but we're going to try. Those lasses are all I have."

Her optimism comes from desperation. Vevina must know Markham won't hand over three women to one man. Still, I respect her efforts to keep them together.

Vevina loops her arm through mine. "I saw you met the governor yesterday. Perhaps you or the lieutenant can put in a good word for us?"

"I'll, ah, think on it."

"There's your husband now." Vevina nods down the way at Jamison, Dr. Huxley, and Commander Flynn exiting the infirmary deep in conversation. Are they discussing the list of settlers Jamison had in his pocket?

A meal bell rings.

"That must be breakfast," I say.

"Breakfast," Vevina says, laughing. "That's the call for midday meal. You've slept half the day away."

Indeed, the sun is too high in the sky for morning. Often after my ticker is recalibrated, I sleep longer to recover my strength.

"Quinn, let's take the cat to our tent."

We make haste to our lodging and set the cat down inside. As he sniffs around, Quinn pours him the last of our water in an empty cup. He rubs against her and purrs.

"What will you name him?" I ask.

"Prince," she says, "like the lost prince of legend."

"A notable name for a brave cat." I pet the feline's long back, from his head to his tail. "I'll refill our water flask. Stay here until I return."

Quinn swings a lock of her hair in front of Prince. The feline bats at the tress and she giggles. I grab my sword, covering it with my cloak, and go to meet my brother.

Chapter Fourteen

Tavis waits in the trees behind Markham's cabin. His physical appearance is torturous. He takes after our father in every way, except his smile. When he smiles, I see Isleen.

"I'm glad you came, Evie."

Tavis is as likely to embrace me as I am to strangle him, so I halt in the tree line a safe distance away. I have no patience for my childhood nickname or this preamble. "Why are you working for Markham?"

"He isn't who you think."

"He's a monster. I saw him kill our parents. You saw his men kill Carlin and Isleen."

Tavis holds my glare. "You should let him explain."

"I'd sooner spit on Mother's grave. Why are you here?"

"I'm Killian's surveyor. When Father returned from their expedition to Dagger Island, he brought maps and charts, proof that the Ruined Kingdom exists on this very isle."

"A children's story."

"History," he counters. "I heard Father tell Mother that he visited the Everwoods, and through there, he entered the Ruined Kingdom. Father found creation power, Everley. The very power that animates our world."

Tavis comes nearer, his eyes alight with fervor. I back away, vigilant about keeping my distance. "Father wanted to bury this knowledge and waste the greatest discovery the realm has made. He refused to turn over all the evidence of his findings."

"None of this justifies what Markham did."

"Is he why you've come?" Tavis asks, forcing me back a step, farther out of the tree line. "I read the report of your sentencing. Streetwalking? Evie. Father and Mother would be devastated."

"No more so than by your betrayal." I steep in my anger to withhold my tears. All these years, Tavis was alive and fighting against my very attempt to avenge him. His disloyalty burns down to the gears in my ticker.

"Everley?" Jamison calls, striding from the direction of the governor's cabin. A few steps behind him follows Markham.

I whirl on my brother. "Did you tell the governor I'm here?"

"Yes, but bringing us all together was Lieutenant Callahan's idea."

My insides tumble to my ankles. Jamison brought Markham to meet with me? How does he know about our connection?

Jamison draws his pistol on me. "Drop the sword, Everley."

"You won't shoot."

"Won't I?" His grip on the trigger does not waver.

A hundred questions bombard me. When did he find out who I am? How long has he known? How much *does* he know? I rake through every word I shared with him, every word he shared with me.

I'm not the only liar.

"Bastard," I say, dropping my weapon. Jamison picks up my sword and shoves his pistol into the waistline of his trousers. "How long have you known who I am?"

Jamison stares me down, revealing no regret. "I began to suspect you were hiding something when you leaped at your sword in the courtroom. I soon recognized the blade as the lost relic Governor Markham has been looking for."

"The lieutenant has always been attentive to details," Markham says, glib despite our stubbornness in not breaking eye contact. He offers me his elbow. "Lady Callahan, will you please accompany me on a stroll? Your brother and the lieutenant will escort us."

Jamison glances at Tavis in astonishment. My head is too full of questions and my mouth too full of venom to speculate why. Swallowing a barb of rancor, I ask, "Why would I go with you?"

"Because you crave answers," Markham replies, his eyes and voice flinty.

He saunters ahead and waits for me to comply. I clamp my teeth down on a growl. Going with him is not a request; it is a poorly veiled order.

Sheer fortitude, even at the expense of my pride, pushes me to follow. We turn down the beach and tour the coastline northward, Tavis and Jamison several strides behind us.

Markham pauses to examine an ivory seashell. "The call of life is nearly deafening at the beach, don't you think?" At my glare, he moves on. "This morning, Tavis told me his little sister was alive. In truth, I didn't realize you were also the clerk from the clock shop until Jamison explained that's where he met his wife. You've come a long way from home for vengeance, Everley."

"You could have made it easier for me by staying in Dorestand."

He dares to smile. "Haven't you asked yourself why I'm here?"

"To steal my father's praise for discovering the isle."

"If only that were true," Markham replies blandly. He blocks my path, his wolfish face as dangerous as it is arresting. "I'd like for you to join me on an expedition around the isle."

I choke on a scoff. "You must be daft."

"Someone with less knowledge might think so," Markham muses, staring at the sea. "I've been searching a long time for the Ruined Kingdom, and I'm close to finding it. Since you sailed halfway around the world to meet me, you must come as my guest."

His invitation might fool a less wary prisoner, but I recognize a command when I hear one. "Why?" I ask, though I've little hope of receiving an honest explanation. "I'm not my brother. You've no chance of persuading me to your side."

"You inherited your father's adventurous spirit and mind for curiosities. You'll come because your need to understand his death is stronger than your will to defy me." He waves Jamison and Tavis to us. "We're going on an expedition. Tavis will come as my surveyor and the lieutenant may escort his wife."

Jamison reveals no emotion, his expression carved from stone.

"What of my sword?" I inquire.

The governor indicates that Jamison should turn over my weapon to him, then he examines the lusterless hilt and long, thin blade. The sword balances perfectly in his grasp. I itch to snatch it back from him.

"I'll keep this for now," says Markham. "Will you join me on my trek, Miss Donovan?"

I hate him, fully and unconditionally. I must obey or he will lock me in shackles and drag me along. "You'll not distract me from why I've come."

"I would be disappointed if I could." Markham steps nearer and lowers his voice. "Join us or I will give Quinn into marriage to the basest convict on the island." Fury singes my tongue as Markham says louder, "Can I trust you to accompany your wife, Lieutenant? It has been too long since I've heard you play the violin."

Again, his invitation is a poorly veiled command. This expedition is just another leg of my sentencing with Jamison as my guard.

"It would be my privilege, sir," he replies, bowing stiffly.

"Grand." Markham flashes his immaculate ivory teeth. "We'll travel by sea aboard my ship." He starts down the beach, my brother trailing after, and calls over his shoulder. "We leave in half an hour. Prepare to set sail!"

I stay where I am, replaying every interaction I had with Jamison after we walked out of the courtroom. Every single encounter I had with him is tainted. "Are you Markham's spy?"

"How could I be?" he retorts. "Killian told me this morning that you're Brogan Donovan's daughter, and I just now learned that Tavis is your brother. I've known Tavis only as Markham's surveyor. Besides Markham serving as your father's expedition partner, I was unaware of your association to either one of them."

I am too overwhelmed to decide if I believe him. "Did you tell them about my heart?"

"No," Jamison says swiftly, affronted.

"Don't pretend my concern isn't justified. You picked me as your wife to keep a closer eye on me."

"That's only part of the reason." He watches the waves, clenching and unclenching his jaw. "Your sword made me suspicious. I thought you had bought it off a trader. For all I knew, you didn't know the weapon was Markham's. I wasn't even certain the blade was his lost relic until I described the hilt to him. Everything I've told you about myself and why I married you was true, Everley. I gave you ample opportunity to be honest with me in return."

"What did you expect me to say?" I counter. "Ten years ago, Markham murdered my parents and siblings and stabbed me through the chest. Until last night, I thought Tavis was dead with the rest of my family."

Jamison searches me for sincerity. "You're saying the governor killed Brogan Donovan? Why would he do that?"

"That's what I came here to find out." My ticker starts to swing out of sync. It will worsen if I do not calm down, so I try to temper my tone. "Markham killed my family."

Doubt lingers in Jamison's expression. "I served under Governor Markham for years, Everley. He's respected by soldiers and sailors. The queen relies on him and he's well liked among nobles. I cannot imagine him massacring a family or stabbing a child."

I haven't had to worry whether my story would be believed. Jamison is the first person I have told, so his reaction matters. I rest a palm over my scarred chest. "Killian Markham stole my childhood, my family, my *life*."

Jamison kicks at a pebble, knocking it into the water. "It's difficult to reconcile the man I know with the one you described."

Hot tears cramp my throat. I have no reasons to deceive Jamison, yet in no small part, I understand his reticence. No one wants to believe monsters are real.

But I believe in monsters. I have seen them take and destroy, suffocate and shred, every sliver of light in the world. Monsters exist, and Markham is the worst sort. He pretends he's charming, but I have felt the coldness of his steel in parts of me that no man has seen or ever will see. He's the vilest, most treacherous monster there is—the kind that feeds off the light.

Jamison steps up to me and brushes a tear from my chin. "I'm sorry. I needed a moment to understand. I believe he hurt you."

His answer soothes decade-deep sores. I needed him to believe me even more than I realized.

"Were you using me to get to him?" he asks.

"It didn't occur to me that I could until our wedding ceremony. But yes, I hoped our marriage would provide an advantage."

His breaths skim my damp cheek. "I want us to trust each other."

Not a moment ago, he disarmed me of my sword and relinquished it to Markham. I've a right to my ambivalence. "Don't come on the expedition, Jamison. Markham wants you to watch me and report to him. Stay here with Quinn."

"I'm not going on the expedition for Markham." Jamison dries my cheek gently. "Don't you want me there?"

"No."

His arm falls to his side. "The governor issued an order. I'm going, all right? I'm going." He stalks up the shoreline for camp.

All at once, I am furious at him, at myself. Why must he meddle in my life?

I stomp after him, spilling sand into my boots. I stop to shake them out and notice Dr. Huxley speaking with a patient outside the infirmary.

"Alick?" I call.

He takes one glimpse at me and hurries inside the tent.

"Dr. Huxley," I call again, quickening my pace. I follow him into the infirmary, weaving between aisles of sickbeds. He halts at a table to organize his instruments. "Alick, please listen. I'm leaving the settlement on an expedition and don't know when I'll return. Quinn needs a responsible caretaker. Will you watch over her?"

He finishes putting away his tools. "You should ask your husband."

"He's coming too," I reply, and the surgeon's posture hunches. "We'll depart shortly."

"To where?" Dr. Huxley asks, ducking out of the tent.

I dart after him. "I don't know exactly. Somewhere on the island."

Alick halts and I bump into his side. His mustache twitches. "Most of the people who have explored the isle have not returned."

"Governor Markham organized the expedition. We're going with him."

Out in the cove, the *Cadeyrn of the Seas* awaits departure. This expedition draws my mind back to when I first left my uncle's home to practice swordplay. The streets of Dorestand terrified me at night. I almost turned back home, then I saw the lanterns of the wharf, and they guided me to the river. That evening I learned my first lesson in vengeance: to slay a monster, one must be willing to pursue it into the dark.

"Dr. Huxley, please," I say. "I respect you and your bedside manner. It would be a relief to know Quinn is in your care."

He removes his hat and tips his head. "All right. I'll look after the lass."

I thank him and hasten to the women's side of camp. As I pass Vevina's tent, I hear male voices inside and peer through a crack in the flaps. She's with sailors from the *Lady Regina*. Their meeting is too formal for courtship, but I've no time for eavesdropping, so I move on to my tent. Jamison is packing the last of our belongings while Quinn hugs the cat.

"He said you're leaving," she says. "Prince and I want to go too."

"Prince will be happier on dry ground with you." I crouch beside her and pet the cat. "Dr. Huxley will look after you and you'll look after Prince. Mind your manners and stay out of the woods, all right?"

Quinn clutches me close, then releases me to embrace Jamison. He pats her back one-handed and tells her to be good. Then, without acknowledging me, he heaves our pack over his shoulder and leaves. Quinn follows us out, cradling her cat. I wave farewell to her and promise we won't be gone long.

Down the beach, sailors load two longboats with baskets of food. Jamison and I pause up away from the surf, where the wind and waves are hushed. He holds out a pair of red gloves.

"Are those . . . ?" I ask, trailing off.

"Vevina cleaned them. She can get blood out of anything."

I decide against asking how he discovered that detail and slip on my mother's gloves. I immediately feel more myself. "You didn't need to do this."

"You're welcome," he says rigidly.

I correct myself. "I meant to say thank you."

"You're welcome," he repeats, his tone gentler.

Claret and Laverick run up carrying individual packs. "We're going with you on the expedition," the Cat says.

"The governor approved our request," Laverick explains.

"Your request?" I ask.

"We're your ladies-in-waiting," Claret replies.

The Fox and the Cat bow, their curtseys abysmal. They are after something, though I cannot figure out what. I point at their bags. "Where did you get all that?"

"We found a few things lying around camp," Claret replies. Her feline features are more pronounced when she's fibbing.

Jamison casts his gaze to the heavens, as though praying for patience, and then goes to the longboats. Markham waits there with Tavis and a group of unfamiliar sailors. They must be the crew of the *Cadeyrn of the Seas.*

I go down to the boats with the Fox and the Cat. They announce themselves as my ladies-in-waiting and are directed to the second longboat. Jamison pinches his lips into a white slash, annoyed that I've succumbed to their ruse. I most certainly have, even though I am entirely befuddled as to what they want.

Markham greets me with an overbright smile. The wind sweeps his hair over his shrewd eyes, his cheeks rouged from the brisk sea air. "I hope you have everything you need, Lady Callahan."

The only possession of importance I own is my sword slung at *his* hip.

He offers to assist me into the boat, but I ignore him and climb in on my own. Markham settles on the bench behind me, and then Jamison and Tavis push us away from the shore and jump in.

They row us across the harbor to the *Cadeyrn of the Seas.* The massive ship sits a third higher in the water than the *Lady Regina* and is longer by at least fifty feet. Her figurehead is a merrow, a mythical creature that is half woman, half fish. The vessel is a floating armory. She has three gun decks and more cannons on the main deck. The weapons are a deterrent to pirates or foreign powers that the crew may come upon during exploration. She is not graceful or stealthy, but what she lacks in agility she makes up for in intimidation. The vessel is a striking exemplar of the queen's power and influence across the realms.

My father used to say a ship is a passport to adventures and a gateway to wonders. But I cannot think of the *Cadeyrn of the Seas* as anything other than another prison.

Chapter Fifteen

The ship speeds along the forested coastline, sails full and bowsprit defiant. Markham oversees the vessel from the upper deck, my brother dutifully at his side. After giving us a brief tour, Jamison parts ways to labor with the crew, and Claret and Laverick disappear belowdecks. I am unaccustomed to servants waiting on me, so they must know I won't ask them for help.

I travel toward the stern, en route for Jamison's and my cabin, and spot Harlow emerging from Markham's quarters. She wears a summery lavender frock and her hair has been curled.

"What are you doing here?" I ask.

"I'm a guest of the governor's."

My chin ticks sideways. "Were you acquainted prior to our arrival to the isle?"

"You could say so." She slings a crafty smile my direction. "I haven't thanked you for disposing of Cuthbert for me."

"For *you*?"

"Quinn was the perfect temptation. All I had to do was suggest he be alone with her while the captain rowed to port, and you three did the rest."

"You encouraged him?" I ask, my jaw lowering by the second. "He could have hurt Quinn!"

"I told you where to find her, didn't I?"

"You said I should search belowdecks."

"And you listened." Harlow strolls off, laughing.

I glare at her as she climbs the staircase to the upper deck and goes to Markham. He places his hand on her back, his touch shockingly intimate. Harlow stares down at me, her grin cutting. I storm into my cabin and shut the door.

Harlow works for Markham. The night we were arrested, she anticipated the raid. She must have known she would receive a transportation sentence to the penal colony, even wanted one. What does Markham need her for? What secrets does she hold? Unless he needs her to help him *acquire* secrets.

I drop onto the bed and cover my eyes. Out of courtesy, Markham had the rest of our belongings moved from the *Lady Regina* for our comfort. He sent Jamison's clothes and violin, as well as our daisy clock. Its patient voice convinces me not to let Harlow upset me anymore.

Someone knocks at the door. Thinking it's the Fox and the Cat, I answer. I am sorely disappointed.

"May I come in?" Tavis asks.

"No."

My brother glances past me into the cabin and then pushes inside. "Is this our clock? I thought it had been destroyed."

"It was. This is the twin Uncle Holden kept at his shop."

"He always was a wonder." Tavis touches the shiny top of the timepiece. "I should like to have my own."

"This belongs to Jamison. He purchased it before leaving Dorestand."

Tavis looks back at me. "You neglected to tell me you'd married. Do you love him?" I shake my head. He studies the clock again, his tone flat. "I was in love once."

"I remember."

"Then you remember our parents ruined it."

Father and Mother disapproved of the young woman, a server he'd met at a tavern. Before Father left on an expedition for Dagger Island, he ordered Tavis to stop courting her, but Tavis didn't get the chance. Father paid the serving girl not to come around anymore, and she bought a carriage ride out of town.

"Is that why you betrayed them? You were heartsick over a woman?"

Tavis touches my personal figurines beside the clock. I carved them on our voyage to the isle and brought them along in my pack— miniatures of Father, Mother, Isleen, Carlin, and him. Tavis does not appear to recognize himself. "We don't choose who we love, Evie. I was hurt, but Father was wrong. He chose to die instead of give Markham what was rightfully his."

"Which was?"

"Killian will tell you. He's requested your and Jamison's company for dinner." Tavis's gaze meanders down me. "Do you own a gown?"

"Do you?"

He laughs, a warm resonance. "I've missed your wit."

I too once enjoyed his humor. When I was little, he would trap me in his arms and I giggled uproariously. Then he would hold down Carlin so I could tickle him. Isleen would roll her eyes at the three of us tossing about the floor. Longing for those simpler days tugs at me, but too much blood has been shed to let Tavis near me again.

I open the door for him. He picks up the figurine of himself and brings it to me.

"Dinner is at seven." He hands me the figurine. "Until then, Evie."

I shut the door behind him and lean against it. My thoughts rotate in tandem with my heart, ticking around and around in a loop of broken memories.

Jamison returns to our cabin hours later with women's garments slung over his shoulder. He spreads out a shift, petticoat, corset, and gown on the bed. The bodice of the dress is low, the cloth a rich burgundy satin with black lace overlay and a square neckline. The sleeves are sleek to the elbows, then billow out with more lace.

"Tavis asked me to deliver this," he explains, and then his voice fills with reproach. "He said you're to wear it to dinner, and if you argue, I've permission to take you over my knee."

I snort at Jamison's critical delivery of my brother's message. "My parents never struck us. Mother could barely beat the dust from a rug and Father doted on his children to no end." I pick up the dress for a closer inspection. My brother always had an eye for fashion. Shame I cannot wear it. "The neckline is too low."

"You might try it on. Tavis said dinner is a formal affair." Jamison removes a two-tone uniform from the dressing cabinet. "I haven't had time to sew the buttons back on my blue jacket, so I'll wear my court regalia."

I hold out the gown again. It reminds me of the dresses my mother wore to the palace for royal engagements. What would she think of me, a lady to an earl? I hope she and Father would be proud despite the circumstances in which Jamison and I wed.

"Will you help me try it on?" I ask. The armor of a lady may embolden me to withstand the evening with Markham.

"Shall I fetch Claret or Laverick? Surely they—"

"They would see my ticker." I undo my shirt buttons and Jamison turns around. I slide the shift over my head and climb into my petticoats. The corset laces foil me. "Could you, please?"

Jamison comes behind me and pushes my hair aside. His body heat sears my neck. He ties each string to the top, then I slip into my dress and he buttons me up. I whirl around, my skirt swinging. The top of the dress barely conceals my scar.

"Well?" I prod.

He examines me thoroughly, giving my question its due consideration, and then replies, "Your brother will be pleased."

Jamison throws off his jacket and sheds his shirt so quickly I freeze. While I pretend not to watch, he puts on a clean shirt and waistcoat, and then I hold out the jacket for him to slide into. He ties his sword to his belt and places his pistol in a drawer.

The clock chimes seven o'clock.

He goes to the door ahead of me and waits. Now that we are dressed and ready to leave, I hesitate over the logic of our evening plans. We're off to dine with my enemy, and I am unarmed.

"Everley," Jamison says, returning to my side. "It's just dinner."

He seems to think this gown has stripped me of courage. I could quickly disabuse him of that misconception by pulling his sword, holding him at knifepoint, taking the pistol from the drawer, and locking him in the cabin. Then I could arrive to dinner doubly armed with steel and gun. But I want to trust I have an ally in Jamison, which startles me almost as much as how dissatisfied I am when he leans away. I nearly had his sword.

Tavis greets us at the door to the officers' dining hall, a wine goblet in hand. He has switched into a lace-collared shirt, a satin necktie, and a trim black jacket. I gape at his likeness to Father, and his jaw sags as he takes me in. A glimpse in a mirror startles me. I take after Isleen. Our sister was a year younger than I am now when she died. Still, our resemblance is undeniable. Tavis throws back his wine and refills his cup, his grip on the wine bottle quaky.

A table has been set with fine linens, crystal, and porcelain ware. Lit candelabras drip hot ivory wax. Harlow sits at the head of the table, puffing on a tobacco pipe. Her red gown dives down the front of the fitted bodice. Someone spent a lot of time tightening her corset. Markham stands behind her, his fingers on her slim neck. He opens his arms in welcome.

"Lieutenant, however did you convince your wife to put on a gown?" he asks.

"I assure you it was her decision, sir."

Jamison and I both sit. Yearning for the security of a blade or tines, I search for knives or a fork and find only spoons. Tavis dines across from us, and Markham takes the opposite end of Harlow.

"Miss Donovan," he says, "you've grown into a lovely young lady."

"You haven't aged a year," I reply. His use of my surname instead of Jamison's hammers in the memory of the life I lost. The life he stole.

Harlow puffs on her pipe, her lips toying with the tip. "Killian is eternally handsome."

Her position on this ship is more complex than I assumed. She and Markham must be partners in more ways than one.

A servant portions out the creamed soup, ladling it from the tureen into our bowls.

"Governor," Jamison says, his spoon deep in his bowl, "I inventoried the male convicts before we left and found one unaccounted for. An inmate, Baylee Rafferty. You may identify him from his snuffbox. It has a crest of his family's tobacco farm on the lid."

"I recall Rafferty," Tavis replies. He finishes another glass of wine and pauses to pour another. "Rafferty was convicted of murdering your sister."

Silence grasps us.

Harlow slurps her soup loudly, thriving on the awkward pause.

"He was falsely condemned." Jamison enunciates so there is no mishearing him. "I spoke with three witnesses who saw the accident. They testified that Rafferty was farther up the road when the wagon tipped onto my sister. They think her horse was spooked by a snake. I have signed reports from the witnesses that attest Rafferty is not to blame."

I listen intently. Jamison did not tell me any of this.

Markham wipes his mouth with his napery and reclines in his chair. "Once a man is condemned, it's impossible to overturn the magistrate's ruling."

Jamison sets aside his spoon, his soup untouched, and adjusts himself in his chair. "Rafferty is innocent. I cannot let him pay for my sister's death."

"Can't you?" Markham replies, his gaze and tone simultaneously sharpening.

"Pardon my boldness, sir," Jamison says. His deference ruins my appetite, so I set down my spoon. "I understand the realm must adhere to sentencings, which is why I'm offering myself in exchange for Rafferty."

Markham points at me. "You've already consigned yourself to life on the isle by marrying a convict."

"Precisely," Jamison replies. "I could serve the years Rafferty was sentenced for, and he could return to Wyeth. The realm's requirement would be satisfied. At the completion of my term, I would return to my service in the navy."

My spine digs into the back of my chair. This was Jamison's motive for marrying me. I'm an anchor he threw to the wind, hoping to stay on the isle and set Rafferty free.

"Has Rafferty agreed?" Markham asks.

"I wished to discuss the matter upon my arrival but couldn't find him." Jamison fidgets in his chair again. "Rafferty was not in camp. I spoke with Commander Flynn and he consulted the prisoners' log. He gave me a list of all deceased male convicts. Rafferty's death was not recorded nor was a headstone erected for him in the graveyard."

Markham shrugs, relaxing into his chair. "You can hardly expect me to keep track of every inmate."

"I know where he is, sir," Tavis says. "Rafferty was with the scouting party that went into the Thornwoods to determine where to break ground for permanent settlement. They were scheduled to return six days ago."

"Have you sent a search party after them?" I ask, drawing Markham's gaze to me.

"Miss Donovan," he says, emphasizing my surname again, "the scouting party mainly consisted of convicts. They and the soldiers with them knew the risks of entering the Thornwoods."

His refusal to accept responsibility scalds. The queen continues to ship men and women to the penal colony without a care for our survival. She and Markham have no heart, but my brother may still have some left of his. "Tavis, our father warned the queen not to colonize the isle. We should return home and forsake this place."

Markham and Harlow vibrate with silent mirth. Their private humor leaves me less than entertained.

"She has no idea, does she?" Markham asks.

"No," Tavis replies. "She was too young, sir."

"Too young for what?" I demand.

"Do you remember Mother's stories about the Ruined Kingdom?" Tavis questions.

"Of course I do, but they were *stories*."

"The kingdom is real," Markham asserts, and Harlow quits chuckling. "Only one man has been inside the gates of the Everwoods since time locked us out over three centuries ago—Brogan Donovan."

Tavis nods. He believes the penal colony is a worthwhile venture.

How pathetically naive.

"I didn't take you for a dreamer, Tavis," I say. "The legend is a myth."

Markham slams his hand down on the table, vibrating the candelabras. "The tale is as real as you and me!" Carefully, as though he did not just rattle the porcelain ware, he lifts the wine bottle and refills my brother's glass. Tavis's cheeks are ruddy from too much wine, yet he dives into his next cup. Composed again, Markham goes on. "Brogan found the gate. We were separated by the Thornwoods and reunited upon his return to the beach. He said the only way to settle Dagger Island was to break the curse."

"How is that done?" I ask, humoring him.

"We reawaken Amadara and restart time."

Restart time? Markham is mad.

"Pardon me, sir," Jamison interjects. "What's your interest in the Ruined Kingdom?"

Markham gazes straight ahead, preoccupied by the flickering candles. "I want to wake those trapped in time and end the curse."

Harlow tings her spoon against the side of her bowl loudly. She sets down her utensil and strangles the stem of her wineglass.

"It's my quest to find the kingdom," says Markham. "I will not stop until I do."

Tavis raises his glass. "To good timing."

"To my queen," Markham adds.

Tavis clinks their glasses together. Harlow throws down her napery and pushes from the table. Markham beckons for her, but she storms past him out of the cabin.

"How long will our expedition take us away from camp?" Jamison asks.

I can see him calculating how many days it will be until we return to the settlement so he can see if Rafferty has returned.

"Our voyage will bring us around the south of the island and up the windward side," Tavis replies. "There, we will enter the Thornwoods."

This excursion is absurd. We are to break a curse? Find the gate to the Everwoods? Awake Amadara and restart time? We're all going to disappear and never again be found.

Markham thinks he can convince me a legend is real and I will forget he slaughtered my parents. He has swindled Tavis, but he won't trick me. This is not a penitent man. He will not admit wrongdoing, and without the truth, I cannot turn him in for punishment.

Tavis can gamble his life away, but I'm not following Markham anywhere else. I'm finishing this tonight.

Markham pushes from his chair and rings a bell, and a server enters with a violin case.

"I think we would all appreciate a lighthearted conclusion to our evening," Markham says. He takes the violin and passes it to Jamison. "It would be good of you to indulge me."

Jamison must be conscious that this is not a request, for he removes the musical instrument from its case and rises. "I believe I recall your favorite, sir."

His long fingers curl around the neck of the violin, his other hand setting the bow to the strings. Markham sits again, and Jamison strikes the first note, a soulful timbre that bridges into a haunting melody. Markham shuts his eyes to listen. I fixate on Jamison, riveted by his fingertips adeptly pressing the strings and the accurate strokes of his bow. He sustains the final note to the fullness of its life and lets the music ascend to silence.

Markham and Tavis clap first, then I join in. Jamison bows and starts to set down his violin, but the governor asks for another song.

Jamison plays into the night, heeding request after request from Markham. The chair beneath me grows harder and the soup I ate begins to curdle in my stomach. I am even more aware that Markham views us as puppets. He knows exactly which strings to pull to make us dance.

Chapter Sixteen

At the close of dinner, Jamison and I return to our cabin. While he puts away his violin, I mull over Tavis's claims about our father. Father boasted that he had made a remarkable discovery, and all these years I presumed his feat was mapping Dagger Island. Could his accomplishment have been validating Amadara's story? Is the gate to the Everwoods cradled in the depths of the Thornwoods?

I rub circles at my temples. I must be tired if I'm seeking truth in Markham's lies.

"I can unbutton you," Jamison says.

"Thank you. Did you take the assignment to the island so you could free Rafferty?"

He finishes with my dress and quickly unlaces my corset. "I couldn't reconcile him paying for a crime he did not commit."

Holding my gown to my front, I swivel toward him. "You're certain he's innocent?"

"As certain as I am that my father was wrong. He didn't care that he sent an innocent man to prison. My mother died of an illness we could not fight, then my sister was taken . . . He wanted someone to suffer." Jamison sits on the bed and slumps forward, elbows on knees. "No magistrate would rehear Rafferty's case. I shouldn't have wasted my time on the courts. I should have come sooner."

Though I am acutely aware of my state of undress, I grasp Jamison's knee. "You came, which is more than most people would do."

"Don't commend me, Everley. I'm simply righting my father's wrong. I'm sorry for involving you in this."

His duplicity doesn't sting. Our marriage offered us both selfish opportunities.

Still, Jamison could have wed any woman aboard that ship. He chose to intervene on my behalf because he has a good heart. He must, or he would not have come all this way to release an innocent man as reparation for a tragedy that was not his fault.

Jamison lays his hand over mine. "You and I aren't so different. We both want to shed our pasts."

We are vastly different. Jamison came to Dagger Island to save a man. I came to ruin one.

"I'm here to make Markham pay."

Jamison rises, our chests so close he can hear my clock heart. "The seconds are ticking by. Don't give him any more of your time."

"You want me to forget what he did?"

"Not forget—forgo. After Tarah died, I realized I couldn't make everything our father did right, but I stopped letting his offenses hurt me. Letting go of my anger set me free."

Freedom from the past is exactly what I'm after, but my wounds are in the present and I carry my prison within me.

Jamison eyes my gaping neckline. "May I?"

Clutching my gown to my chin, I hold still as he bends and rests his ear over the ticker. Each beat echoes through my head as though my own ear is pressed to my chest. He straightens and touches under my chin. The tick resonates there like a regular pulse.

"You're a marvel," he says.

"No—"

"Yes. These years you were given are a gift. Don't be so distracted with what keeps you alive that you neglect to live."

I duck my chin, burying it in my loose dress. Though I am still mostly covered, I feel completely exposed.

Jamison withdraws. "I'll turn around now."

Once his back is to me, I undress and get into bed quickly. He makes a bed on the floor and lies down. Before long, his breaths slow to shallow pulls and he drifts off.

I get up and dress in black trousers, a shirt, and a cloak. As I take up Jamison's sword, why I have come returns to me stronger. A decade of biding my time has pushed me to this night, this choice, this opportunity to emancipate myself. Markham's day has come, and I am ready.

Night has slunk aboard the ship and hunkered down for a rest. Low-lit lanterns swing in the billows that fill the sails and power our journey. The quiet deck is disturbed by a light ringing. My trouser pocket has a small lump in it. I reach in and take out the bell that belonged to my regulator. Jamison must have slipped it into my pocket. Smiling to myself, I tuck the bell away.

A shadow falls across the planks before me. Markham stands on the upper deck, overlooking the bow. I sink into the shadows and climb the stairs. As I approach the helm, I unsheathe my sword.

"Father Time is a cruel trickster," Markham says. "He makes us wait for most everything we desire. Have you patience, Everley?"

"I'm all out of patience with you. Why did you come to our home? What did you want?"

"Would you believe I sought redemption?"

"What does it matter what I believe?"

"You won't stop hunting me until you have your answers." He unsheathes my father's sword. I bend into my knees, preparing to spring at him. He grabs lower on the hilt and rotates it so the blade points at him and the hilt at me. "Take it. Satiate your hunger. But beware. Ambition has a putrid aftertaste."

"You'd let me dispatch you?"

"You seek release, do you not?" He extends the sword closer. I replace Jamison's rapier in the scabbard on my hip and take my father's steel. It feels right in my hand, like my gloves did when I put them on again. Markham does not draw another weapon to defend himself. "Now that you have your blade of choice, end this."

I wait for my fury to respond, but this is not how I envisioned our encounter. I'm unprepared to slay an unarmed man.

Markham steps forward, and the tip of my sword touches his vest. "Brogan stood in the way of my redemption. I'm so tired, so very tired. I've sought peace longer than you can fathom." A half step, the blade pressing into his clothes. "Finish it, Everley."

He must be mocking me. He doesn't think I will cut down a defenseless man. Maybe he's right. Though he killed my family in cold blood, I didn't imagine this moment would include outright butchery. Even so, freedom lies at the end of my sword. Or is Jamison right? Can I still walk away? Or have I gone too far to turn back?

"Ah, you've something to live for," Markham says. "Love perhaps? You've given your heart to Lieutenant Callahan?"

"He has nothing to do with this." I don't love Jamison, but I did let him into my head, and he's jeopardized my judgment.

"Both of us bring loved ones into this stalemate." Markham smiles sadly. "You're grasping your salvation by a thread. Taking my life will destroy your spirit."

"You already did that." My memories of that night slither in around me. I am seven again, and he is standing over me with his sword. Every hour has come to this. I am one grand sweep from escape. "You ruined my life."

"That was not my intention. I'd intended to end it."

I plunge the sword into his chest.

Markham gasps as the blade sinks deep, impaling him. I follow the impetus of fissured sinew, his body recoiling against steel, then step back. He grasps at the hilt of my weapon. With inhuman strength, he pulls the sword from his chest.

The blade is clean. I wait for blood to spread across his chest and stain his ivory shirt. His heart does not break, nor does he crumble.

Markham caresses the edge of the sword and then sheathes it at his hip. "Do you see now that your ambition is futile?"

"H-how . . ."

Markham bows regally. "Prince Killian Markham of the Kingdom of Amadara at your service."

"It cannot be." The world tilts as though the ship is capsizing, but it's only me. All reason and rationale fall around me, dropping me into an eddy of disbelief. It's a moment before I stop sinking. "You . . . cannot be him. The lost prince and Princess Amadara are characters in a story."

"I call her Ama," Markham replies, devastation marking his brow. "Losing her and our home ruined me. I need not sleep, nor can I eat. Food tastes of salt and wine of ash." He lifts a pocket watch, its craftsmanship old. The second hand is frozen between the eleventh and twelfth hour.

"I know clocks," I say. "You could have removed or broken the gears."

"Clever, but no." He carefully opens his buttoned shirt. He has no injury or scar from my stabbing. But I saw the blade go through him. "Everything I love, all that I am, is trapped in time with my beloved Ama."

My mind whirls in a million directions, striving to comprehend. "Father Time banished you from the Everwoods and into our world where time exists. You should have begun to age as soon as you arrived."

"On her dying breath, Ama tore time to save my life. Father Time cannot violate her blood sacrifice; thus, I am stuck in between worlds."

His voice is so full of agony, it crackles. "I exist in between the beat of a clock, continuously locked in the middle of nowhere."

The tumbling sensation returns. Everything is upright except for me. I am plummeting through an endless loop of madness. "You would have been banished three hundred years ago."

"Three hundred and forty-nine. Immortality is beneficial for one purpose—counting time." Markham's stricken gaze lowers to my chest, as though he can hear my heart.

Even after seeing his torso unmarred, I cannot accept he is Amadara's husband. "The lost prince was flawed, but he wasn't wicked. You're—you're a monster."

He touches his chest, offended. "You pursued me across the high seas, endeavored to take my life, and *I* am the monster?"

The world lists further. All the time I spent, the sacrifices I made, the preparation and training. All of it was for naught. I can never avenge my parents. Never see this man destroyed. I failed my family. Failed my father.

"You're like Brogan, thinking your intentions are noble and your deceptions are defensible." Markham's voice rises, his color waxy. "Brogan Donovan was a thief and a traitor. Given the chance, I would exterminate him again."

I ball my fist and swing. My knuckles crunch against his cheekbone. Markham absorbs the hit without defending himself. I shake out my hand and strike again, my concentration transforming into a rage of fists, my vision a blur of red. He must hurt, cry, *bleed.*

Markham grunts when I bludgeon his lip. Still no blood, but he feels pain.

He should feel pain.

I unsheathe my sword. We will see how immortal he is after I carve him apart.

He draws his flintlock pistol and pulls back on the hammer. "I've been more than patient, Everley. Drop the sword."

I cannot determine if he's bluffing, and I would rather not find out, so I release my weapon. The sword lands with a clang. My chest heaves so hard, my lungs may burst. I cannot inhale enough air to fill me. It is with pure defiance that I compel my ticker not to stall. What powers are protecting him? His eyes are clear, his skin unmarred. He is the epitome of handsomeness, the princeliest of men. My own knuckles bleed and darken with bruises.

Tears spill over my lashes. I was a fool to think I could defeat him. That I could be whole. I start down the stairs on rickety knees, my vision smeared. Markham pursues me like a bad dream.

"Go away," I rasp.

"I need your assistance."

"You'll get no more of my time. I've wasted more than enough on you."

Markham pins me against the handrail and presses the pistol under my chin. "I need someone Father Time and the Creator favor. Soon after I fled my kingdom, I lost my sword here on the island. I searched and searched to no avail. Centuries later, your father came upon it. Tripped over the damned thing, to be precise. Of all the hundreds of acres on the isle, and all the years I spent searching, Brogan stumbled upon my sword his first journey into the Thornwoods. The sword of Avelyn chose him for reasons only the Creator knows."

My father's sword, the one Markham is holding, is the sword of Avelyn? The Creator gave the sword of Avelyn to Father Time to guard the Everwoods. In the legend, it was the weapon the prince wielded to cut into the heartwood of the elderwood tree, thus carving into his princess's heart.

Markham has again revealed his madness. He's a prince. And my father's sword is ancient? I could spit in his face for the audacity of his lies.

And yet . . . his appearance contradicts my doubts. He has not aged in a decade.

"I believe Father Time may favor your father's bloodline." Markham wipes away a tear dangling from my chin with the end of his gun. "You will help me return to my kingdom."

"You have Tavis."

"Your brother wasn't left the sword of Avelyn, a fact I was unaware of until after I spared his life. Father Time chose *you.*" Markham tears open the top buttons of my shirt. I jerk the neckline shut too late, and his finger hovers over my clock heart. "Eternal life has taught me to recognize Father Time's hand and train my ear to his call. Who built this magnificent machine? It could not have been your uncle. His crafts-manship is too basic. I would like another glimpse at it, if you'll spare me the curiosity."

"Fall on your sword," I answer, holding my shirt closed. He has abolished my purpose for coming here. He won't also rob me of my pride.

"Perhaps I'll look another time." Markham strokes my jaw with the end of the pistol. "You must be very special for the sword of Avelyn to have selected you. It must be your clock. The sword senses its master within you, Time Bearer."

He speaks as though the sword picked me, when, in truth, the day my father came home from Dagger Island, I lusted for it. The sword represented his adventures and travels, both things I wanted. My bond with it was born from my love for him, not a higher calling as Markham would have me believe.

He speaks quickly, manic in his conviction. "I can sense when the sword is near. I felt it in the Thornwoods and in your uncle's clock shop. All those clocks deluded me into thinking I was sensing Father Time, but the sword was with you." His face splits into a monstrous smile. "Everley Donovan, you're going to lead me home to the Land of Youth."

Dread lances through me. He wants me to return him to his land, his people, his *Otherworld.* "I won't. I cannot."

"Have you forgotten who I am?" he asks, his tone dead quiet. "The lieutenant came a long way to plead Rafferty's case. I can help or hurt his cause."

"Leave Jamison alone."

Markham lowers his pistol and splays his fingers across my collarbone. His hair falls into his feverish eyes. "Will you risk your love so I may return to mine?"

"That's what you want? To reunite with your princess?"

"I wish to undo a wrong. I cheated time, much as you have. To break free of my debt, I must release Amadara. I will give you the same riches I promised your brother. Land and a title when I return to my kingdom."

"Your incentives are meaningless."

His fingers bite into my neck. "I wouldn't discard my generosity. Cooperate or the lieutenant will know terror and pain. It has been a long while since I have keelhauled someone."

"Keelhauling" is a word my father would whisper to my mother so we children couldn't hear. I searched out the meaning in a book and have never forgotten what I read. A brutal practice by mariners, the victim—usually a convict or prisoner—is tied to a line looped beneath the vessel, tossed overboard, and dragged under the ship's keel from one side of the vessel to the other. Most men are cut up by the barnacles along the hull, resulting in lacerations that lead to infection should the man live that long. The majority of the victims drown.

Markham has me suspended on a wire of merciless steel. Only I am no longer hanging from his clutches alone. He has strung up Jamison beside me. This is why Markham brought him along, to use him against me.

"I'll go," I say, "but Jamison will know nothing of our agreement."

Markham's lips hover over mine, his grip on my neck loosening to oily petting. "We're alike, you and I."

"I'm nothing like you."

"Oh, you are. We'll both do anything to protect the ones we love."

His unrattled answer in turn rattles me. My affections for Jamison are minimal, far from love. But I don't want him brought further into Markham's web. This is my past, my problem, my purpose for coming here.

Markham *will* bleed.

He lets me go, his smile an arrogant slash. I throw on my hood and stalk into the dark. At my cabin door, I crumple against the wall and will myself to stop shaking. Jamison may be awake inside, and he cannot see me this way or he will know something is wrong.

Everything is wrong.

Markham has the worst possible advantage. I've no sense if everything else he told me is true, but I felt my blade go through him and saw his unscathed flesh. Out of all the preposterous claims he made, his inability to perish is legitimate.

A brisk wind teases my cloak and chills me. I cannot wait to compose myself before going inside or I will be out all night. I slip into our cabin so depleted not even the shadows pacify me. Jamison is still fast asleep. I lie down and stare into the dim, too numb to cry. My heart ticktocks at a normal rate, both of us at a loss for what to do other than survive the night.

For one glorious second, when my sword was embedded in Markham's chest, I had triumphed. I was unchained from my debt to my family, and the time I stole with my clock heart was rectified. It is not enough that he took my family and crippled my future. He deprived me of justice.

Exhaustion finally relieves me of my anguish. Killian Markham may be eternal, but so is my hatred. And he may be delusional as to whether he is the hero or monster of his story, but he is unmistakably the monster in mine.

Chapter Seventeen

My ladies-in-waiting are nowhere to be found. After searching belowdecks, I finally come upon them in a quiet place on the forecastle, huddled over a book in the morning sunshine.

"What are you doing?" I ask.

Claret closes the book and tucks it beside her. "My lady, do you need something?"

She says "my lady" with an impertinent tone that doesn't bother me in the least.

"Actually, yes." They look at each other in amusement. They thought I wouldn't ask anything of them while they were aboard. "I came to speak to you about the expedition. I heard from the crew that we'll arrive at the drop-off soon. I want both of you to remain on the ship. The Thornwoods will be treacherous. I don't want either of you hurt."

"But we have to go," Laverick protests. "The expedition is the reason we came."

"You came to explore the island?"

Claret stands, hugging the book to her chest. "We came for the same reason Governor Markham is here. To hunt for treasure."

I bluster a laugh. "That's a tale I haven't heard."

"It's true," Claret insists. "We overheard soldiers discussing a secret treasure at camp. We went searching to find out whether it's real and found this." She opens the book to a portrait of a woman with sunny hair, huge light-green eyes, a slim neck, and creamy skin. Her beauty is like a rose in full bloom; it would be impossible to overstate her perfection. Under her portrait is a name written in fine penmanship—*Ama*. I turn the page to a picture of my father's sword; the title reads *the sword of Avelyn*.

"Where did you find this?" I ask.

"We may have found it in the governor's quarters," Claret says.

This must be Markham's personal sketchbook. He called Amadara "Ama," the same caption beside the portrait of the woman. "You shouldn't have taken this," I say.

Laverick snatches the book back. "The governor has a large library of texts. He won't notice it's missing. We'll return it later after we study the drawings inside. Some of them are of the Ruined Kingdom."

"See for yourself." Claret opens the book again and flips through page after page of pictures of countryside scenery. "Look how vivid and detailed they are. The person who drew them must have spent time in the kingdom or knew someone who had."

My tongue curls into the back of my throat. It won't be long before they associate Markham with these drawings or realize that my weapon mirrors the sword of Avelyn. They might already suspect.

"Where does it mention there's a treasure?" I ask.

Laverick turns to a picture of a stone castle surrounded by forestlands. A river slices through the middle of the quaint village within the castle's compound. A well-dressed couple stands in the window of the highest tower, she with lustrous hair and he a proud demeanor. I read the caption beneath.

Land of Youth.
Blessed of Father Time and ruled by Princess Amadara,
the Land of Youth is the wealthiest in all creation.

Laverick points to the caption. "See, the kingdom is wealthy. Their coffers must be overflowing with gold."

"Or jewels or fine furs or ancient relics," Claret adds. Her attention drifts away as though she is imagining various forms of treasure.

The caption does imply the kingdom has untold riches, but I'm still doubtful that there's a hidden treasure. "All right, you two. You found the proof you wanted. Now put the book back before the governor finds it missing and keelhauls us all."

"You should see one last picture," Laverick says. She turns several pages to a charcoal sketch of a solemn young man.

My heart gives a significant tick. No nameplate or caption identifies him, yet I recognize his character from the feeling of his presence. Father Time is unmistakable, as his power has dwelled within me for years.

His thick black hair and youthful face are startlingly familiar. Though he appears sterner and more severe than I visualized, that may be the interpretation of the artist or the grace of my own vision. Father Time's pensiveness grants him an air of wisdom and agelessness. He could belong to any century and world. He is unbound, ancient yet eternal.

Markham captured his persona with a critical, unforgiving eye. This is a portrait of someone he has met and is well acquainted with. Either he has an astounding imagination or the drawings in this book are accurate representations of real people and places. I don't want to accept that he's the lost prince. Then I would have to consider that Amadara truly danced in the Everwoods and the myth about her tearing time to save her prince is not a tale. It is history.

Laverick nudges me. "The young man in the portrait feels like someone you know, doesn't he? Claret and I stared at his portrait for an hour this morning. We cannot recall where we know him from."

I study Father Time's brooding expression. He really does exist—my ticker has professed the validity of his power for a decade. An unspoken side of me hasn't doubted his authority, yet it is different to see evidence that a guardian of time watches over us.

I close the book. "Return this immediately."

"Don't you want to see the other pictures?" Claret asks. "There's one of a village—"

"We're rowing to land soon. You have to put this back before we leave."

"You mean you won't be angry at us for coming with you?" Laverick asks.

"Would it stop you if I were?"

Claret pretends to consider my question. "Well, if we're being honest . . ."

I push the Fox and the Cat toward the governor's cabin. Markham stands at the middeck near the longboats. He and his crew are preparing for our departure, well within sight of the door to his quarters.

"What now?" Claret whispers.

"You're the con artists," I answer. "Think of something."

"We'll distract him while you return the book," says Laverick.

I shrink back. "Why me?"

"Claret and I are always together. The governor will be suspicious if we aren't seen side by side." Laverick's claim has as much merit as a dead sea rat has voice, but we're speedily approaching the drop-off location.

"All right," I grumble, grabbing the book. "Keep him busy."

The Fox tosses her long auburn hair behind her shoulders and links arms with her partner in crime. "You have three minutes."

The Fox and the Cat stroll to Markham and engage him in conversation. While his back is turned, I dash into his quarters and shut the door.

The cabin is quiet and empty, no servants in sight. Since we ate in the officer's dining hall yesterday, this is my first visit to Markham's personal quarters. They are plainer than I anticipated. The bed is made without a single lump or misplaced crease. His furniture and shelves are organized and clean. No personal emblems are displayed on the desk or bedside table.

Life at sea and tight quarters require that sailors be tidy and travel with minimal possessions, but Markham's cabin is barer than Jamison's. He displays no pictures or maps on the wall, no boots by the door or tobacco pipe near the untouched decanter of whisky. The washbasin is so clean it shines. Next to it are a full bottle of shaving oil and a sharp razor that look as though they haven't been used. He spent months aboard this vessel traveling back and forth from Wyeth, yet I see no signs of ownership or permanency. He could vanish at any moment and leave no trace of himself behind.

Bloody bones, I should have asked the Fox and the Cat where they found the book. I see no gap on the shelves where it would go. The bookshelves are packed with texts about geography and nautical exploration. Thinking Markham may have hidden the book in his desk, I open the drawers. The first two are full of parchment, ink, and quills. The inks are the same colors I saw in his detailed sketches in the journal.

Shoved to the back of the top drawer is an older-style book similar in size and thickness to the one I have. The outer cover is creased and stained from wear. I set the journal in the drawer and pick up the second book.

A strip of leather binds it closed. I unwind it and open to the first page. The passage is dated three hundred and forty-nine years ago.

I finally located the mainland, though I know not where. The skiff drifted many months across the high seas. Starvation and dehydration nearly took me, but time is merciless and would not let me perish. The curse pursues me everywhere I go. I wear its mark like a brand. I don't yet know how to break free. The gate to my beloved home is far from this foreign shoreline. How will I find you again? How will I undo what has been done?

I miss you, Ama. I swear I did not know this would become of us. Dearest love, please forgive me.

"Drop anchor!" a sailor shouts outside.

I jump onto my toes and listen for someone to come in. All the footsteps go past the door. I turn to another date in the journal, a few days after my father returned from Dagger Island.

I behaved horribly, Ama. I am sick with shame. I fear my need to return to you is hardening my heart.

A friend betrayed me. He was the only person in decades who I entrusted with the unabridged truth of our downfall. He understood my need to find you and wanted to help me. Together I believed we could break the curse. But greed overcame him. After all I'd done, he intended to cut me out. I couldn't allow him to do that, Ama. I couldn't let him go to you and leave me behind. The thought of him returning to my home without me drove me mad. I had to silence him. I had to keep him from the treasure.

My eyes burn from not blinking. I cannot pull my gaze from the page. Given the date of the entry, Markham must be referring to my father, but he has not used his name or referenced him as his partner. For me to turn this in as evidence, I need specifics.

After he was gone, and I was stained in ash and blood, I wished I could leave this life. Please don't think me weak for seeking an end to my wandering. I know your suffering is beyond comprehension, but I am weary of this prison of flesh. My every attempt to join the stars has been foiled.

Father Time is torturing me. He did this to us, Ama. His jealousy and spite divided us. I will undo his treachery. On Mother Madrona's hallowed crown, I swear I will return.

"Find anything of interest?" Markham asks from the open doorway. He enters and shuts us inside.

"I—I didn't mean—"

"Of course not. You invaded my quarters, searched my desk, and read my private journal by mistake. What an unfortunate mishap for you." He strides over and sees his journal open to the passage I last read. "That was a low day for me. Your father and I had countless discussions about my kingdom. While Brogan pretended to sympathize with my plight, he was plotting to return to my world without me."

"Nothing he did merits your killing him or my family. My mother and siblings never did anything to you."

"Unfortunate casualties." Markham slams the journal closed. I bury my fear under my skin and it rises in gooseflesh. "Brogan was weak. You're stronger than him, Everley. Out of everyone aboard this ship, or at the penal colony, or in the realm, and perhaps in all the worlds, you more than any other person understand why I couldn't let him stand in my way. You know what you want and you let nothing block your path."

His compliment rankles. Stubbornness is not a quality I would shine up and wear like a medallion. "Unlike you, I don't feign to have good intentions."

"Your integrity may be what I admire about you most." His finger trails down my front to my clock heart. The ticktocks boom as his mouth leans near my ear. "Clocks are fragile pieces, as delicate as the time they mark. Think on that before you invade my privacy again."

"I will find a way to kill you."

"I have every faith you'll try." His dry lips brush against my earlobe, and my insides sour and slosh. "But you won't succeed today."

"Are you going to pull your pistol on me again?" I ask, hungering for the excuse to jam my elbow into his nose.

Markham pulls back and lifts my hand to inspect my skinned knuckles from beating on him last night. "Don't be in such a rush to hurt yourself again. I need you whole."

I yank from his touch. "You're worried about bruises? You're taking us into the Thornwoods. This expedition can only lead to more suffering."

"You're a child," he answers hotly. "Walk the worlds more than three centuries and you will know true despair."

His journal entries return to my mind, foremost his anguish and hopelessness. I cannot comprehend his ingratitude. My ticker could give out at any second, breaking beyond repair. He need not dread dying before fulfilling his aspirations. He does not live in fear of departing too soon.

"Don't envy me, Everley. Too much time is a curse." Markham opens his pocket watch and reads the frozen hour. His tone turns melancholy. "It's the limited time we have that makes life precious. Eternity is a lonely bedfellow."

I sense his thoughts are on Amadara. He loves her, and that love will compel him into the Thornwoods, putting me and our party at risk. Does selfishness negate love? How much blood must a man spill before he is irredeemable?

Markham snaps his pocket watch closed, his head down. The light streaming in from the windows calls attention to a tear sliding down his cheek.

"Leave me," he says.

My astonishment holds me there. Monsters do not cry. They stalk and howl, feed and ravage, rampage and kill. They do not weep, especially not in front of their prey. But his solitary tear, so average, so human, disintegrates my doubts.

Markham *is* the lost prince of legend. He will lead me and a thousand more people to our graves so he may return home to his princess and break the curse on the isle.

I wobble out of his quarters into the sunshine and gulp down briny sea air.

"Evie?" Tavis asks.

I didn't notice him leaving the neighboring cabin. He pulls me against him and leads me to mine. We sit on the bed in weighted contemplation, my inner turmoil rising to an unbearable pressure. Silence can speak for itself, but right now, I need my brother to explain.

"You know Markham's real identity," I state flatly.

"I didn't at first. After that night, he took me in as his apprentice. It wasn't long before I observed his strange habits. Killian doesn't sleep or cut his hair or grow tired. He hardly eats except for the occasional apple. And he doesn't bleed."

"I know," I grumble, rubbing my sore knuckles.

"You must understand, Evie. Father had his reasons for discovering the Ruined Kingdom. Before he left home, he promised Mother he would return with a treasure that would guarantee his retirement, but he came home empty-handed and needed to go back to retrieve it. He and Mother were making plans for him to return to the isle." Tavis's voice becomes younger sounding, like when we were children. "Isleen and I were in town purchasing gifts for Mother's birthday when we saw Markham and his men. I mentioned that Father was eager to return to Dagger Island with him. Not until later did I find out that Father intended to go without Markham, without the aid of the navy, and without permission from the queen."

I stay quiet, aghast that Father would double-cross the realm.

"Killian said he would visit the manor to speak to Father about it. He came that night for his sword, but Father wouldn't give it up. He said he needed the sword to direct his path to the gate. Killian called his men in from where they were waiting outside. I promise I didn't know their argument would escalate."

I blink slowly, all my tears currently dried up. "He spared you."

"He thought I could lead him to the gate with the sword. His men had searched our manor and couldn't find it."

"No," I say, remembering it differently. "Markham had no time to search. He stabbed Father and then started the fire."

Tavis lowers his chin to his chest. "I saw you on the floor beside Mother and Father, Evie. I called to you, but you didn't move. You were in shock, so stunned you weren't even crying. Markham's men searched the manor for nearly an hour, tearing everything apart. They couldn't find the sword, so they dragged me out and set the fire. I begged Markham to spare you, but he needed only one of Father's children. He selected me because I was older."

My brother's timeline of that night creates a gap in mine. "I—I don't remember seeing you. I heard the gunshots—"

"I fought back and the soldier fired wide. Carlin and Isleen were already gone." Tavis's voice trembles. "You asked if I dream of her. I do. Every night for years, Isleen and Carlin and Mother return to me. You did as well, but since you've come to the isle, the dreams of you have stopped."

He didn't mention Father harassing him in his dreams. Tavis really does blame him. How he can find him culpable but not Markham astounds me.

"I've missed my family," Tavis says, reaching for my hand.

I shy away, too sickened by him to allow his touch. I believe my brother didn't anticipate what Markham would do or how that night would end. But Tavis's betrayal wasn't surviving. It was siding with our family's destroyer.

Jamison throws the cabin door open and halts in the threshold. "I, ah . . . I can come back later."

"Tavis was just going," I say.

My brother stands gradually, straightening like an old, fragile man. He tips his hat in farewell at Jamison and strides out.

Jamison shuts the door behind him. "Pack up. We're rowing to shore."

"I want you to stay behind."

He wipes his brow, damp with perspiration from working on deck. "We discussed this already, Everley."

"The trek could worsen your sore knee."

"I can keep up."

Fear strangles me and won't let go. "I don't want you to come."

He throws the pack on the bed and sends me a quizzical expression. "Why not?"

Because I don't trust Markham not to use you against me. I don't say this, of course, and instead shorten my reply. "I don't trust Markham."

Jamison's mouth and eyes stretch in comprehension. "Are you trying to protect me?"

"No." My answer was a reflex, but am I?

At seven years old, I woke with my newly installed clock heart and my uncle told me my parents were dead. I vowed never again to rely on another person for protection or let them rely on me. Life was definitive then. Myths were stories, my father wasn't a traitor, princes were not murderers, and monsters could be slayed. I miss those days of certainty.

"You shouldn't come, because I cannot be sure what dangers we'll face," I explain.

"Nor can I, but I'm still going."

Jamison resumes packing our bags. My mind floods with confessions about Markham's possible princedom, my father's secret return voyage to the isle, and the mysterious treasure. I won't tell him any of this unless I know all of it is absolutely true.

Nothing will feel certain again until I find the Kingdom of Amadara and look upon the ruined world myself.

Chapter Eighteen

Our expedition party stands at the frontier of the Thornwoods. Claret and Laverick, Markham and Harlow, and Jamison, Tavis, and I heft our gear in preparation for infiltrating the heart of Dagger Island.

After rowing ashore, we hiked up the rocky peninsula to the tree line. The women followed my example and exchanged frocks for breeches, shirts, and waistcoats, along with cloaks, boots, and packs full of water flasks and hardtack. Harlow wears the masculine garb with flair, a yellow kerchief tied at her collar and her hair tied up under a wide-brimmed hat. She and Markham make a striking pair, despite her ignoring him. She must be holding a grudge from their exchange at dinner.

We are indeed on the windward side of the isle. The gusts toy with our hair and clothes, pushing against us. I am already perspiring, the day stifling despite stormy clouds masking the sun. An occasional raindrop splatters on my head as I peer into the crooked trees. The Thornwoods do not smell of clean pine or warmed dirt, but like a bog—stinky feet and wet peat. Birdcalls and the whir of insects spill from the ferny undergrowth. The evergreen canopy stretches so high I can imagine the trees truly do hold up the sky.

A throb seeps up from the ground, as subtle as a rabbit's pulse. The faint resonance does not disturb me as much as the way Markham looks carrying my sword. He had a servant polish the gold hilt, so the green tinge has been replaced by a splendid gleam, bright as the first eventide star. Though I am reluctant to accept that the weapon is the hallowed sword of Avelyn, the noble relic would give authenticity to his pedigree.

Markham draws my sword and crests the Thornwoods. Harlow follows him armed with a rapier. I start to set out, but Jamison grabs my pack and holds me back.

"We should have a signal in case we're separated," he says. "Do you know how to whistle?"

"Tavis taught me." I glance at my brother carrying his walking stick. Laverick and Claret go around us into the woods. "I have a good sense of direction, Jamison. I've never been lost before, and I've memorized the map of the isle."

Markham calls from ahead. "Come along!"

"Another moment!" Jamison answers, and then says to me, "Good sense of direction or not, if we're divided, whistle and I'll come." He pats my shoulder, as though committing me to memory, and then we head into the trees.

Tavis trails us, the last party member in line. Up ahead, Markham slashes at branches and ferns. The spare cutlass I borrowed from the weapons stockpile on the ship is clunky and uninspiring, but complaining about the wretched blade would be pointless. Harlow would delight in my whining and Markham would know how much it still irritates me that he has my sword.

The rain begins to fall in earnest, dampening our cloaks and boots. I pause and look back to gauge our progress. The trees obstruct our view of the sea, sealing out the salty breeze and trapping us within the dense, fetid Thornwoods, where every direction appears the same.

"Markham," I call, "how do you know which way to go?"

"Direction is unreliable in the Thornwoods, as the paths are ever changing. You must look for evidence that we're on the correct course. The Thornwoods showed your father the way. It will do the same for you."

The Fox and the Cat swivel toward me, inquisitive yet mystified. Why am *I* searching for our path? Jamison must be wondering too, but none of them press me, probably because I appear just as perplexed. Markham and Harlow start off again.

I whisper to Tavis, "The trees will show me signs?"

"Don't worry. I came prepared." He shows me the circumferentor at the top of his walking stick—a surveyor's compass. "This will show us which direction we're traveling." He swings the stick in a small circle. The needle does not budge. He jiggles it harder, but there is still no movement. "It worked on the beach."

"I believe you," I say. "Bad luck follows me everywhere I go."

I march over beds of pine needles and steer around sticker bushes. The evergreens are a tedium of razor prickles for my cloak to snag on. Each of us pauses periodically to untangle ourselves from the crooked thorns. A few sparrows and squirrels stir in the hushed woodland. Otherwise, most of the creatures have the sense to seek shelter from the rain.

Every few paces, I listen and search for a sign that we are traveling in the correct direction. My only consistent impression is of the gentle pulse throbbing up from the ground and out from the trees, pressing into the deepest cogs and gears of my ticker. If the woodland is communicating with us, and the trees have voices, I cannot understand their language.

Our party slogs on. Laverick and Claret make a game out of our travel by playing "walk as I do." Harlow puts a stop to it when Claret does a rather ingenious impersonation of Harlow batting her eyelashes at Laverick standing in as Markham.

"Governor," Jamison says, "we came this way."

Markham dries his face, wet from the rain. "How can you tell?"

Jamison points out a score in a tree root. "I marked this over an hour ago."

"Eiocha's stars," Harlow swears, dropping her pack.

Claret chews her lower lip, and Laverick sits on a log to massage her calves. My brother fiddles with his jammed circumferentor, and Jamison shifts his weight to his good leg to hide his limp. I have no idea how long it has been since we left the beach, but we cannot waste our strength walking in loops.

I grab Markham and drag him aside. Harlow is still close enough to listen to us. Markham will likely repeat what I say, so I let her eavesdrop.

"Let me lead," I say.

His lips pucker as though he's sipped sour tea. "I'm not lost. The Thornwoods is finicky."

"Maybe having me with you isn't enough. Maybe I have to hold the sword."

His wolfish gaze narrows. "You nor the sword will leave my sight."

As if he would let me wander off. A while back, he hovered uncomfortably close when I relieved myself in the bushes.

Despite his reluctance, we switch weapons. As my fist curls around the hilt of my sword, a knot between my shoulder blades unwinds. Markham walks away swiftly with the stubby cutlass. His pistol is tucked in his pocket, so he will get no sympathy from me. I return to the others.

"You got your sword back," Jamison notes.

"Looks good strapped to her hip, doesn't it, Lieutenant?" Claret says.

Jamison and I flush, and the Fox and the Cat snigger.

Harlow and Markham exchange quiet, heated words, and then she storms off to sit under a tree. Their relationship is confusing. What does Harlow gain from helping him return to his princess? What has he promised her?

Markham catches me staring and makes a shooing motion. He relinquished his weapon to me, and now he expects me to guide us to the gate.

I scour the area for hints of our location. The woodland is a wash of gray and green, a gloomy and daunting landscape. The ground is fairly level. We have not gone far enough inland to reach the mountains. I don't believe the Thornwoods will provide a clear sign, so I pick a random route on impulse and follow my intuition. It has yet to lead me astray.

"This way," I say, waving my party forward.

My optimism sustains me for an hour or two. Trusting my inner compass will not fail me, I trudge onward, but our eerie surroundings challenge my concentration. I snag my arm on a thorn, cutting it and tearing a hole in my cloak. I cannot seem to focus on where to go, because all I want to do is leave these foul woods. After a third hour of nothing, my ticker starts to beat off rhythm and everyone's pace drags.

We stop for a drink from our water flasks. Runoff from the passing rain drips from the canopy and peppers my head. My frustration grates at me. I haven't seen any suggestion that we are or aren't on the right track.

"I told you the Thornwoods was unlike any other landscape." Markham is not gloating. He also seems disappointed in me.

He rests on a rotting log and shakes a pebble from his boot. I sit beside him, preoccupied by my incompetence in finding my way.

"How long did it take my father to discover the gate?" Frustration shortens my tone, making me sound as irritated and tired as I feel.

"I couldn't say. The Thornwoods distorts place and time. The light is always desolate, that of an overcast day, and the trees impede us from viewing the sky. The nearer we are to the gate, the less time shifts."

"That's impossible."

"Then explain to me why we have wandered hours and the light hasn't changed." Markham gets up and cases the trees, pacing like a lone wolf in a cage.

Nightfall should settle upon us soon, but the longer we stay here, the less convinced I am that it will. In the legend of the Ruined Kingdom, the forest surrounding the gate to the Everwoods was cursed to prevent the prince from returning. Did the curse on this woodland include manipulating time?

I peek down the front of my shirt and a hot tickle crawls up my neck. The second hand of my heart is ticking in place, thumping the same second on repeat.

Here in the Thornwoods, time has no power.

My thoughts return to Markham's expectation that I will lead us to the gate. I assumed my inner compass was an instinct I was born with, inherited from my father. But could the promptings come from my clock?

Jamison stretches his leg and rubs his bad knee. Our wandering cannot continue. I have to obtain proof that we're on course. I find Tavis at the edge of the group still fiddling with his surveyor's compass.

"Any luck?" I ask.

"No," he sighs.

"Shouldn't you have known it wouldn't work? I thought you had been on expeditions on the isle with Markham before."

"Once," Tavis says, his tone and countenance darkening. "I didn't have the compass then. Our party of twenty men walked for days without a sign of the gate. After what was probably our twelfth night— it's difficult to determine how long we were traveling—our party was attacked by a strange beast and the men fled in every direction. Only Markham and I found our way back to the beach." Guilt emanates from Tavis's bowed posture. As our father's son, he was assigned to guide the party to the gate and failed.

"Why did you come back?" I ask. I would be hard-pressed to return after that.

"I came to be with you."

His sincerity renders me speechless.

Tavis tenses, suddenly alert. "Did you see that?" He points to the copse of trees about fifty strides ahead of us. "There."

Two golden eyes flash in the underbrush and vanish before I see what they belong to. My brother pinches my sleeve and drags me back to the group.

"Time to move," he announces.

"We're waiting for a heading," Markham says. He holds me accountable for our lack of progress. Though I fear what he will do when his impatience runs out, I am also afraid of the eerie yellow eyes my brother and I saw.

I search the misty forest, gripping my sword for encouragement.

Father Time, we're lost. Markham won't let us leave until he thinks I've done everything I can to lead us to the gate. Actually, I don't think he intends to let us leave at all. Send me a sign or a way out of this nightmare.

My ticker thuds harder. Not faster—stronger.

I venture forward a step and the ticktocking builds as I approach a tree. The sword vibrates and warms. A splash of color draws me to the tree roots, where a single perfect daisy grows.

"Odd," Jamison says. "I've only seen daisies grow in clusters."

"That's not the only thing strange about this place," Claret replies. "Did anyone see any flowers before now?" We all shake our heads. "Nor have I, and I've an eye for pretty things. This little flower doesn't belong here."

Her opinion endorses my own. The Thornwoods is too harsh a terrain to produce blossoms.

"I think we should look for another," Laverick suggests.

I don't know how I discovered the first flower, so I repeat my actions and aim the blade past the daisy. A vibration runs up my arm from my sword. I step around the tree and walk until the sword warms and quivers again.

"Here," says Tavis, kneeling by another daisy. "Do it again, Everley."

Once more, the sword directs me to a flower several strides away.

"They're making a trail for us," Markham says. He plucks the daisy and inhales its summery scent. "I'm coming, Ama."

My amazement continues as the sword buzzes warmly in my grasp, leading me from one daisy to the next. I don't know how I'm doing this, but I am too grateful to finally have a direction shown to us that I dare not question or doubt the source.

Twenty-four daisies later, our gait slows to a slog. Nighttime still has not fallen, but I drop my pack and declare it is time to retire. Markham doesn't challenge me. He collected the daisies in a bouquet and sniffs them occasionally. By all appearances, he's a prince besotted with his princess. From Harlow's scowl, she's waiting until he puts the flowers down so she can crush them under her heel.

We dine on tasteless hardtack. Along with the absence of time, we've lost the warmth of the season. My cloak and gloves ward off the worst of the cold. Harlow tries to start a fire with her striker, but the damp moss and kindling will not ignite.

Tavis keeps a lookout while Jamison spreads out the bedrolls. Buzzing insects have taken flight, and chirping resounds around us, strident like a discordant violin note.

"What's that?" Claret asks, her eyes huge.

"Crickets," says Markham. He scrapes thorns off a trunk and settles against it. He will be on watch while the rest of us sleep. Harlow sits beside him and tucks against him for warmth.

I lie down with my sword, my bedroll adjacent to Jamison's. As we tracked the trail of daisies, he became quieter and quieter. He stares up into the forest canopy, his concentration broken by yawning. The crickets' chirps swell, their lullaby clamorous. Not bothering to try to stay awake, I let fatigue drag me under.

In what feels like a matter of minutes, Markham nudges my side with the toe of his boot.

"Wake up," he says, "We need to move."

The crickets have not quit chirping.

I bury my face in my arms. "Let me sleep."

"You'll have to make do. It's unsafe to linger in one place too long."

He wakes Jamison next, who glances about bleary-eyed, and Harlow rouses the Fox and the Cat. Claret sits up in a drowsy daze, while Laverick rolls over and ignores us. My brother is awake, his bedroll folded and put away. I haul my sore muscles up, but only because I need a private moment in the bushes.

I leave my bag and wander to the edge of camp. Markham sends Harlow after me to ensure I don't take off with the sword. I walk faster to make her task of keeping track of me more difficult.

Just beyond the sight of camp, the cricket song ceases.

I go still, my senses jumping. Directly ahead, two yellow eyes glow in the undergrowth. They are the same pair of eyes Tavis pointed out hours ago. My heart rebels against my stillness, ticking faster. Something is hunkered within the fountain of ferns, and its measured breaths are cavernous. Whatever hides there sounds large, larger than me.

Very cautiously, I retreat a step. The beast snorts in response. Gooseflesh skitters across my scalp.

Harlow barrels through the undergrowth. "You can't lose me, Everley. Your red gloves make you easy to spot."

"Stay back," I say, waving her away.

"Don't tell me what to do—"

The ferns before us undulate in violent ripples, patches of tan hair visible amid the greenery. My ticker beats the same second over and over, sprinting in place.

"What is it?" Harlow asks, her voice horrorstruck.

"I hope not to find out. Maybe if we retreat slowly, it will leave us alone."

Harlow strides backward at an urgent pace.

"I said slowly!"

The beast bugles and crashes out of the underbrush. I stumble back and land on my bottom. Harlow races for camp, and the enormous four-legged creature rears on its hind legs. Its powerful elklike body fills my view. A pair of antlers curls high and forward, their ends tapering to vicious points over irate eyes.

I can scarcely believe my sight. Centicores live in the highlands of the Land of Youth, but we do have myths about the territorial beasts in our world. One common story tells of children playing too far from home and coming upon a centicore grazing. All that was found of them were their shoes. How did a centicore get here from an Otherworld?

The beast rears up and tosses its massive curled antlers and drops less than ten strides away. The centicore bugles again louder, a gut-shaking cry. I cup my ears and shudder.

"Everley!" Markham cries from off in the woods. "Everley, come back to camp!"

I carefully rise to my feet. The beast paws its front hooves, its head down.

Jamison and Markham crash through the foliage behind me. They pause about thirty paces back with their pistols loaded. I stand right in their firing range, between them and the centicore.

A shot explodes, whizzing past my head. The lead ball strikes a tree near the beast. Markham's aim went wide. The centicore drops its antlers and charges at us. I sprint into the Thornwoods to flee Jamison's line of fire.

A cracking boom resounds through the trees. I slow to see if Jamison's aim hit the centicore, and the beast bounds right after me. I take off again faster.

Heavy gallops draw nearer. I circle back around to find camp, giving Jamison time to reload, but I am swiftly lost in the labyrinth of briars. I don't look back to see how close the centicore is at my heels. The beast is fast and spry, made of agile strength and muscle—it will outrun me in no time.

Taking advantage of my smaller size, I weave between tightly packed trees to slow it down. Unfortunately, I slow myself down too.

I pick a straighter course and speed up, leaping over tree roots and rocks. The sound of the centicore galloping in pursuit stays within range. My chest tightens, my heart ticking madly. My side aches and legs burn. Low tree branches scratch my face, and the thorny tree trunks discourage me from climbing to safety. I hope to find my way back to my party, but neither camp nor my comrades are visible.

My pace starts to lag. The centicore's noisy stampede is falling behind. The beast must be tiring as well. I duck behind a tree and press my hand over my exploding heart. My regulator would be ringing like the bells on the palace chapel. I hold myself together one breath at a time.

A shadow streaks across my side vision and then hot pain ignites across my side as I'm flung forward. I hit the ground and my sword is thrown from my grasp. The centicore vaults on top of me, landing with a bone-jarring wham. All air whooshes out of my lungs as its hoof slams my torso. I shove against its breast, hand full of wiry hair. My other hand reaches for my sword, but it's beyond my grasp.

Square teeth nip at me, just shy of my nose. I push against the centicore's maw. Spiky horns bear down, close to goring. I scream as the beast snaps at my jugular.

The echo of my scream comes back to me. The centicore's eyes glaze over and it slumps on top of my legs. Five frantic ticks later, it still has not moved. I panic, shoving and wiggling to pull free. I squeeze out from under it and crawl away. Markham stands over me, his sweaty hair matted to his forehead.

I run my fingers over my ticker. A line snakes down the glass, cracked but not shattered.

"Everley!" Jamison calls.

I hear but don't see him.

Markham looms over me and drops my sword at my side. "Don't run off again."

Jamison shouts for me once more. I catch my breath enough to whistle. Jamison run-limps to us. His pistol is shoved into the waist of his trousers, and black powder stains the front of him. My ribs ache from where the centicore kicked my side and landed on me.

"Are you hurt?" he asks.

"Just bruised. Help me up."

He grips my wrists and hauls me to standing. Markham yanks his cutlass from the centicore's side. Its lopsided mouth hangs open, its tongue drooping out. Nausea dangles in my belly as the stench of blood fills the forestland.

"Thank you for getting to her in time, Killian," says Jamison.

He would not praise Markham if he knew the beast couldn't have harmed him. Markham spared me for his own benefit, or rather for the benefit of the sword. My only satisfaction is knowing he must have thrown a fit when I ran.

I scoop up my weapon and loop my arm around Jamison's waist. "How's your leg?" I ask.

"No worse than your bruises."

He plucks pine needles from my hair, and I brush more off my cloak.

"Evie!" Tavis calls from nearby.

Jamison whistles, and another whistle answers. He and Tavis exchange signals until the remainder of our group comes into view. My brother bends over, breathless. Claret drops Jamison's and my packs that we left behind. Harlow goes right to Markham and they embrace. He says something quietly in her ear, and she hugs him harder, both equal in their affection.

Laverick pokes her toe at our dead attacker. "I thought centicores were beasts of fable."

"They hail from an Otherworld," says Markham, releasing Harlow to inspect the beast's antlers. "This one must have come through a portal."

"There are portals?" Jamison glances around as though he might see one.

"All portals are hidden at the highest peaks of the tallest mountains or in the darkest depths of the seas, places mankind rarely roams." Markham tips over the centicore's hoof. It's as big as my hand. "Travel between the worlds is best through the Everwoods."

"The queen doesn't allow belief in the Everwoods," Claret says quietly.

"She discourages worship of Madrona," Markham explains. "The Everwoods is the divine forest of Eiocha, thus a part of Progressive doctrine."

"How do you know so much about the Everwoods, Governor?" Laverick asks, her green eyes fixated on him. She is as cunning as her namesake the fox. He must lie well or she will suspect him.

"Queen Aislinn commissioned me to explore outside our realm, which includes investigating the Otherworlds. I intend to prove they are more than myth." Markham saws off the tip of the centicore's antler, collecting a keepsake as proof of his discovery.

His lie is so entangled with the truth of his explorations and assignment from the queen to expand her realm that Laverick appears convinced. She even asks him to saw off the end of the second antler for her.

Jamison retrieves our packs. Our bedrolls are missing, as well as his powder horn and water flask. The Fox and the Cat step away to relieve themselves in the underbrush while Jamison and Tavis inventory our supplies.

Harlow clucks her tongue at my wild hair and dirty clothes. "You don't look like a shop clerk now."

I am too wound up from the centicore attack to stop myself from snapping back. "Why did you come along, Harlow? Was it to serve as Markham's mistress?"

Her eyes brighten shrewdly. "You think you know everything." She grabs my shoulder companionably, her voice deceptively soft. "But you didn't know that Cuthbert was Killian's man. Nor did you know that Cuthbert was sent to watch over me on our voyage to the isle." Her fingers dig into my flesh, pressing down with bruising strength. I repress the impulse to shove her face-first into a prickly shrub. "You want to know my place here? I've already shown you. I belong right where I am, at Killian's side." She lets me go and strides to him.

He takes her hand in his and says, "We've enough rest. We're trekking on."

Such a surprise. The immortal deems us fit for travel.

"Claret and Laverick aren't back yet," Jamison says.

He shouts for them, and when they do not respond, Tavis and I holler for them as well. My imagination swiftly plays against me. Uncle Holden was wicked about scaring me into obedience by telling me stories of giants and elves and sorceresses. If the centicore made it through a portal from an Otherworld, other beasts could also call the Thornwoods home.

"Laverick and Claret probably got turned around," says Tavis.

"They left that direction," replies Jamison. "We'll take a look. Everyone stay together."

Markham steps out in front of him, jawline hard. "This is a waste of effort. We cannot be deterred from our expedition to search for a pair of streetwalkers."

"Then stay here and wait for us," I say.

Hoisting my sword, I set off with Tavis and Jamison. Markham will not let my blade out of his sight, so it is not long before he and Harlow begrudgingly follow.

We call out for the Fox and the Cat, all of us on alert for any other creatures lurking in the woods. I fully anticipate another surprise attack, so when we enter a grove of nettles and Jamison motions for us to stop, I am unprepared for what we discover.

Chapter Nineteen

A sign is nailed to a tree at eye level. The square-cut piece of lumber is washed white and inscribed with an elegant bold script. I touch the bluebell flowers painted beside the words, "Cottage of Souls."

"What do you think it means?" I ask Jamison.

"Precisely what it says." He gestures ahead at a roofline partly visible through the evergreen boughs.

We creep through the underbrush and come upon a bigger surprise— a lovely little cottage. The exterior is immaculate, with flower boxes overflowing with pale-pink flowers, a river-rock chimney, shining windows and painted shutters, and a low white fence. Sunshine filters through the leafy trees, the dappled light adding an inviting coziness. In front of the quaint home, a swing made of rope and wood dangles from a lower branch of an apple tree, and a wooden bench is set among tufts of wild lilacs.

"What is this place?" Tavis asks.

"I've no recollection of it," Markham replies. "I haven't come upon it before."

"Is it real?" I ask. We haven't been in the Thornwoods long, but I already have a sensible amount of distrust for this place.

"Oh, I'll go first," Harlow says impatiently. She shoves past us to the gate.

"Wait," Jamison calls. "We should keep looking for Laverick and Claret. The owner may not wish to be disturbed."

Markham beckons Harlow back to his side. "The lieutenant is correct. We cannot allow ourselves to become distracted."

"But the sun is shining," Harlow says.

Freckled sunlight streams through the trees and dances across the cottage. I, too, miss the sunshine and would like to see more of this refuge from the briars, but we must be on our way.

The Fox and the Cat stroll out from around the back of the cottage, their arms loaded with vegetables. "You found us," says Claret.

"Come in," Laverick adds. "No one's here."

Harlow does not delay to go through the gate. Markham enters after her, gripping a single daisy that must have survived our run through the woods. I step onto the stone path, half anticipating the cottage and its surroundings will vanish. Instead, I am bombarded by golden light and a timid breeze that smells of lilacs and sweet grass.

Big yellow butterflies flit from bloom to bloom. Tavis holds out his hand and one of the winged beauties perches on his palm. Jamison pads up to the cottage and squints through a circular window in the front door. Through the main window, the inside appears dim and nothing moves.

"Look at all the food we found," says Laverick. She carries an armload of freshly picked carrots, peas, and apples. "Around back there's a vegetable garden and more fruit trees. Our garden was half as good as this one when I was growing up."

"The well is full of cold, clean water," Claret announces, chewing the end of a carrot. "We drank a bucketful all by ourselves."

Harlow lifts the pail and sips from the ladle. The drink must be good, because she offers Markham a taste. He declines, his interest fixated on the apple tree. Though it is too early in the summer season for ripe fruit, the boughs are laden with large red apples.

I sit on the bench amid the lilacs, their scent light and floral. The seat was crafted with care. The grooves and notches are plumb and the wood sanded and treated with lacquer. A shiny apple hangs off a lower branch and grazes the top of my head. As I grab for it, Markham snatches my wrist.

"Don't eat that," he says, letting me go. "You don't know why it's here."

I prepare to argue that I don't know why any tree is where it is, but the "it" he refers to includes more than this fruit tree. It is peculiar that this charming cottage is nestled in the Thornwoods. The apples appear delicious, especially after I've eaten hardtack for the last two meals, but the fruit and its tree belong to the owner.

"Any clue who lives here yet?" Tavis asks Jamison.

"I can't see anything." He knocks on the front door and waits.

We crowd around the threshold. Laverick sidles up to my side, crunching on a snap pea. "Want one? The vegetable garden is brimming. I doubt they'll be missed."

"Have you tried an apple?" I ask the Fox.

"No, that's next."

"I wouldn't," I say. "The fruit is rotten."

Markham nods, not surprised at all by my response. I cannot quite understand why I'm lying, except that I should be wary of anything that he fears.

Jamison turns the handle and slowly opens the door to the cottage.

"Is someone inside?" Claret asks from the back of the group. She rises onto her tiptoes to see over our heads.

"You said no one was here," Markham reminds her.

"We didn't go inside," Laverick replies. Her disapproving tone implies that would be a violation to the owner. She doesn't think raiding someone's garden is wrong, yet going inside the house is trespassing. I suppose even thieves have a moral code.

Jamison steps into the single-room, one-floor cottage. Most of the interior can be surveyed from the front door. It is furnished with simple, well-crafted pieces: a chair, table, and bed. Though small, the space is cheerfully decorated with clean blue curtains, a patchwork quilt, and fresh flowers in a pitcher vase. Not visible are books, letters, pictures, or any other materials that could present clues about who lives here.

In the corner kitchen, between the hearth and washbasin, are one plate and glass, and one of each utensil. The owner must live alone—and whoever they are, they were home recently. The floor is newly washed and the windowsills dusted.

Jamison picks up a basket by the hearth and brings it to us in the doorway. It is full of a variety of objects: a broken pocket watch, a pipe, coins, a whisky flask, and several snuffboxes. He inspects a silver snuff-box with a crest engraved on the lid.

"What is it?" I ask.

"This has the Raffertys' tobacco farm crest on it, and these are Baylee's initials." Jamison shows the snuffbox to Laverick and Claret. "This belongs to a man I know. Are you certain you didn't see anyone else around the cabin?"

"Hello?" a tentative voice calls.

We turn around so fast we bump into each other. A maiden in a simple pink day dress exits the woods. Her deep-brown eyes are the same color as her hair, an arresting contrast to her snowy skin. The maiden leads a donkey alongside her on a rope. Chains of pale-pink flowers wreath both their necks.

She stops inside the gate, her smile radiant. "I thought I heard voices. Welcome to my humble cottage."

Jamison edges to the front of the group. "Our apologies for intruding."

She dismisses him with a wave. "Help yourself to anything you find. Would you like some bread? I baked it fresh this morning."

Laverick and Claret jump to accept, but Markham speaks over them.

"We're just leaving," he says shortly.

"You look like you've been traveling. You should stay and rest awhile." The maiden's voice has a musical lilt that is gentle yet persuasive.

She lets go of the donkey, which grazes on the lilacs, and then she plucks a big red apple from the tree. "I'll bake us a pie."

"We aren't staying," Markham replies.

His abruptness startles me, as does his white-knuckled grasp on his daisy. Though it may seem ridiculous to fear an unarmed maiden who adorns her donkey with flowers, anyone who frightens a man who cannot perish is someone to avoid. Jamison identifies the same signals of unease from Markham and prods us from the cottage, pushing us along the path.

The maiden trails after us, offering her apple. "You don't have to wait for me to bake a pie. You can take a bushel with you." She speaks pleasantly, but the more we rebuff her hospitality, the tighter her features.

"Instead of feeding us," Jamison says, "tell me where you got this snuffbox."

The brown-eyed beauty bats her lashes at the silver container. "I come across odds and ends during my walks through the forest. The woods are full of secrets."

"Did you see the man it belongs to?" he presses.

"You are the first souls I've seen in ages." She loops her arm through Jamison's. The movement is so naturally possessive, I prepare to draw my sword. "I insist you stay for a pie. I cannot eat it on my own."

"We really must be going," Markham says, opening the gate.

The gate flies closed again and latches. A trickle of fear flows through me. No wind pushed the gate and no one touched it.

The maiden hooks her fingers into Jamison's arm. Her other hand lifts the apple. "Try a bite, and I promise you won't wish to leave ever again."

Markham confronts the maiden with his cutlass. I view every single one of the nearly 350 years he spent walking our world in his assertive glare. "I see what you are now. Let us go, old hag."

The young maiden cackles, a broken rasp like nails raking across a brick.

The cottage and property transform as though someone is peeling off a mask. Leafy trees become unsightly thornbushes. Grass and flowers wither to barren ground and weeds, and the tree swing rots to a snarl of dead vines. The only vegetation unaffected is the apple tree, which, still vibrant amid the dreary foliage, is likewise disturbing. As the scenery changes, I am struck by the stench of decomposing flesh and plug my nose.

Her once-picturesque cottage dissipates to a rundown shack. The cracked windows, crooked shutters, and holes in the roof are comprehensible, but not conceivable are the walls constructed of bones. Stacks of bones, all types and sizes, compose the shack walls, fence, bench, and chimney. Someone muddied them together with layers of clay.

The donkey transforms into a mongrel of the same size that barks at us. Instead of a chain of flowers around its neck, the dog wears a chain of teeth. Jamison backs up and almost trips over a massive skull half buried in the ground like a yard ornament.

Laverick and Claret gasp and drop their harvest of vegetables. The carrots and peas have become lumps of mud. They clutch their bellies as though they need to purge, and Harlow covers her mouth and gags. The well in which she stole a drink of water reeks of festering slurry.

The cackling maiden sheds the illusion of her youth, and in her place stands a hag. Though she is old, her posture is impeccable and her carriage strong. White hair hangs to her waist in thick cords. Stripes of dried blood streak beneath her cloudy eyes and down her squished nose. A helmet, the skull of a beast with two horns, covers her head. Her neck and wrists jangle with chains of assorted teeth, some pointed, some curved, some square.

Those yellow butterflies Tavis admired shift into crows. The large birds, at least two dozen, hop closer. One of them perches on the old hag's shoulder. A small satchel is slung across her torso crosswise. Along its bottom, in place of tassels, dangle severed toes.

"Let us pass," says Markham.

The hag pets her crow's breast. "My children will pick your bones clean, and from them, I will build a shelter for my mongrel."

Markham puts away his cutlass and thrusts out his daisy. "Everley, the sword."

Though I have never seen anyone look more ridiculous than him, I draw my blade.

The old hag hisses. "Your symbols have no power here."

"Is your life worth maintaining that assertion?" Markham maneuvers so the two of us are side by side, me with my sword drawn and him with his daisy. It appears the two are equally threatening. "Tell us how to find the gate and I will be forgiving."

The hag snarls and then bites out her reply. "The pathway has not been revealed to me, but I know where you will find the helmsman. The merrow king is waiting for you under the wave, O lost one. Bring him what he seeks and you will have your prize."

She opens her arms and her crow children take flight. The flock encircles her in a tunnel of whooshing black feathers and sharp claws. We duck down and cover our heads. The cawing crows disperse, taking off into the thorny woods. In the commotion, the old hag has vanished.

The bone-chilling silence shoves at me, prodding us to hasten out of this shrine of death. I hurry ahead of the group, stepping over the graveyard of bones strewn about the dirt. Markham cuts in front of me, his stride even faster.

"What was she saying about the merrow king?" Jamison asks, right behind us.

"Ravings of a madwoman." Markham shoos off a straggling crow and kicks open the gate. We keep up with him, speeding away from the gruesome shack.

"How did the old hag trick us?" I ask.

"She lures in prey with a glamor charm and then poisons them. When eaten, the apples from her tree are paralyzing. One bite could have rendered you immobile."

I recall how close I was to consuming one before Markham stopped me. "How do you know about the apples?"

"I have lived many, many years," he answers so only I may hear. "I did not let them go to waste."

We pass the cottage sign. It still reads "Cottage of Souls," but the message is scrawled in blood, and instead of painted wildflowers, it's decorated with bloody fingerprints.

Once the old hag's home is far behind us, our party pauses to gather our breaths. Laverick, Claret, and Harlow rinse out their mouths with clean drinking water. Jamison rubs the engraved lid of the snuffbox and then shoves it in his breast pocket.

My sword vibrates and warms in my grasp, indicating our next direction. The call to continue directs me to a daisy. I pluck the tender blossom from a bed of moss and tuck it in my pocket. A flower that can frighten a hag is a flower I want on my person.

I maneuver through the bristly brambles in search of another little flower, more uncertain by the moment about whether they are guiding us somewhere I truly wish to go.

Chapter Twenty

Since leaving the old hag's shack, our party has been collectively morose. Understandably, Claret and Laverick have been sick to their stomachs. Harlow and Markham speak in private often, and Jamison continuously checks his pocket to assure himself that he hasn't lost Rafferty's snuff-box. Tavis and I lead the group, following the magical trail of daisies.

"Do you know why the old hag was afraid of the daisy?" I ask.

"Yes," Tavis replies, sounding perplexed. "Don't you remember, Evie? Mother and Father taught us."

"I don't remember. I guess I was too young." It isn't fair that Tavis had more years with them, and from those years, more memories.

"Daisies symbolize purity. For the Creator to descend to our world, she would have had to give up her throne as goddess and dwell in impurity, so she placed Madrona here in her stead." Tavis checks that Markham is out of hearing range, then says, "In the legend, it's said that Father Time cursed the isle and banished Markham. I heard once from the prince himself that Madrona corrupted the island to protect the gate under the authority of Eiocha. Daises represent their unity."

This interpretation is more logical—and disturbing. All three deities fought to keep Markham from the Everwoods. For some reason, one of them is helping us. "Who is leaving us the daisy trail? Madrona, the Creator, or Father Time?"

"They are all of one mind. A daisy from one is a daisy from all."
Tavis stops abruptly. "Did you hear that?"

I still and hear the rush of water. We side-foot down a ridge to a
river, our packmates trailing us. A daisy blooms on the riverbank, our
seventieth flower since the cottage, and still no gate.

"Where to now?" Laverick asks, scanning the murky water.

Markham plucks the daisy and twirls it between his fingers. I point
the sword upstream, downstream, and across the water. Nothing. That
doesn't make sense, unless . . . I aim the sword down at the river and
it warms and vibrates. I push out an irritated breath. Not in a million
worlds am I going in the water.

"Well?" Tavis questions.

"We need to cross to the other side," I say. "We'll walk alongshore
and find a shallower channel."

No sooner do I finish than a daisy appears upstream, floating on
top of the water. It surfaces out of nowhere and dances downstream.
The flower spins in front of us and sinks.

Markham grabs my wrist and aims the sword at the river. The hilt
heats up and tremors. He growls in my ear. "Deceive me again and I'll
do to your husband what I did to the centicore." He lets me go and lifts
his voice. "I've walked this channel before. We'll wade in."

Fear plants me on land.

"Sir," Jamison says, "we don't all need to go into the water. Everley
and I will follow along on foot."

Claret dips a finger in the river. "It's cold. I'll stay with them
onshore."

"I'm not keen about cold water either," says Laverick, scrunching
her nose.

"None of you can remain on the riverbank," Markham barks. "Get
in or be left behind."

He strips off his boots and stockings. Tavis joins him, removing
layers and stuffing them into his satchel. He wades in first and balances

his pack on his head. With his other hand, he judges the depth around him with his walking stick. At the center of the river, the water rises to his upper thighs.

"This is the deepest point," he says.

Markham shoves his shirt into his pack. "If I remember right, the water doesn't rise above chest level."

"You'd best be certain," I say. "Don't forget you need me."

His shirtless torso presses against my arm. "I'm not likely to forget your usefulness, Miss Donovan. You'd be wise not to forget mine." He lifts his pack overhead and wades in.

After an impertinent sneer at those of us stalling, Harlow trudges in as well. Stripped down to her shirt and trousers, she hisses at the abrupt cold but does not pause.

"Everley, you can follow us along the bank," Jamison says. "I'll carry the sword into the river." His offer is thoughtful, but he cannot take my place. The sword has ordered me into the water, and my defiance may prolong our quest.

"The river isn't too deep," I say, my confidence weak. As long as my ticker isn't submerged, I will be all right. The glass face seals out some water, including perspiration. "I'll be careful."

I remove my boots and stockings. Claret and Laverick follow my example, undressing down to their billowy shirts and breeches. The Cat grumbles the whole time, bemoaning the impending frigid water. I leave on my waistcoat. My shirt will become sheerer when wet, so the thicker cloth will conceal my heart.

Jamison removes all his clothes except his trousers. My gaze roves over his broad chest, golden skin stretched over sleek, firm muscles. I catch Claret and Laverick doing the same and shoot them a withering glower. They smirk at one another, unrepentant in their ogling.

Markham snaps at us to hurry along. He and Harlow are already shivering. Tavis waits in the thigh-high water, and I hesitate at the bank. The last time I entered any water was the night before my parents died.

Mother bathed me in their washtub and Father combed my hair by the fire. While my tresses dried, he told my siblings and me petrifying tales of the isle. He later stroked my head and said I had no cause to worry. Dagger Island was far away, and I was safe in our home.

Time is the foulest trickster.

Jamison consolidates our belongings into one pack and hefts it for us. Balancing my sword, I wade into the frigid water. The stony riverbed digs into my feet. One loose or slippery rock and I am doomed. I subdue my dread by concentrating on each step.

At the center of the stream, Markham twirls the daisy he plucked from the bank. Harlow stares daggers at the pretty little flower.

"Which way?" I ask.

He sniffs the daisy and tosses it into the water. We watch as the flower bobs downstream. Then suddenly, as though the river has switched directions, the daisy pinwheels back, passes us, and travels upriver against the current. Gooseflesh showers me from head to toe.

"Mother Madrona," Laverick breathes.

Back home, she would be sentenced to burn for uttering blasphemy. Here in the wilds, halfway around the world, where Madrona's power dominates more than any ruler's, she prays to the only authority that's relevant.

Markham and Harlow track the daisy upstream. Claret and Laverick go next, arms above their heads, holding their daggers and packs. I slog along between Jamison and my brother.

"Everley," Jamison says, "when we get out of the river, you're going to explain what's happening. I'm trying to be patient, but if one more daisy appears out of nowhere, I may explode."

He still hasn't guessed Markham's true identity. Why would he? Not in all the worlds would anyone assume he's the lost prince. I didn't want to tell Jamison or the Fox and the Cat, but the longer we spend in the Thornwoods, the more their ignorance feels like a risk.

Trees line the river. Their swaying boughs pause when we approach, then restart as we move away. The lull in birdcalls and creature chatter is more apparent from water level, a unanimous quiet that alarms us into silence. No forest I have traversed has been more aware of man's presence. The very river shifts in reproach at our invasion. Currents slice past my legs like fingers on the verge of plucking us up and tossing us to shore.

Our spinning daisy leads us into waist-high waters. I lift onto my tiptoes, legs quaking and feet aching. A steep incline extends far above the riverbanks. We enter the gulch, the water creeping up to the bottom of my rib cage. Any deeper and it will be more efficient to swim.

Laverick and Claret stop and go very still.

"Something brushed past my thigh," says Claret, her rolling r's more pronounced when she is afraid.

"I felt it too," replies Laverick.

She and Claret stay frozen while Tavis and Jamison survey the surface for signs that what the women felt wasn't a fish or a frog. Farther up ahead, Markham halts and then spins in a circle.

"What are you doing?" I call.

"The daisy disappeared," Harlow answers.

I search the high riverbanks for another flower. We're at the bottom of a ravine, the worst place to return our hunt to dry ground.

Harlow and Markham swivel toward a ripple approaching them quickly from upriver. Something skims the surface, bulging the muddy water.

Markham draws his cutlass. "Get to land!"

He and Harlow swim hard for the bank. As the swell races after them, I take out the daisy I tucked in my pocket and grip it for protection. Markham glances over his shoulder at his silent pursuer—and then they meet.

Water spurts up as Markham is dragged below. Harlow goes still as a statue just feet away from where he went under. Claret and Laverick shriek and thrash toward the steep riverbank. Tavis readjusts his grip on his walking stick and high-steps for shore. I start to return to land as well, my gait more cautious to avoid slipping in.

"Harlow!" Jamison calls.

She's unresponsive. He tosses his pack to shore and shouts for her again. As I lumber ahead of Jamison, every movement in the river feels adversarial. Claret and Laverick scramble up the embankment, clawing at loose dirt and pebbles. I'm in shin-high water when a tight binding wraps around my ankle and wrenches.

I twist as I fall, landing on my backside in the shallows. Tentacles shoot out of the river and grasp blindly at the embankment. The Fox and the Cat scream and kick. One of the tentacles, a slimy greenish feeler, has captured my ankle. I swing the daisy to ward it off, but the tentacle tautens and pulls me farther into the water.

"Enough of that," I say, discarding the flower.

A swift drop of my blade liberates me. I rise, drenched from my navel down, and the daisy is crushed in the mud.

Jamison slices at the tentacles, his rapier gleaming as a righteous beacon. Tavis cudgels the invader, wielding his walking stick like a staff.

Claret and Laverick have scaled out of reach. I begin to join them when Markham resurfaces, gasping. He rolls in uproarious waves, fighting against a thick tentacle coiled around his neck. Harlow returns to herself and stabs at the cloudy water. Her blind aim strikes his stealthy attacker. The tentacle releases Markham and the two quickly splash to shore.

I back up out of the water. Shivers course through me in violent surges. My heart clunks, a gradual unwinding.

Be calm. Be machine. Be indifferent, like time.

The water quiets, the surface glassy. Jamison and Tavis do not wait for another strike. They swim for safety. Markham and Harlow fight a path up the ridge. Laverick and Claret crest the top and look down. My brother reaches the embankment and starts up.

I hold back for Jamison. He's nearly to shore when tentacles shoot out, wrapping his arms and legs. He arches his back and swings wildly, but they pull him under.

"Jamison!" I wade back in as far as I dare.

He bursts from the depths, writhing against the tentacles around him. They snake up to his neck. I cry up to Markham. "Help him!"

He stops up the incline. "Climb to me with the sword!"

"We aren't leaving without Jamison!" I eye the river. The water isn't too deep out by him. I'll wade in and—

The tentacles roll him under and out of sight.

Quiet accompanies the leveling of the surface. Any splash or bubble is reason to hope, but no signs of life below manifest. He has been under too long already.

I start into the river with my sword.

Markham slides down the embankment and hurls me back. "You will not risk yourself." We grapple with the blade, jerking it back and forth. "Remember who you are, Everley. You're no hero."

I stomp on Markham's instep and he stumbles back. Sword raised, I wade into the water. Tavis side-foots down and splashes to me.

"You can't, Evie." He glances at my ticker hidden behind my wet waistcoat. Markham must have told him about my clock heart. My brother pries the sword from my grasp and dives in.

Standing at the water's edge slathered in mud, I scour the surface. Markham grabs my long hair and wrenches me back.

"Foolish girl. We cannot lose the sword!" He shoves me hard and I fall into the shallows, up to my wrists in chilly water.

Panic lashes across my middle. Time holds me captive, each tick another moment Jamison and Tavis don't have air. Each second drills through me, robbing me of my own breath.

The water erupts, and I shield my chest from a shower of spray.

A grindylow ascends from the river depths, Jamison entangled in its tentacles. Tavis stands before them both, the monster twice his height. The grindylow, a water creature that hails from an Otherworld, is the color of the river, a muddied mix of browns and greens. Round blank eyes sit on the outside of its bulbous head. Dozens of tentacles shoot out from its thickset body, and spiky fins run along the ridge of its humped back and oblong face.

The grindylow peels its mouth open, exposing razor teeth from gill to gill. Markham backtracks and clambers up the rise.

My brother confronts the creature and slashes Jamison free. He drops into the water and comes up gasping. Tavis maneuvers between them and stabs the grindylow in the side. The monster screeches, a garbled, high-pitched shriek. Tavis holds it off as Jamison staggers to the riverbank. I guide him out, and he collapses on the bank.

He pats his breast pocket. "Where's the snuffbox?"

"The what?"

"Rafferty's snuffbox. It's gone."

The grindylow shrieks and thrashes its head. I heft Jamison to his feet and push him to climb the embankment. Claret and Laverick call to him, encouraging him upward.

"Everley!" Markham hollers from above. He's almost to the top. "The sword!"

His concern for the blade and not my brother incenses me. If he cares so much about the security of the weapon, he should be down here.

Tavis splashes to the bank, and stringy tentacles sweep at his feet. He flies forward and hits the rocky ground.

I take back my weapon and step in front of him. The grindylow glides closer, sliding lithely at the surface, its head above water and its tentacles twitching. In shallower depths, the monster starts to climb out of the river, walking on tentacles. The grindylow spreads its lips in a vainglorious grin and lunges, teeth bared. I jump sideways, leaping over its feelers, and rotate. Double-fisting my sword, I drive the blade through its plump middle. The beast screeches, a pained whine. I withdraw my blade, and it limps back and then dives underwater.

Tavis scrambles up the slippery bank. I keep my sword raised for another strike, but the river soothes to a croon as the current journeys off into the forest. Something silver in the mud catches my eye. Rafferty's snuffbox. I shake off the water and pocket it.

Claret and Laverick help Tavis up the incline. I throw Jamison's pack over my shoulder and slip up the muddy ridge, the grindylow's shrieks still ringing in my ears. Near the summit, Markham reaches for me. I hold on to the sword and clamber up the last few feet on my own.

Rolling onto my back, I lie between my brother and Jamison.

"Are you—?" Tavis starts.

"I'm alive," I reply. "Jamison?"

"Just grand."

Laverick and Claret pass around the water flasks. I sit up to drink and take in our sorry state. Mud covers our battered bodies, our faces pale and tired. Markham and Harlow are already re-dressing, pulling their stockings and boots on over their dirty feet.

"Get up," Harlow says. "The lot of you can recover on the trail."

"We're not going anywhere yet," I counter. "We need to rest."

Markham tucks in his shirt and shakes water from his hair. "You will move when I tell you to."

"Had you helped us fight the grindylow, we might listen to you," I reply.

He replies with a rigid jaw. "I've waited nearly three hundred and fifty years, and on the cusp of my return home, you dare to thwart me?"

I rise on bare feet, hoisting my sword between us. "If you think that was a threat, just wait until you hear what I have to say now that I'm standing."

Markham reels back to strike me. I double-fist my sword and glare down the blade at him. Though I cannot wound him, the gratification of stabbing him would not be a waste of strength.

"Killian," Jamison says, his brow knit tight and his voice quiet, "how have you waited three hundred and fifty years to go home? Isn't home Wyeth?"

Markham withdraws from me and lets Jamison's inquiry go unanswered.

Tired of his ambiguity, I answer on his behalf. "He's been lying to you about who he is. He isn't just a governor for the queen. Killian Markham is the lost prince from legend. The gate we seek that will lead us to the Everwoods will in turn let him into his kingdom in the Land of Youth. Or so he says."

"It's not postulation," Markham says. He bows, a stiff bend at the waist. "I am Prince Killian, husband to Princess Amadara and king of the Ruined Kingdom."

Jamison holds very still, and then he lies back down again, his hands on his pumping chest as though he suddenly cannot catch his breath. Harlow wrings out her cloak, everything about this unsurprising to her. Laverick and Claret make up for her dispassion with gaping mouths.

"You're the lost prince of legend?" whispers Claret.

"You mean *the* lost prince?" Laverick finishes.

"It's not as impressive as it sounds," I say dryly.

"Ha!" Harlow snorts. "Where are your crown and title, Everley?"

No one laughs. My brother is understandably unmoved by this revelation, yet it is Jamison's reaction I am most preoccupied by. He sits up again, his demeanor even paler. I cannot read him. Is he astonished by Markham's identity? Wounded by his leader's lie? I wait for him to challenge this information or demand to know more. He hangs his head and says nothing about this fusion of myth and reality.

Markham tugs down his waistcoat. "Now, if everyone is recovered, I wish to return home to Ama. We may not succeed if we do not find the gate soon."

"What do you mean?" I don't recall any mention of there being a time limit on finding the gate to the Everwoods.

"Time cannot stand still forever," Markham answers, his tone clipped. "The tear in time in my world will eventually cave in on itself. My kingdom, my whole world, will collapse, and Amadara with it."

The Fox and the Cat fall into somber silence. They do not have all the information, not even half, but the significance of our mission is evident. Our failure to assist Markham on his journey home will lead to the destruction of a world.

Jamison rubs his forehead, as if he is massaging a terrible headache. He still has not looked up at me.

"Killian," Tavis says gruffly, seemingly bothered by our sudden time limit, "what would you have done had Everley not been sentenced to the isle?"

"Her arrival was inevitable," Markham replies simply, his arrogance absolute. "Misfortune worked against me for centuries. What you call bad luck is time shifting out of accord with one's wants and needs. Luck was bound to turn in my favor eventually. Time always heeds to persistence and determination."

By some absurd chance, I understand his reckoning. The very tick of my heart propelled me to find him, which in turn led me to the isle. My uncle calls this process dovetailing. He selects two pieces of wood that do not fit together and carves out notches until they knit in harmony. Time does not bend to our will as Markham thinks. We merely wait until our moment arrives. This philosophy has spurred me on for a decade. I always knew that someday Markham and I would reunite.

Jamison lifts his chin and opens his mouth to speak. Another moment passes before he finds his words. "How do we know you're not lying?"

"A lie serves its master." Markham holds out his empty hands. "I gain nothing from revealing my greatest vulnerability."

That may be true, but Markham is in the ideal position to deceive us. Only he escaped the fissure in time. Only he could have told the outside worlds *The Legend of Princess Amadara*. As the author of the tale, he could have manipulated the story to suit himself. All or nothing of what he told us could be true.

"My deepest apologies, Lieutenant." Markham lays a solemn hand over his heart. "Your wife insisted I not tell you. Out of respect for your marriage, I left the details of our excursion for her to recount. My regrets to you all."

The Fox and the Cat accept his apology with nods. They were the lost prince's supporters before his revelation, and even if they do not fully believe who he is yet, they want to.

Jamison tugs on his shirt and boots while I fish my own boots and stockings from his pack. Regardless of my constant glances at him, he ignores me. Dressed and ready to travel on, he asks, "How long do we have, Killian?"

Markham weighs his inquiry before he replies. "The closer we are to the kingdom, the more unstable the tear will become. Envision a tattered rope bridge suspended over a chasm. Brogan snuck across without damaging the integrity of the bridge. But the more people that pile onto the bridge, or the more often the bridge is traversed, the sooner the brittle ropes will snap and collapse."

Jamison accepts this answer without balking. "Which way do we go, Everley?"

His cold tone shrivels any gladness I felt that he's acknowledging me. "I'm sorry, Jamison. I would have told you—"

"Which way?" he repeats.

"I'll consult the sword," I mutter.

Claret and Laverick heave on their packs. Besides theirs, all our packs except Jamison's were lost in the river. Both his and Markham's pistols were rendered useless by the water, and Tavis lost his walking stick, the current having swept it downriver. The Fox and the Cat pull away from the group, excluding me from their quiet conversation. Though I wait for someone to come with me, no one offers to help me locate the next daisy. I am on my own.

Chapter Twenty-One

My sword directs me down a trail of daisies that bloom like new stars in the duskiness. Claret and Laverick whisper behind me, their discussion indistinguishable except for the word "prince" every so often. I have no interest in eavesdropping, my concentration on heeding the sword's promptings.

Ahead I spot a break in the woods. I duck through the gap and stop. We have come upon a lake, the sky above overcast and mountains in the distance. Trees crowd up to the still, dull water. My companions join me, Jamison limping a little.

"Children of Madrona," Claret groans, "I'm still damp from the river."

The island has more hidden pockets of peril than the alleyways of Dorestand. I refuse to aim the sword at the lake's flat surface and find out if we should go in. No matter what, I won't go in.

"Is this area familiar to you, Markham?" I ask.

"Your father and I were separated at the river. That was the farthest I've gone."

"Look there," says Tavis.

Daisies are mixed into the reeds by the lakeshore. Thank the Creator, we aren't going near the water.

We track the flowers around the lake in a single-file line. Tavis stays as close as my shadow, his nearness driving my thoughts to our father. I cannot fathom why Father would leave his wife and children to return here. He was not motivated by riches or treasure. His curiosity for answers and hunger for adventure were his downfall. In that, I hope we are not alike.

"I don't expect you'll forgive me, Evie," Tavis says, his voice weary. "I know you aren't proud of what I've become, but it would mean a lot if you'd remember me as the brother I was and not as I am now."

His request compels me to compare this man to the brother I remember. "I think I prefer you now. You're more forthright than you were, and you went back into the river to help Jamison. I'm not sure the old Tavis would have had the courage to do that."

I glance over my shoulder, assuming my brother will be pleased. His brow puckers and he rubs his chest as if pained.

"I should have been with you all these years," he says. "You needed me, and I let you down."

Exhaustion frays at my resentment. I haven't the strength to hold on to my anger, not here, not with so many other worries requiring my care. "I still need you, Tavis. I hope you'll choose me this time."

A long pause stretches between us, disturbed only by our footfalls. Finally, he answers. "I will, Evie."

The pathway deviates from the lake, back into the woods. Our party seizes the opportunity to wash away the dried mud before parting from the water, in which time the Fox and the Cat finish their conspiratorial whispering and query the prince.

"How did you manage to hide for so long?" Claret asks. Whereas I am suspicious of his tricks, she seems impressed by his centuries-long ruse.

"By not hiding." Markham's reply triggers a round of "aaaahhs" from the con artists. Harlow beams with pride, as if fooling others is worth boasting over. "No one anticipated the legend was authentic, which made changing identities simple. I moved around every decade or so and took a new name. My greatest detriment was my inability to age. My state position in Wyeth is the longest post I have held in the public eye. This is also the only time I've used my given name. With time running out, I needed to return to myself."

Laverick appraises him. "Does the queen suspect who you are?"

"Queen Aislinn is blinded by her own ambitions." Markham trails his touch down Harlow's arm. "I've also hired assistants over the years who've dispelled rumors about me that were too near the truth."

A question jumps off my tongue. "Was my father too close to your falsehoods?"

"Brogan had his own secrets," Markham replies.

"*He's* not here for me to question," I say.

My brother shakes his head at me to disengage. Again, Markham is unruffled. "I gave your father several chances," he says.

"How many chances did you give my mother?" I take a charged step forward. From the corner of my eye, I see Jamison grip his sword.

The governor, the prince—no, my parents' killer—replies quietly, "Brogan could have saved your mother, but he let her die."

I charge Markham, slamming him toward the water. He stumbles to the lakeshore and teeters on the brink of falling. I grip his collar, uncertain if I will toss him in or impale him. "What about Isleen's final moments? Your men used my sister and knocked out my brother for trying to stop them."

Harlow drags me off him. "Everley, control yourself."

"What do you gain from this?" I ask, shoving her off me. "Your prince wants to reunite with his princess. Once he does, he'll let his men use and discard you too."

"There are other ways to be used and discarded," she says.

"You'd know that better than I."

"That's enough." Markham tugs down his waistcoat, the epitome of propriety. I sense the Fox's and the Cat's alarm and confusion but feel no inclination to expound on my rage. "My patience is ebbing. Everley, I've been forthright with you, yet you continue to punish me for your father's deceptions. I tolerate your misplaced animosity because I know who I am. Despite your ingratitude, I have given you the same chance as your father to explore wonders and discover worlds. Don't squander my gift."

"You've no remorse for what you've done," I say, tears grinding my teeth. "You can pretend you're something else, but I see you for what you are. You're a monster."

"Which of us is wielding the sword?"

His pious smirk undoes me. I swing my blade to slice his stupid, handsome face. Jamison's rapier connects with mine, stopping the blow.

"Everley," he says lowly, "you're better than this."

"I'm really not."

I push against him, steel against steel. Claret and Laverick stand ready with their daggers. Tavis's fists are balled. They will fight alongside me—*they* have loyalty—but a mutiny will solve nothing. Markham will still be indestructible and a charlatan. We will still be lost in the Thornwoods, and I will still rely upon my clock heart, which, at the moment, is closer than ever to breaking.

I withdraw my sword and stalk uphill into the woods.

Markham yells for me to come back. The evergreens muffle Jamison's reply, his voice infuriatingly level and reasonable. I storm farther into the trees. These woods are full of threats at every turn. I would still rather be out here than spend another moment near that liar. Markham can play the poor lost prince, but he *is* a monster.

And yet, the longer I am with him, the less certain I am that he's the only one.

Footfalls resound behind me.

"Everley, wait." Jamison's plea urges me faster. "I cannot keep up. Slow down."

"Do I need to defend myself?" I ask, halting. "Or can I put away my sword?"

"I interfered on your behalf." He hikes up to me, lunging over heaving tree roots. "Taking Markham's life means more to you than your own."

"I cannot kill him. The lying bastard was honest about two things: he's the prince and he's trapped in time. Markham is immortal."

Jamison comes closer, compelling me to lower the sword. "You didn't think it was important that I know? You'd hang for killing the governor. I was preparing myself to attend your execution."

"My thoughts have been elsewhere. Tavis says our father was culpable in his own death." My voice hitches, then drains to a rasp. "If Father could have saved us, why didn't he?"

"Sometimes there's no good explanation."

"There's always an explanation."

"The solution you want might be wrong." Jamison's clear eyes pin me, obviously aching in pain. "After Tarah's death, I returned home on leave. My sister was long dead by the time I arrived. The marquess sent for me after her wake. My fury was so great at him for not taking better care of her that I struck him with all my might." Jamison balls his fist and stares at it, as though he carries the memory in his knuckles. "My father huddled on the floor weeping, so drunk he couldn't stand. His weakness incensed me. I hit him again and again . . . When he was bloody and unconscious, I was so ashamed of what I'd done. I had beaten the man who for years had beaten me. I couldn't be like him, not his marriage, not his selfishness, not his temper. With his blood still on me, I vowed to change."

I start to ache for Jamison, for his loss and sadness, and then an image of myself plunging my blade into Markham returns. I was unashamed then, and I still am. Something must be wrong with me to have no compassion.

"Jamison, I'm not you."

"I don't want you to be. My father disowned me. My relatives want nothing to do with me. I lost everything, Everley. I don't want you to lose everything too."

Jamison reaches for my sword hand, and I recoil.

His tone hollows out. "All I want is your trust."

"I warned you I'd make a poor wife."

"So you did." Jamison inhales a long, slow breath, and those morning-sky eyes beam at me. "I promised myself that my life wouldn't emulate my father's in any way. No woman ever tempted me to go against that vow until I met you."

My chest pangs. I have never felt more undeserving of someone's kindness. "I cannot change who I am," I say, patting my heart. I cannot discount the ticking hunk of wood in my chest, my life force, my compass. "I'm sorry, Jamison. Even at my best, I'll always be a little broken."

"Over here!" Claret shouts from somewhere off in the trees. "We found something!"

Jamison reaches for my hand. This time, I let him take it. "You're more than the girl with a clock heart. You're Everley Donovan, born into this world to do great things." He tips his head against mine, his forehead to my temple. His deep voice curls into my ear. "You are not broken."

Markham appears downhill. "Callahan! Everley! You must come see this!"

I lean against Jamison, wanting so badly for what he said to be true. But then why am I afraid of not making the most out of each moment? Why am I seldom content where I stand? I pull from his grip and trudge downhill to Markham.

"Finished sulking?" he asks.

"Want my blade in your gut?"

He chuckles darkly. Oh, how I long to put him in a grave.

Jamison ambles down to us, his manner reserved. I send him a brief smile, so he will know that I may be angry, but not at him. Markham leads us parallel to the hillside. The land levels off and trees thin out. Our party stops at the opening to a bowl-shaped canyon filled with daisies.

Thousands of the yellow-and-white wildflowers stuff the field within the gorge. The meadow is as long as the *Lady Regina*'s main deck and twice as wide. Flat, rocky cliffs on both sides soar straight up, higher than bell towers.

Across the meadow, on the closed-in side of the ravine, the massive stone wall is draped with legions of ivy vines. The barrier is so tall it could obstruct a giant. In the center of the rock face is a small divide like a slot canyon. An iron gate two doors wide is wedged between that narrow opening. Ivy has coiled around the bars and filled in the gaps, hindering our view of the other side.

"This is it," Markham says with a bright laugh.

Harlow beams at him and grabs his arm to revel in their accomplishment. The two of them are positively giddy. Jamison squints at the gate as though it's an illusion that he expects will disappear, while the Fox and the Cat wear expressions of eagerness like they have spotted a profitable mark to steal from.

My brother and I gape in rapt amazement. Until seconds ago, the entrance to the Everwoods existed only in storybooks.

"It's real," Tavis whispers.

"Mother would have loved to see this." My sword thrums, vibrating in double time with my ticker. The amalgamation of their warbling makes me light-headed. The feeling reminds me of Father's homecomings. I could hardly sleep the night before he came home. First thing in the morning, I would dress and wait for when it was time to go to the docks. Mother was up and ready for the day, more excited than me. When we first saw Father walking down the gangplank, Mother would run to him. Watching him scoop her up and swing her off her feet made me feel airy all over, like I was the one flying. The same feeling emanates from the sword and collects in my clock heart.

This blade—my blade—is the sword of Avelyn. It must be. I cannot otherwise explain how steel could radiate joy.

My sword wants to go through that gate, and I want to take it there, but the field has an unnatural tranquility that puts me ill at ease. The rock faces are vertical, the flat stone terrible for climbing without rope, which we lost with Markham's pack.

"Well," he says, "shall we?"

"Something isn't right," replies Jamison. He picks up a stick and throws it into the field. The instant the stick hits the ground, dozens of black dots leap up around it.

"What in the name of Madrona?" Harlow says.

Jamison flings another stick and the same explosion of life occurs.

I crouch down and part the nearest crop of daisies. On the floor of the meadow, concealed by the flowers, crickets swarm. Tavis, Claret, and Laverick all inspect the sections in front of them. The crickets, as long as my forefinger, are everywhere. Jamison tosses another stick farther out, and more crickets burst from the flowers.

"Ow," Tavis says, jerking his hand away. His finger is bleeding. "One bit me."

Markham pokes a stick into the flowers. Some of the crickets hop away, while others snap at the wooden intruder.

"Grand," he drawls. "Flesh-eating insects."

We stare across the expanse at the gate. My sword has not quit vibrating. I point it at the iron doors, and it warms and shivers more quickly. I should have known this would not be as simple as walking up to the gate. Nothing on Dagger Island is as it seems.

A cricket strays outside of the flowers. Harlow slams her foot down on it, producing a sickening crunch. Markham watches the drab sky with centuries' worth of frustration. He could cross the meadow alone and suffer through the cricket bites, yet he stays. He must need me to pass through the gate; otherwise, he would have taken the sword and left.

Claret and Laverick sink back and carp about the crickets. Tavis pinches the bridge of his nose, the same motion our mother used to chase away headaches when her children were squabbling. Jamison contemplates the field as though it's a puzzle.

"We came all this way," Harlow states, referring not just to our trek through the woods but to the voyage across the sea, "and now we're going to let crickets stop us?"

She picks up a stone and hurls it at the daisies. It strikes the flowers, then bounces and slides to a stop. No crickets leap from the meadow floor. Jamison edges forward, peering at the thrown rock. He takes a pine cone and tosses it in the same direction. The pine cone lands near the stone, again without disturbing the crickets.

Nothing on Dagger Island is as it seems.

Sheathing my sword, I speak to the group. "Everyone collect stones and pine cones. There may be a path across. We just have to find it."

They all listen except Harlow, who crosses her arms over her chest. Jamison removes his cloak, turns it inside out, and folds it into a sling. We load our pickings into it.

"Harlow Glaspey," Markham says, his arms full of pine cones, "help us or be gone."

She stomps into the trees and returns with a bundle of sticks. Once the sling is brimming, I grab a handful of dirt and sprinkle it on the closest flowers until I find a section where no crickets hop out. I expand the width until they do.

"This area is clear," I say. "It must be our way across. We'll use the pine cones and stones to test which direction to go."

"I'll go first," Markham says.

He hefts the bundle of rocks, stones, and twigs over his shoulder and steps into the field. His feet crush the dirt-covered blooms. No crickets are riled. He casts a handful of stones ahead of him until he finds the next clear patch of land. Over and over, he uses the ammunition to test and mark a zigzag path. More than once, he disturbs the crickets and suffers their wrath. He does not let their bites slow him down.

Halfway across the field, he pauses to consider the sky. I was so intent on his progress, I did not notice the light changing. The gray dims rapidly, spreading out from an inky cloud hanging over the gate.

"The curse is trying to keep him out," Tavis says. "We need to cross *now*."

Markham begins to toss stones and pine cones haphazardly. Harlow embarks down the established route, then Jamison and I follow. Claret holds on to Laverick and they enter the ankle-high daisies, followed closely by Tavis.

The field is wider than it appeared from the outskirts. Winding through the switchbacks goes on forever. By the time we close in on Markham, the murky heavens have deepened to onyx. We catch up to where he stopped, over halfway across, and view the problem. He has run out of ammunition.

"Find things to throw," I say. "Anything you can spare."

"We've no time," Markham counters, gesturing at the sky.

He lunges for my sword, knocking Harlow out from between us. She stumbles toward the edge of the path. I grab her before she falls in, and Markham gets ahold of my sword.

Jamison grabs the back of Markham's shirt and swings him around. Markham jabs the blade at Jamison. He staggers back, letting go, and Markham sprints into the field.

Crickets explode around him, bouncing and flying.

"Killian!" Harlow shrieks.

He doesn't stop. The wave of agitated crickets sets off ripples of jumping and chirping that spread across the meadow. The insects rain down on us.

"Get to the gate!" Jamison shouts.

We dash into the fray. My brother streaks after us, the Fox and the Cat holding hands while running. Harlow reacts the slowest, her figure speedily masked by the swarm.

Crickets crowd the sky, obscuring the failing light and blocking our view of the gate. They land in my hair and on my clothes. More crunch under my feet, the whir of their wings deafening.

Pain erupts from my scalp, my ear, my back. I battle down my revulsion, my ticker driving into my sternum. They are feeding on me.

Jamison and I run headlong into clouds of them. His knee gives out, but he catches himself before he falls. I throw my arm around him and we stagger through the wall of insects. More crickets bite through my clothes. Jamison and I arch in agony.

"Everley! Jamison!" Tavis calls for us from ahead.

We follow his voice to the gate. Midnight swirls around us, pushing down from the deadening sky. Markham yanks at some sort of square lock with tiered inner dials, a cipher of peculiar digits inset in the metal around them. The mechanism binds the gate shut. He gives up on solving the cipher and strikes at the lock with my sword.

Jamison swings his pack at the crickets. Out in the field, they form shifting flocks that swoop over the flowers. Harlow breaks through the curtain of crickets, batting wildly. Claret and Laverick appear in front of her. One of them trips and they both fall. Harlow speeds right past them. A barrage of crickets descends, covering the Fox and the Cat. Tavis plows back into the field for them. At the same time, Harlow arrives.

"You left Laverick and Claret," I say.

Harlow leans against the wall, winded. "I made it. They can too."

"Everley!" Markham calls. "The lock is unbreakable. We must cipher the code."

Welts spot his forehead. I would be glad that his good looks have been spoiled—punishment for this brutal chaos—but the same bites cover me. Unlike mine, his heal soon after they rise.

I inspect the keyless lock and twist its three-tiered dial. "What are these signs?"

"Our calendar. Year, month, and day."

"It's a clock," I say. The workmanship is unlike any I have seen. This timepiece was crafted by someone with a very complex understanding of time. "The cipher must be a date. Try when you were locked out of the kingdom."

Markham turns the dials until the correct year, month, and day line up with an arrow at the top. He wrenches down.

The lock does not open.

Tavis calls out from close by. Through the cloud of crickets, I discern pillars of shadows. My brother carries Laverick on his back, Claret lurching alongside him. Jamison shouts their names and guides them to us. Bite wounds riddle the trio. Laverick's injuries are the worst; her face is so swollen, I would not recognize her if not for her reddish hair.

Markham curses. He attempted another date on the dial and failed.

"Try a date you spoke to my father about," I say, striking at crickets. "He unlocked the gate with information you gave him."

Markham stares sightlessly at me while he scrolls through his memory. "I told him about the day I entered the Everwoods and met Amadara."

Harlow blanches. The date of significance involves his beloved. It is also the day the prince took Amadara from Father Time, who I am almost certain is the craftsman of this lock. Markham spins the dials to line up the numbers. Tavis and Jamison knock crickets off Laverick, who can scarcely stand. More insects leap from the field onto us. An immense swarm heads our direction, a shifting haze in the night.

I back up against the gate. "Markham, hurry!"

The swarm barrels toward us, their beating wings thunderous. Jamison and I swing at the first arrivers. Our whole party retreats to the gate and presses against the ivy-draped bars.

"Markham!" I yell.

Darkness descends in a blinding barrage of wings. I shield my face from the chomping crickets. Just as all the light has been taken, the gate behind us opens, and we pitch backward into oblivion.

Chapter Twenty-Two

I'm weightless, neither falling nor flying, standing nor sitting. My limbs and hair float around me, my body suspended in a blinding wash of light, not sunshine yellow but silver like moonbeams. I smell pine and moss, wild berries and fresh dew. And I'm warm, warmer than I've felt in years. My fingertips are toasty, the normal tingling replaced by a generous current of heat.

The radiance fades and I return to the ground.

A bed of moss cushions my landing. I clutch at my chest, gasping. Warmth lingers in my hands, similar to residual heat from a hot bath. My ticker vibrates against my palm. I close my eyes and savor the rare seconds without wintery pain.

"Everley?"

I roll onto my side. Jamison is lying next to me, and our wounds have healed. His eyes are the bluest I've seen, as vivid as blueberries. I could stare into them forever.

Forever.

The word resounds through me. I scan the leafy canopy, mottled moonlight streaming through the branches. Markham blocks my view, the sword of Avelyn in his grasp. I prop myself up onto my elbows, feeling a fool for ever doubting his birthright. Standing before me in this lush forest, he exemplifies the prince of legend.

"Where are we?" I ask.

"The Everwoods. The tunnel to my kingdom is on the other side of the garden. Get up. We need to move."

Markham goes to rouse the others. The entirety of our group made it through the gate. Each of us is still on the ground, staggered and awestruck by our surroundings.

Moonlight twinkles across the tender greenery. Starflowers decorate the forest floor, their pastel petals every color of a sunrise. Majestic elderwood trees tower over us, their boughs leafy and their wide trunks a russet hue. I have seen depictions of them in books, but they are much taller in person. A breeze streams through their branches, wind song as gentle as a lullaby. As the name suggests, seasons do not visit the Everwoods. These waxy leaves are everlasting.

Butterflies dart around the climbing blossoms, radiating sparkling light. One flits past us and I see its body is shaped like a woman. They aren't butterflies or moths, but sprites. This one has long green hair, horns like a caterpillar, and twisting purple veins throughout her iridescent wings. The sprite blinks her doe eyes at Jamison, then darts off into the night. Even the darkness between the trees is welcoming, cozy pockets of shadow.

Something small runs past us. Jamison bends forward and picks up an orchid. Someone laid the azure bloom on the ground near my feet, and that person is still nearby.

A little man, no taller than the length of my foot, peeks out from behind a knoll of tree roots. He wears a robe of leaves over his portly body and a crown of twigs on his bald head. The second our gazes connect, the gnome disappears.

I've scarcely accepted what I saw when the petals of the orchid Jamison is holding open. The blossom transforms into a tiny young woman with a pointy chin and ears.

"A pixie," Jamison says.

Pixies are common creatures in stories. They are to myths what clouds are to the sky. She has two smaller wings that are turned downward and a set of larger wings angled up and out from her slender back. Though the pixie is blue, wings and all, she has more childlike features than the sprite's, as well as short hair and a mischievous smile.

"She's lovely," I say.

Jamison extends a finger to touch her. The pixie trills a string of high notes, her tone unmistakably indignant, and zips off.

These creatures belong in storybooks, to worlds beyond our own. Myths say that the Everwoods is an ingress to the seven worlds. Some say this bridge to all life exists on the moon, others in the heart of an acorn, while most say this eternal garden of creation is all around us, veiled from sight, and only the pure in heart may see it.

Jamison picks a fat raspberry from a briar-free bush and pops it in his mouth. He moans and immediately grabs another. "You must try this."

"Are those safe to eat?"

"Where else can you trust a berry than in the Everwoods?" He offers me one. The sweet sourness permeates my mouth.

"It tastes like a perfect August day."

"Didn't I say?" Jamison picks more and eats them, staining his lips red.

I inhale the moonlit air. It smells fresh without being musky and frosty without being cold. "Can you believe we're here?"

He touches a pink carnation. The blossom transforms into a pixie that flies away. "It's better than a dream."

Now that I have seen the Everwoods, I appreciate why Princess Amadara wished to roam here and never leave. But I myself don't want to linger. Until moments ago, I thought this place and its Creator were an allegory for how life came into existence. I'd rather not be found trespassing in Eiocha's domain.

Claret and Laverick help Tavis to his feet and take turns thanking him. They have healed as well, which above all, Laverick is thankful for. She was in an awful condition when we left the meadow. Jamison and I get up next, him still favoring his bad knee. Only the wounds we sustained in the Thornwoods, those inflicted by the curse, have vanished, which makes sense. If old injuries had healed, I would not still need my clock heart.

"The little imp snuck into my pocket and stole my fire striker!" Harlow says. She runs past us to a tree and sticks her arm down a burrow at its base. A second later, she yanks her hand out. "It pinched me!"

"Gnomes are fond of shiny things," says Markham. "I'll replace your striker."

"The striker was my father's. It's irreplaceable." Harlow revolves on her heels and stalks off to kick at flowers. Pixies flee the path of her rampage, shooting away to safety.

Harlow's mention of her father stuns me. She never speaks openly about her family or upbringing.

"Who was her father?" Laverick asks. She, of course, is swift to meddle.

"He was my former assistant," Markham replies, his tone griefstricken. "We were mates in the navy. He passed away from illness while we were at sea. Years later, I heard Harlow's mother had been arrested for streetwalking and had died in prison. Harlow had been living on the streets for months."

"You saved her," says Claret, commending him.

Markham answers loudly, so everyone can hear. "Harlow was succeeding on her own. If not for her aid guarding my secrets, my identity may have been found out."

Harlow doesn't respond, though she does quit stomping on the helpless flowers.

Markham gestures with my sword. "This way. Stay close."

He tromps into the trees, scrutinizing every shadow. Though I cannot tell what has agitated him, he must be anxious to find the doorway to his world.

We navigate through the pathless underbrush farther into the forest. Claret and Laverick walk close together. The humming pixies and countless pairs of eyes observing us from every level quiet them. Harlow maintains her distance from Markham, who plows through the undergrowth unaffected by her coolness.

Tavis and I gawk at every wonder. The ancient elderwoods are colossal. Nothing could feel more indomitable, yet they shrink from us, lowering their roots to the ground and lifting their branches to evade our touch.

"Do you think we'll see Mother Madrona?" Claret asks Laverick.

"I should hope not." The Fox gives the next elderwood a wide berth. "She could be any of these trees."

"Maybe she's listening," says the Cat. "Maybe the trees and animals do have spirits. Do you think so?"

"I think I'll never eat meat again."

I would laugh, but making light of creation power would be disrespectful, especially here. I cannot refute the elderwoods' eminence. The warmth I felt upon arrival radiates from their spirits. They are filled with the call of life. I hold back from my party and lay my palm against a tree's velvety bark.

Anguish pulses from its core, so strong my head reels. The sadness flows to my chest and pools around my heart. I distinguish a single sentiment in the deluge of emotions—the elderwood tree is in mourning.

More trees lend their voices to the one I'm touching, all imparting the same sorrow. The conclave of trees seems connected and unified. I rest my cheek against the gentle bark. *Why are you in pain? Who hurt you?*

Shadows stir in front of me, and in them, a young man appears. All but his face is concealed by the dim. I step back, meaning to run, but stop. The austere gentleman, so grave and serious, is not a stranger.

Father Time I know, and he knows me.

He knows my woes and scars, my past and present, and more intimately, my clock heart. His attention ensnares me. His all-seeing stare probes past flesh and machine, cracking open my soul and exposing my innermost secrets. My lust for vengeance is plain for us to see. I joined this trek to discover answers about my father and prove I can be courageous like he was, but my bigger incentive is to punish Markham.

I cover my chest to conceal the ugliness. In this spotless bridge between our world and the next, the intent of my heart has never felt more monstrous.

Jamison jogs back to me, our other packmates gone ahead. Father Time vanishes as though the wind picked him up and swept him away.

I check down the neckline of my shirt. The crack in the glass face of my clock has spread. More alarming is the minute hand spinning like a windup pocket watch. Earlier, when I felt my clock's vibration, I thought nothing of the absence of its ticktock. My clock heart is pushing onward. It is time that has stalled.

Jamison adjusts my shirt and waistcoat to cover my ticker. "Are you all right?"

"Well enough. We need to go."

I do not add where the inner warning stems from. All I know is that Father Time didn't collect on the years I owe him. I don't want to give him a second chance.

We hurry to catch up to our companions. They are too engrossed by the animated garden to notice our temporary absence. As far as I can discern, I'm the only one who saw Father Time. He must be whom Markham is wary of. The last time they saw each other, Father Time banished him.

My brother treads to my side. His approach wakes a group of sprites from a shrub, and the dainty creatures shoot off into the night.

"Father walked here," Tavis says, contemplating the flowering vines cascading down an elderwood's trunk. "He must have been fascinated, the explorer that he was. I understand his desire to return here now."

I prefer to think our father viewed the forest as I do. He would have known as soon as he entered that he was unfit to dwell here. Every regret, every misstep, every transgression against another, would have been a needle in his soles. We all fidget and glance around with the same out-of-place feeling.

Except Markham.

He continues without a care for the blossoms underfoot or the trees he brushes past. As I think ahead to his time-frozen world, my unease spreads. Markham was vague about what happens next. He spoke of treasure, restarting time, and reviving his princess. Never once did he divulge how he would reverse the curse.

I search the shadows for Father Time but do not see him again. A constant flurry of winged creatures dart about, the sprites more agile than the pixies, and the pixies more playful. Gnomes peek out from their burrows and, on occasion, run across our path like scurrying rabbits. The main mystery of the forest is which of these magnificent elderwoods was the first tree in all the world, Mother Madrona herself. Naturally, Markham does not point her out. I wouldn't be surprised if he took a longer route to avoid her.

Before long, we arrive at a thick hedge on the outskirts of the woods. Markham plucks a pixie off a tree branch and shakes her. Shimmering dust rains from her wings like stardust and lands on the greenery, and then a hole opens near the ground at the roots of the shrubbery.

"Impertinent vermin," Markham says, flinging the pixie.

She dashes off in a stream of light.

"The poor darling!" says Claret.

"Pixies are the rats of the Otherworlds. If it weren't for the magical properties of their dust, we would exterminate them all." Markham wipes excess dust off on his trousers. "In concentrated dosages, their dust makes things vanish. A convenient talent when one needs to create a door."

Tavis bends over to examine the cavity in the shrubbery. "This leads to your world?"

"Don't let the portal's appearance dissuade you. We will be in the Land of Youth in moments." Markham kneels on the ground. "Brogan told me what we can anticipate on the other side, but be vigilant. Our arrival may exacerbate the tear in time."

He crawls into the tunnel, and Harlow goes in after him.

"Is anyone else disturbed by the magical hole?" Jamison asks.

I am more concerned about what we will find on the other side. We are leaving the Everwoods for a time-starved world. That is far scarier than a tunnel. My ticker has survived the Thornwoods and the Everwoods, but I have no way of knowing how it will respond to the Land of Youth.

"We'll go next," Laverick says.

The Fox and the Cat enter the opening one after the other. Tavis and I stare each other down. Neither of us wants to go next. At last, my brother concedes and crawls in.

Jamison eyes the heavenly woodland. "Something feels amiss. I don't know what."

"This entire expedition is lunacy. But aren't you curious what we'll find on the other side?"

"I could live without knowing." He passes me the bell from my regulator. I slipped it into his pocket before we left the ship. "We're going to survive this so I can teach you how to hide that better. Keep it for luck."

"Will this bell save me from tragedy?" My lips quirk. He has no idea that the function of my regulator was to do just that.

A movement in the woods diverts his attention.

"What is it?" I ask, slipping the bell into my pocket.

"Nothing. Go on. I'll be right behind you."

I bend down and peer through the narrow tunnel. A grayish light waits for us at the far end. Is this how Princess Amadara snuck into the Everwoods, by means of pixie dust and enchanted passageways?

Keeping the girl princess in mind, I crawl through the tunnel and into an Otherworld.

Chapter Twenty-Three

Tavis helps me climb out of the portal. Our party has gathered at the base of a tree on a grassy hillside. At least one detail of the legend is wrong: Princess Amadara could supposedly look out from the balcony of her castle and see the Everwoods. But the forest is gone, no hedge or elderwoods in view.

Markham has lowered to one knee. He presses a palm on the ground, his head bowed in triumph. The lost prince has come home.

Far as I can see, the Land of Youth is equivalent to ours in design. Ground under us, heavens above, and sky in between. The similarities of this foreign territory do not prevent me from fretting. We are far away from our world, and I've no idea how to get back except for the way we came. I memorize the tree and our surroundings.

Jamison climbs out of the portal last and takes stock of our destination. No one speaks, all of us waiting for direction from our guide.

Markham rises and motions for us to be still. He treads away from the tree while we hold our breaths and wait for the world to cave in on us. I envision a rope bridge snapping and all of us plummeting into an abyss.

I tug my gloves higher. The weather is not cold enough for our breaths to stain the air silver, but the night is crisp under the tarnished moon.

After several steps, Markham beckons us. "Come along. The tear is holding for now. Remember, low voices and light feet. We should be all right."

His reassurance is thin comfort.

We trample through the grass as carefully as seven people can. The field is unsettling without any wind; nothing moves. A deer with curling antlers and stripes across its midsection has lowered its head to graze. Flies and moths hang in the air as if on invisible threads. The stillness is absolute, as though we're traipsing through an oil painting.

My clock thrums as it spins, a reassuring vibration amid the stasis, yet every so often, the whirling hiccups. The minute hand is snagging and tripping over something. I cannot figure out what, so I pick up my pace as much as I dare to speed along our progress.

Markham pauses to overlook the valley. Far off, across more fields, housetops crowd up to a stone castle, the whole village surrounded by trees. Something blue zips across my side vision. I stop and peer through the knee-high grass. Everything should be still and quiet, so the thought of something else awake with us pushes me closer to my comrades.

We go carefully down the hill toward odd-looking trees. Nearer to them, I see they are a forest of men. Statues of soldiers spread before us, bedecked in armor and bearing spears and battle-axes. At least three hundred men are congregated near a river. All of them—skin, bone, hair—have hardened to wood. I have admired many wooden figurines in my life. None were this realistic.

Claret knocks on a soldier's chest and a hollow thud resounds. "Who did this?"

"Our army was preparing for battle against another kingdom when Amadara—" Markham presses his fist over his mouth in despair. "When people are held captive by a break in time, creation power dims and flesh and blood decay. This wooden state occurs when a spirit is trapped in a body where time has ceased."

A curious pattern of logic. Time bows to creation power. That's reasonable, given that the Creator oversees Father Time. What does that mean for my clock heart? It's still sustaining me. I wish I knew for how long.

Laverick looks into a soldier's blank eyes. "They're not dead?"

"Dormant," Markham says. He grips a statue's shoulder, his expression aggrieved. "We may start to feel the effects soon as well. Let's keep moving."

We travel through a cluster of soldiers and past their cavalry. They were watering their mounts at the river when Amadara tore time. The soldiers' horses have also turned to wood, and the river around them is eerily stationary. I am tempted to touch the water or the horses, but I dare not disturb either. I cannot fathom how time can stop an entire river from flowing.

"Are your foes from the neighboring kingdom locked in time as well?" Jamison asks.

I startle at his curiosity. The legend tells of the impending war, but doesn't clarify the fate of their enemies, and I did not think to inquire.

"Yes," Markham replies flatly. "The tear impacted my whole world."

"How many people live here?" Claret whispers.

Markham turns away from the cavalry, toward his castle. "Too many."

Harlow strokes the back of his head to soothe him. I despair to think that these soldiers are trapped inside themselves, alive and aware of their slow decay from flesh to wood. Amadara could not have known the consequences of saving her prince. Even Markham, bastard that he is, could not have foreseen that harvesting the heartwood from the Everwoods would amount to unending torment for countless innocents.

We trail the inert river downhill through the wooden regiment. Markham pauses at every other man, addresses them by name, and pats their shoulder. They were his soldiers and comrades, his brothers-in-arms.

As we near the end of the field of soldiers, his stride quickens. The castle waits, its towers illuminated by moonlight. Upon the highest tower, the roof has been broken by the top of a tree.

"Onward to my beloved," Markham says, leading the march to his castle with my sword.

The village seems deserted. Cobblestone roads span between tight rows of thatch-roofed cottages. I expect to see more wooden people, children and families, servants and clergymen. Not a soul wooden or otherwise is immediately in sight.

"Where is everyone?" Laverick asks.

"Why are you whispering?" Claret replies.

"Why aren't you? This town is frightening."

Jamison veers from the group to a cottage. He rubs his elbow across a dusty window and waves me over. He steps back so I can see through the streaked glass, his lips in a grim line.

My muscles jump under my skin at what I see. A child lies in bed, frozen in sleep, while his mother sits near. They are both wooden. Whatever brought her to his bedside is a secret that has long since been locked away. Did he have a nightmare? Was she singing him a lullaby?

More mysteries whisper through the static village. An old man stands frozen in the open door of a cottage. Is this his home? Or was he visiting? A woman was lugging a heavy basket down an alley. Where was she going? What brought her out at night?

My mind spins along with my heart clock. Markham believes the spirits of his people still reside in those wooden shells. I hope he is wrong and they are unaware of their confines, sleeping soundly in this lull in time.

I quit glancing in windows and doorways. Part of me wants to turn around. I'd rather endure the biting crickets again than follow Markham another step. But my father saw something in this place that was worth returning for. I cannot leave until I view this bleak kingdom from his perspective.

We start across the arched bridge over the river. Water would have flown by the castle and flung itself off the side of the hill in a dramatic waterfall. Instead, the river is stuck midleap, the airborne water frozen. Untouched by what must have been a powerful current, the stone castle clings to the hillside, a grand overseer for all the kingdom. Battlements crown its many towers and staggered rooftops.

Our stone path connects to the lowered drawbridge, which we take to the outer curtain. The portcullis is almost up, a welcome gesture if not for the wooden guards gripping the pull chain in the gatehouse. We slide past them and Markham opens the iron yett, letting us into the large inner courtyard surrounding the keep.

Along with guards and servants, animals are stalled by the wooden scourge. Horses do not flick their tails, and a cat's hunt was thwarted, its hind legs set to pounce on a mouse. As we pass through the stables, I duck from a spider dangling on a strand of web. The sanctity of life stops me from plucking it down to study the slenderness of its wooden legs. It is not a figurine to play with.

The entry to the keep is closed. Jamison and Tavis open the door and Markham slips inside. We file in after him, Harlow more reluctantly than the rest. The musty air settles in my nostrils as Markham goes to the wall and lights a torch. He travels the exterior of the room, lighting others. Jamison and Claret each pluck one up.

The great hall is as still as a coffin. Moonlight sneaks in through a window high above, illuminating the large room and double-wide stairway leading to the upper floors. We pad across the red carpet to the pair of matching dining tables that are as long as the room. The table legs are carved with daisies. I stoop to admire the artistry and spot a white bear rug before the hearth at the far end of the hall. Candelabras decorate the tables, and tapestries hang on walls opposite each other.

Over the hearth, a banner with a crest spans to the ceiling. It is a white mare beneath an elderwood—the Creator and Madrona. The antiquated furniture and architecture belong to another time and place. There's something distinctly foreign about the rounded doorways, bright carpets, and wide molding.

Markham runs his fingers over a high-back chair. He suits this bygone era, when people hung tapestries and needed arrow slits in their walls. Without a word, he strides to the arched stairwell and bounds up.

"Killian, wait!" Harlow says, dashing after him.

The remainder of our party hurry to follow. At the upper landing, we stop and listen. Harlow calls for Markham above us.

"This way," Laverick says, following the sound of her voice.

The Fox and the Cat round a corner and shriek. Something hits the ground, and wooden pieces scatter over the stone floor. Tavis drags me back. Jamison draws his sword and charges around the corner. I shake free of my brother and edge forward.

A wooden guard lies on the floor, his arms and legs broken into chunks.

"I—I didn't see him," Claret says.

"We didn't mean to knock him over," Laverick assures her.

Jamison crouches over the guard and picks up a lump of his shattered leg. My mouth parches, repelled by the wooden cadaver. The insides of the man are hollow like a rotting log.

Tavis steps over the fragmented remains of the guard. "Markham is headed to the top of the tower. That's where he shared a chamber with Amadara."

Farther down the hall, we pass a chapel with a stained-glass window. It is a duplicate of the crest in the main hall of Madrona and the Creator, a white mare beneath an elderwood. Laverick and Claret duck inside and peruse the chapel.

"Don't disturb anything," I say.

Claret eyes the collection plate. "We're going to take a look around. We'll catch up soon."

We leave them to rummage around while we continue down the hall. Jamison limps to another stairway. Tavis and I start up, but he stalls to rub his knee.

"Go ahead," he says, offering us the torch. Tavis and I swap a glance, then my brother slides his arm around Jamison and starts to climb. Jamison goes along, but grouses. "I can make it on my own."

"My sister thinks I should help you."

"She didn't say a word," Jamison replies.

I push out a sigh. "Be quiet and let him help you up the stairs."

"You make a fitting husband and wife," Tavis remarks, his tone light. "Our mother and father would have approved, Lieutenant."

A weighted pause overtakes the stairwell. I am both relieved that I cannot read Jamison's expression and wish to the stars that I could.

The stairs end at a set of doors defended by a pair of castle guards with spears. Markham jiggles the lever. When it doesn't open, he claws at a brick in the wall. Harlow is so still she could be a statue. Markham pulls out the loose brick and reaches into the hole behind it. He emerges with a golden key.

"Killian?" Harlow asks, a breathy plea. She seems to be seeking a promise of reassurance. For what, I cannot say.

"It will be all right," he replies.

Markham straightens his waistcoat and inserts the key into the lock. The noise of the bolt sliding echoes through the stairwell, then a deafening click. Markham pulls up the lever, pushes in the door, and mutters something to himself.

Only after he goes in do I decipher what he said.

"I'm home."

Harlow lifts her chin and marches in, and then the three of us follow. Jamison and Markham set our torches in the sconces. Feminine cloth and gold leafing trim the elegant furniture. A silver comb and hand mirror rest on a vanity. Across the door is a balcony, the doors hanging open, and in the center of the room, a grand bed. I only know it's a bed because of the four posts still standing. The mattress, canopy, pillows, and other bedding have been consumed by an elderwood.

The fingerlike roots of the tree snake across the floor, buckling the stone. So thick is the trunk that the center occupies the bulk of the wide straw mattress. Low branches cover the ceiling, yet only the bottom portion of the tree grows within the castle walls. The top has pushed through the roof and spilled into the night.

A tree growing so successfully in the middle of a bedchamber may be the most spectacular sight I've seen yet.

Markham strides to the grand elderwood and touches the velvety tree trunk. "Amadara, I'm here. I've come to set you free."

He draws my sword, and gripping it with both hands, slices into the tree. The gleaming blade goes through the trunk with little resistance. Claret and Laverick find us in the tower, their packs hanging lower and their pockets thicker than when we left them. They gape at the prince sawing into the elderwood. We all remain at the edge of the chamber while he chops through the outer bark.

He punctures the exterior of the trunk, and an inner cavity opens. Markham lays aside the sword and peels off the velvet bark in great strips, ripping the hole wider.

A hand appears inside.

"Help me," he says, pulling at the outer layers faster.

Tavis goes to his aid. Together, they dig open the center of the elderwood and uncover an arm and torso. In another few moments, the hole in the tree trunk is large enough to crawl into.

"Careful," says Markham.

He and my brother reach into the cavity and pull out a young woman. She is as stiff and pale as white pine. The two men struggle under her weight but manage to lay her on the floor without dropping her. Unlike the guard in the castle hall, the princess has hardened to solid wood.

I edge forward beside my brother. Princess Amadara could be a wooden statue or an expertly crafted doll. Her exquisite features are so lifelike she could stand up and move about without a puppeteer or strings. She does not seem much older than me. Her face is composed of angled features balanced by a soft chin and full lips. It's no wonder Father Time fell in love.

Markham traces her high cheekbone, his gaze wandering over her face. "Do you dream of me, my love? For I have dreamed of you."

He leans down and tenderly presses his lips to hers.

I fidget at the intimacy of the moment. We are intruding upon their privacy, yet I cannot stop myself from watching.

Tears run down Tavis's cheeks for the reunion of the husband and wife. Markham's hands will always be bloody, but the horrors outside this castle feel far away compared to the hope the sight of the prince and princess instills.

Love is unstoppable.

Love can break the bounds of death.

My hand seeks Tavis's. He looks at me in astonishment. I have not yet sought his touch or affection. I have been too afraid of what it would mean to move on. No matter how trivial or insignificant, my touch is my best offer of forgiveness. A promise that I would seek him through the eternities.

The prince kisses his princess's cheeks and forehead several times each. Tears brighten Harlow's angry eyes, her chin quivering. Laverick weeps too. Even Jamison's gaze shines with withheld tears.

"So beautiful," Claret says, wiping her wet cheeks.

"How do you wake her?" Tavis asks.

Markham stands above his wife, his countenance drawn down. "No power can repair the damage left by a fissure in time. Once time is torn, the lives under its care are lost forever."

Before I can ask him to explain, he picks up my sword, lifts it over his head, and plunges it into the chest of his sleeping princess.

Chapter Twenty-Four

Time buckles beneath me. My heart does a little jump, skipping ahead and then whirling, then skipping, then whirling once more. The sequence of stops and starts, the incredulity and dread, leave me woozy.

I need a moment to think and breathe. Per usual, time doesn't care what I require.

As Markham hacks farther into his princess's chest, my unbelief blinds me to what I am seeing. What is this insanity?

I seek my companions' reactions for understanding. Harlow's lips twist in a wicked smile, but the others are no less shocked than me. Claret and Laverick appear near to fainting, embracing one another as though to hold each other up. Tavis covers his eyes and mutters "no, no, no" under his breath. I relate to Jamison most, his expression locked in horror. It is the look of someone who has identified a monster—a blend of abject terror and wrecked innocence.

Monsters exist and, apparently, so do monstrous princes.

The princess sheds no blood. Markham butchers her surgically, as my uncle would section a portion of wood for crafting, splintering away the rough outer layers and cutting into the hard inner core. He goes no deeper than the length of three or four barleycorns into her left breast and then saws out a small section where her heart once beat. Out of spite or warped sentimentality, the shape he chooses to carve is a heart the size and width of an acorn.

"This," Markham says, holding up the wood for all to see, "is the greatest treasure in all the worlds. Others have sought riches and gold, jewels and priceless antiques. The heartwood of an elderwood tree contains the power to animate life."

Harlow strides to his side. "I'm sorry I doubted you, Killian."

He kisses her and murmurs against her lips, "I promised we'd be together."

Markham's honeyed words for Harlow, when not long ago he was professing devotion to Amadara, snap me from my shock. I tremble all over, my ticker jumping sporadically. The image of him carving out the princess's heart will never leave my mind.

The heartwood must be the sought-after treasure from his kingdom. This expedition was for him to finish what he started in the Everwoods. He returned to his world so he could gain creation power.

And he still has my sword. I *want* my sword back.

"You're vile," I say. "I should cut you down and leave you here to rot. You never meant to wake Amadara."

"I couldn't," he replies, sweeping out his arms. "Amadara ruined time. Not even Father Time could reverse her destruction. He no longer has power here. Releasing Ama from this living tomb was a mercy. She's at peace."

"She's in *pieces!*" I yell.

A sudden quake shudders the castle. A pulse of agony strikes the middle of my chest. I double forward onto my knees, my clock heart wrenching. Markham and Harlow lean against the tree for support. Tavis weaves on his feet while the doors to the balcony swing closed and then open again. Laverick and Claret brace themselves in the doorframe. Behind them, the sky is staggering. The moon is tilting from its perch and steadily dropping toward the horizon.

As soon as the quake stops, the pain in my chest ebbs but leaves a wake of gooseflesh.

A second stronger quake hits, and the agony recommences. The tree branches swing and sway as though a gust of wind is barreling through the tower. I stay down as furniture skitters across the floor.

The Fox and the Cat have crept out of the chamber onto the balcony. Stones from the hole in the roof shower down, and Tavis bends over me to shield me from the debris. Jamison covers his head until the shaking peters out. I can breathe again, but the deadening cold senses my weakness, and the tingling in my fingertips spreads.

Tavis straightens from where he stands over me. "What have you done, Killian?"

"The rope bridge is falling," Markham replies.

The tear in time is collapsing. The pain in my ticker must be tied to the incoming obliteration. Time is falling apart, and with it, the one thing that is keeping me alive.

Tavis is pasty, his countenance drained of color. All his strength goes to his voice. "You're destroying your world."

"Oh, don't look aghast, Tavis." Markham loops his arm over my brother's shoulders and embraces him as he would family. "Time eventually turns on everyone."

I see him raise his sword, see him turn it on my brother. Yet I am too slow to react, to scream, as he plunges my sword into Tavis, straight through his middle. I experience the blow as though I am the target, the pain paralyzing. Tavis releases an awful noise that should never be made by anyone. I make a similar moan of agony as Markham extracts the blade in a clean swipe.

Tavis drops to the floor, bleeding out before me. I kneel by his side and press down on his wound. My gloves are sticky and wet in seconds. On a burbled exhale, his gaze washes to blankness and the call of life within him goes silent. I cannot tell if the anguish in my clock heart has restarted or if it didn't ever cease.

"Don't weep, Everley," says Markham. "Access to creation power may only be obtained through blood sacrifice. Tavis would have wanted it to be him."

Markham wipes my brother's blood across the heartwood. The blood soaks into the wood and it glows, strengthening in brightness. A wave of light ripples out from the heartwood and cascades through the castle, out the door, across the balcony, and expands to the rest of the kingdom. Within a moment, the golden surge overtakes the field beyond.

Laverick and Claret step nearer to the edge of the balcony to see. Below them, the waterfall unfreezes and gushes down the cliffside. As the shining wave stretches to the horizon and travels on, the glowing heartwood dims.

Markham lowers his treasure. "Guards!"

The castle guards stationed outside, formerly wooden statues, step into the room. Their appearance has not transitioned back to flesh. They are wooden, like giant replicas of the figurines I lovingly carve. Each movement is mechanical, rigid and meticulous. They cross their spears, blocking the door.

Jamison helps me get up onto my wobbly knees, then stand. We back up toward the balcony, closer to the Fox and the Cat. The terrible quaking returns, fiercer and angrier. The minute hand of my ticker is slowing and the pain screwing deeper. Time is vanishing, and with it, the power that has driven my heart is vanishing too.

"You've awoken your army?" Jamison asks.

Pain blurs my vision, so I cannot see out at the fields. Jamison holds me upright and prevents me from sinking to the floor again.

"My men would have perished," replies Markham. "I have given them a second life. Flesh is weak. In this form, they are strong."

A shudder from the land sinks the moon faster. Segments of the castle crack apart, and debris streams and bounces around us. Agony cranks into my chest, swelling in cruelty.

Another quake loosens the balcony, severing free the stones under the Fox and the Cat. The whole partition collapses, and they tumble out of sight, their screams swallowed by the revived waterfall.

Jamison and I retreat from the torn-off ledge. The wooden guards stomp up behind us, their spears forward.

"Lay down your weapon, Lieutenant," says Markham.

Jamison drops his rapier. The next quake pushes a fresh stab of pain into my chest. I gasp, clutching my clock heart. Jamison holds me up and stares daggers at Markham. "Will you sacrifice us too?"

"No need. I'll leave the collapse of time to finish you. When the moon collides with the horizon, this world will disintegrate." Markham signals at his castle guards. "Seize them."

The wooden soldiers drag us to the elderwood. The tree wilts and withers to gray, yet another life Markham has taken. Jamison swings at a guard. His fist slams into his wooden chest and goes no farther. He grimaces, like he has punched a wall. One of them strikes him in the middle, and Jamison slumps over, wheezing. They manacle our arms over our heads to low-hanging branches, so high that our feet dangle.

Harlow saunters up to me. "This is how you and I part, Everley."

The castle walls decay, another one tumbling loose, and weakening moonlight rushes in. I rely on my bindings to hold me up, my head hanging and my hair in my face. The pain in my chest threads apart my focus. My clock has outlasted the lull of time, but it will not outlive its collapse.

Harlow opens the top of my shirt to reveal my sputtering clock heart. "I imagined it bigger," she says.

From the corner of my eye, a blue light dashes in from the doors to the balcony and disappears behind the vanity. My sight is focusing in and out, eroding to splotches.

"It's time to leave," Markham says to Harlow.

I glare at him through the curtain of my hair. "My father was right to keep you away from here."

Markham strides up to me. "You still don't understand. Brogan knew this world was unsalvageable. We intended to harvest the elderwood's creation power together. He betrayed me, Everley. He failed us both." The prince tucks my hair behind my ears so I have nothing to hide behind. "Your father's greed killed your mother and siblings. He could have saved you all, yet he chose to die instead of share the treasure with me."

His harsh words drain the last of my strength. I slump forward, too stubborn to let his and Harlow's final view of me be with tears.

"Come along," Markham says, locking elbows with her.

They depart, the guards following them out, and leave Jamison and me shackled to the tree as the world shakes apart.

Chapter Twenty-Five

Markham's rapid footfalls down the stairs carry from the tower into the chamber. I sag forward from the tree, my toes skimming the ground. As soon as the noise of Markham's departure ceases, a swell of rage floods me. I wrench at my bindings and yell at the sinking moon.

A quake hits, crippling me with a fresh flood of agony. Each rumbling tremor lengthens and strengthens. The roar rises through the floor, widening the cracks in the stone.

In the following quiet, Jamison jerks against his shackles.

"I'm sorry," I say.

He quits resisting his confines and slumps forward. "You didn't know."

"I knew he was a monster, and yet when he held Amadara, I believed him. I believed he loved her."

"Maybe he did love her once." Jamison's voice mellows to a reflective timbre. "I didn't want to change you, Everley. I just wanted you to be free of him."

"I wanted that too."

A tremor hits the castle and the floor splits open between us. Branches wane as the tree leans in our direction. We try to scramble from its path, but our bindings lock us to the plummeting elderwood. Trunk and boughs tip toward the floor as branches crash around us. The top of the tree rips through the ceiling as it bends, its roots buckling the stone.

Jamison and I are pulled under a tangle of leaves. My branch snaps as the tree lands on the torn-up floor of the chamber. The top of the tree breaks through one wall and hangs partway out of the tower. A tidal wave of green immerses me. I go still, then slip my shackles off the broken branch and climb to the surface of the greenery. Out the huge hole in the ceiling, the moon has nearly sunk into its grave.

On the far side of the tree, Jamison tries to free himself from his branch. I need something to trigger our locks.

"The tool kit," he says.

I unbury his bag from under debris and dig out the kit. My fingers tingle and my joints quiver. I jam the recalibration tool into his lock and jiggle it open. Jamison frees me next from my shackles, then stuffs the tool kit in his pack and puts it on. We help each other over the cracks in the floor to the stairway. Big chunks of steps are missing and crumbling apart, the staircase too precarious to use.

More quaking starts and does not stop, one long sustained rumble, one never-ending stream of pain. I lean against the doorjamb while Jamison searches for another way down from the tower.

A pixie flies out from behind the vanity and hugs a bough of the fallen elderwood, her little wings drooping. She must be the light I saw more than once since we came to this world, having followed us from the Everwoods. Jamison sneaks up behind her and snatches her in his fist. She squeaks at him and kicks her little feet.

"I'm not going to hurt you," he says. "We need you to make a doorway to the Land of the Living. We need to go home." The pixie sticks her chin out in defiance. He lifts her to eye level. "We'll all perish if you don't help us. Can you create a door that will take us out of here?"

The pixie points out the balcony and makes a motion like a door opening.

"There's a portal?" he asks, and she nods. "Will you show me?"

Jamison loosens his fist, and she flies out the balcony door. We stumble across the vibrating floor, around gaps and crevices, to the ledge. The pixie flutters her iridescent wings over the rushing waterfall. She points down, and then once more, makes the motion of a door opening and shutting.

"Oh, no, no, no," I say. Markham told us the portals are in undesirable places. A waterfall suits where one could be hidden. I dare not consider where it will spit us out on the other side.

"Is there another option?" Jamison asks.

The pixie points off into the hills by the army of wooden soldiers. The moon is a moment away from splintering. We will never get to the other portal.

Jamison's solemn gaze holds mine. "Everley . . ."

The tower starts to disintegrate around us, shaken apart by another quake. The pixie flies into Jamison's breast pocket to hide. I lock hands with him, and we leap.

Suspended in midair, we're cradled by the same warm hand that welcomed us into the Everwoods. The hand slows our fall, as though we're dropping through hot molasses, and then we burst the bubble and smack gushing water.

I lose Jamison's grip on contact and plunge under the surface. Though I can hold my breath longer, my heart clock immediately floods, knocking me breathless. The gears lurch to a halt, and my limbs seize. A current hurls me about over and over again as I sink farther into the deep.

Arms drag me up to the surface. Air presses upon me, but my sleepy lungs will not draw a breath. Water tosses me about in hard, wet slaps, and soon, the cold quits hurting. I stop preparing for the next wave of pain and embrace the quiet.

Amid the emptiness comes a pervasive calm. I sit up, but my body stays beneath me and I float out of myself in spirit form.

Even as a spirit, I have a clock for a heart. Below me, Jamison is hunched over my body on a beach. The pixie sits on his shoulder, watching him work on my ticker. Beyond them lies a blur of green and blue, land and sky. I float up, so high that I breach the treetops and swim in the clouds.

Across the isle, I see the white tents of the settlement. North, up the same western coastline, another group congregates.

Who are they?

My clock heart spins, and then my spirit soars up the seaside. Markham and his army of wooden soldiers emerge from the Thornwoods and gather on the shore. He evacuated from the Land of Youth through the second portal the pixie pointed out.

His mammoth ship is anchored offshore. The last time I saw the *Cadeyrn of the Seas*, it was moored on the windward side of the isle. He must have anticipated his return from his fallen world. All along, his plan was to awaken the wooden soldiers and lead them here.

He and his army begin marching down the shoreline toward the settlement.

What does he have planned?

In answer, my clock heart whirls, and my spirit leaps across great distances, flinging me like a streaking comet. The moon and sun fall away, and then suddenly I'm floating over a fallow field.

Two armies confront each other on opposite ends of the open area. Markham directs his troops from atop his horse, brandishing the sword of Avelyn. His battalion comprises fearsome giants. The monsters of legend tower over the catapults and are even bigger and uglier than my imagination.

Across from Markham's legion of giants, a second militia has gathered. Smaller in number, their soldiers include men and women as well as some giants and a mixture of mythical beasts. Within their ranks are so many fantastic creatures, I cannot fathom where they came from or how these forces were united.

The hodgepodge military is captained by a woman astride a white mare. Her helmet and shield conceal her face and hair. The captain extends her sword and leads the charge against their enemy. I have no sense what her army battles for, but I am invested in their victory.

What will happen should they lose?

Again, my clock heart spins and my spirit jumps across a great distance. I arrive at a location I haven't been, a hilltop overlooking apple orchards. Servants toil in the field below, picking fruit and packing it into bushels. Among the workers, I recognize Vevina and Quinn. The lass is older, closer to my age. Markham sits in a throne on a dais above them, the sword of Avelyn at his side.

The severed head of his adversary, Father Time, is displayed on a pike for the field workers to view. And above in the heavens, worlds explode, shattering to dust.

Something tugs on my spirit. I want to stay and see which worlds have been demolished, but I'm dragged through a backdrop of black punctuated by stars. When I halt, my spirit is again hovering over Jamison.

The pixie looks up and grins at me, then I am sucked down into my body.

Tick . . .

. . . tock.

Heat surges in, scattering the icy hollowness. Air, sweet and pure, sneaks past my lips. I lean on my side and cough up water. When I roll onto my back, Jamison engulfs my vision.

"Good creation, I thought I'd lost you." He gathers me in his arms. My dry eyes ache from sand and sun. I close them and listen to my heart ticktock between us. Its song is my call of life.

"How?" My voice is hoarse, like I swallowed buckets of ice.

"The daisy clock," Jamison says, rebuttoning my shirt. "Before we left the ship, I took out its innards. The glass face of your clock is still cracked, but the gears work."

He dismantled the daisy clock and gave me its working parts.

I slide my fingers into his damp brassy hair. His hand trails down my back and pulls me closer. Cold water splashes over our feet. We are lying on a beach, in the path of the fledgling waves. Dawn has risen on the eastern side of the island, the horizon awash with fiery hues. The sun gains strength as she rises to her throne above.

Up from the breakers, sitting on a log, the pixie hums to herself. Her wings are tucked behind her, her little legs crossed at the ankles. Two pairs of fresh footprints lead from the sea up to the trees.

"Do you think those tracks were left by Laverick and Claret?" I ask. "We should have a look around."

Jamison assists me up the beach to the scattering of driftwood where the pixie has perched. I sit down to rest and she stops singing to herself.

"Thank you for helping us," he says. The pixie flies up and wags her finger at him. "My apologies for holding you against your will. It won't happen again." She sits down and ignores us. "I guess that means I'm forgiven. Wait here, Everley."

Jamison follows the tracks up the beach, searching the seashore for evidence that the Fox and the Cat did indeed enter the portal and return here. I would search for them too, but I don't want to tax my newly repaired ticker.

I remember everything that happened while my heart clock was flooded. Floating out of my body and flying, visions of wooden soldiers and giants and apple orchards. They couldn't have been real.

But the images were vivid—and plausible. Markham reanimated the castle guards. He could have roused his brothers-in-arms and evacuated them out of the Land of Youth to the island. Until I eliminate the chance that what I saw was a bad dream, I have to presume the vision of the future was real.

Jamison trudges back. "Their tracks disappear at the tree line. I doubt they went into the Thornwoods. The curse isn't broken." He plunks down on the log and flicks sand from his hair. "Given the placement of the sun, we're on the southern end of the island. Claret and Laverick must have gone west toward the settlement."

His geographical assessment matches the map of the island I memorized. It also fits the location of Markham's troops and the direction of their marching. They were on the northwest end of the isle heading south.

"Jamison, I think Markham is on the isle." I quickly summarize having seen his army while I was incapacitated. I don't tell him about the battlefield or the dais over the apple orchard.

He ponders to himself, his countenance contemplative. "Your spirit left your body and flew across the sky." He doesn't sound skeptical, merely confused.

"I don't know how I did it. I only know what I saw. Do you think Markham plans to attack the colony?"

"It's possible. Now that he has his treasure and his army, he could do anything." Jamison curses to himself. "His army of wooden soldiers are brutes. When I struck the castle guard, I thought I'd broken my hand."

My concerns mount for the settlers, especially Quinn. "We should get back to camp."

Jamison shoulders his pack. I rise slowly, testing the vigor of my clockwork heart. After all the wondrous things I have seen, I hoped I would gain an understanding of how my ticker functions and sustains me. What has increased is my gratitude for the extra time I have been given. I live for Tavis, and Amadara, and every other soul in the Land of Youth whose time has expired.

The pixie flies ahead, bucking the strong winds. Every bit of me aches, from skin straight down to bone. Even the hair on my scalp twinges. The pixie waits for us far in front. We catch up and she zips ahead again.

"Blue's an impatient thing," Jamison says.

"Blue?"

"It doesn't seem right not to give her a name."

"How do you know she doesn't have one? And suppose she doesn't. Your first choice is 'Blue'?"

"You name her, then," Jamison says.

The pixie hovers in the air as we trudge up to her. She and I cannot communicate through speech, but it is as plain as the scowl on her face that she considers me inferior.

She lands on Jamison's shoulder and trills a tune that is far more complex than any birdsong. He grins at her.

Good sin. He's smitten.

"'Blue' will do," I say on a sigh.

As we trudge farther up the shore, Jamison passes me a dagger from his pack. "Take it, Everley. It's the only one I've got."

His gesture warms me—he knows I'm less apprehensive when carrying a blade—yet his relinquishing our only weapon to my care also sobers me. We have to reach the settlement before Markham and his army.

Chapter Twenty-Six

Blue zooms ahead and waits for us in midair, her arms crossed and toe tapping. She will have to tolerate our infirmities. Jamison's knee hasn't had a rest in countless hours, neither of us have had proper sleep in I don't know how long, and my heart clock may be ticktocking, but the new gears are clunky. The ticks feel sharper, as though the minute hand is flinging itself forward. The alteration is slight and I sense no physical repercussions, but I am coddling the replacements parts. The daisy clock was beautiful sitting on a shelf. But does she have the strength to run more than time?

We catch up to Blue and she perches on Jamison's shoulder. We climb a rocky outcropping and take in the view of the settlement huddled in the cove. No wooden army is in sight.

"Are we going?" I ask.

Jamison's awareness has drifted out to sea. "A storm is coming."

Indeed, a curtain of gray suspends across the watery horizon. We quick-foot down the outcropping and up the beach. The *Lady Regina* remains anchored in the bay. I watch for Markham's ship to cruise into the harbor, but as we get closer to the tents, neither his ship nor his army have come.

As the winds serenade us, I smell breakfast—hotcakes and bread. Hunger pains warble through my stomach. Jamison halts and offers

Blue the front pouch of his pack to hide in. She flits inside and he pulls the flap down over her head.

"We need to get everyone on the ship," he says. "Send the women to the beach. I'll gather the men and the longboats."

I grab his arm, making him stay. "Good luck."

On impulse, I lean in and kiss his cheek.

Jamison gives me a closed-lipped smile. "Good luck to you as well."

He squeezes my hand and jogs off to the settlement. I select another path and go straight to our tent. Quinn is playing with Prince on the floor. Dr. Huxley keeps her company while sorting through his medical supplies.

"Everley!" Quinn throws her arms around me. "You're back!"

"Pack your things, we need to leave." I scoop up her cat and pass him to her, then stuff her wooden figurines in her bag. Alick rises in alarm. A gust billows the tent walls and howls over the roof. "We need to round up as many people as we can and board the ship. Governor Markham has turned against us."

Claret and Laverick burst through the door, Vevina after them. With all of us inside, the tent is cramped.

"You made it!" Laverick cries.

"Jamison and I went through the same portal," I say. "How did you find your way back?"

"We remember the map of the island from the lieutenant's cabin," Claret answers, setting down the sack slung over her shoulder. "We came to warn everyone about Markham, but no one believes us. Not even Captain Dabney."

Vevina sets her hands on her hips. "The captain thinks an immortal prince is hogwash, but I didn't trust the governor. He's too charming."

"It helps that we showed Vevina our bounty." Laverick pulls a bronze candlestick from a sack. Also inside are a handful of strange gold pieces and the silver collection bowl from the castle chapel.

A slight vibration shakes the ground. Over the wind, another tremble comes. Then another.

"We have to hurry. Markham brought the wooden army from his world and they are marching this way." I push Quinn toward Alick. "Get the sick and wounded to the beach. Quinn, stay with Dr. Huxley." She holds Prince close and pets him. "Vevina, you and I will evacuate the women. Jamison is alerting the men. Women go in the longboats first. As soon as you fill a boat, row out to the ship. Return as many times as you need for the others. We will try to hold them off, but if there are any strong swimmers, suggest they not wait."

Vevina draws a dagger. "I guess I'll be needing this gift from the captain."

"We'll each require a weapon," I reply calmly to avoid hysterics from Quinn. She has stemmed her distress well so far.

"This is a penal colony," Alick interjects. "Half the men aren't armed, and those of us who are have few weapons to spare."

"Laverick and I will find something," says Claret.

They leave to scour for a defense, and Alick extends his rapier to me.

"Trade me for the dagger," he says. "I'm not much good with a sword."

I do not know if that's true or if he's being generous, but we exchange weapons. I hug Quinn, squishing Prince between us, and send her along with Alick. Vevina and I leave the tent, and she claps loudly for the women to gather. Many have left their own tents to discuss the vibrations.

As I usher women outside, I spot a daisy in the middle of the path. A second daisy bobs in the wind not far away. Then even farther, in direct line with the others, a third and fourth flower.

I follow the row of daisies to the tree line. Ferns swish and branches sway, bullied by the drafts. The stormy horizon has shut out the sun, casting pale shadows over camp. I stop before a patch of daisies and still. A slight kick of my ticker nudges me to peer into the woodland.

My gaze locks with another's.

Father Time is partly concealed by a pocket of trees. He has come to collect on his debt. I could run, but that would be pointless. I cannot hide from time.

I brace myself for the conversation I have been evading for almost decade and traipse into the underbrush, halting so I am still within view of camp.

"You found your way." His voice is as smooth as a well-oiled clock. "We have waited a long time to meet you, Time Bearer."

I search for the partner he speaks of, but only Father Time slips out from behind the trees. As with his ageless features, his clothes are time-less and elegant: polished boots, charcoal trousers, fitted gentleman's jacket, crisp collared shirt, and plain black neckerchief. His lean limbs, straight shoulders, and trim waist lack distinguishable attributes. He is a paradigm, the original form for mankind, if on the shorter side.

He strides to me, daisies sprouting at his feet. His gaze is level with mine, our height equal, his eyes the shade of an evergreen. His spidery lashes could rival any lady of the court's. His feathery hair sweeps across his forehead and hugs his neck, neither too short nor too long. With a willowy finger, he taps my ticker, and a jolt goes through me as my heart clock quickens.

"Please don't collect on the time I owe," I say. "Not yet. I must stop Markham's army first, then we may settle my debt."

"Everley, you owe us no debt."

"Then I must make amends for my family. My father—" My voice breaks, testing my dominance over my ticker. "The Donovans have been dishonorable to the Everwoods and Princess Amadara."

"Amadara was indeed Majesty of the Trees, but Prince Killian was jealous of our friendship and has not told the whole truth of the events. Perhaps someday we will share the tale with you as it truly transpired."

Father Time steps nearer. My racing heart levels out and the gears glide effortlessly. His presence is a balm for the ticking in my chest. "Brogan Donovan did not defy creation power. Upon his return to the isle, he was to deliver the sword of Avelyn to us in the Everwoods."

"But Markham said—"

Father Time's expression turns stony. "Prince Killian has told many falsehoods. You have seen the insidious aftermath of his corruption and foresaw the calamity that will befall the Otherworlds."

For a moment, I am at a loss, and then I recall the spirit journey I took while Jamison was repairing my waterlogged ticker. "My visions were real?"

"You sense their truth and fear their validity. A single lie can break a spirit or destroy a dream."

"But if I saw the future, then I also saw what will become of you."

"That is our fate should you fail." Father Time's reasonable tone of voice belies the urgency of his warning. "You must take back the sword of Avelyn, Everley. We already lost one world. We cannot lose another. If we've any hope of defeating Prince Killian, you must have it."

"Who is 'we'?" I ask, checking the small grove. "Are you not alone?"

"Time is infinite. We are not here nor there. We are everywhere and in everything. It is easier for the mortal mind to confine us to a single figure, so we choose this form."

Right now my mortal mind is muddled by a cluster of emotions. I have countless questions for him, ponderings and worries that have kept me up at night and haunted me during private moments of the day. "My Uncle Holden said you brought me back to life. Did you save me? Did you help him install my clock heart?"

"Do you not believe your uncle?"

I blink fast, taken aback. I didn't anticipate he would ask my opinion on the matter. "I—I don't know."

"The time will come when you will be ready to receive the answer, then you will know." Father Time does not fidget or gesture when he speaks. His confidence exudes a supernal stillness. "Do not fret over how much time you have left, Everley. You will have enough to accomplish the task we have set forth."

I still have a hundred questions about my clock heart, but his reassurance convinces me that I can set them aside. The army's approach is nearing an end, the beat of their march strengthening as they come closer. "What do I do about the heartwood that Markham stole? Can I stop his army?"

"The heartwood is not invincible. Prince Killian must stay within sight of his troops and carry it on his person for the army to remain animated." Father Time waves his palm over the nearest tree trunk and the thorns transform to little flowers. He plucks a daisy and examines the ivory petals. "The blood sacrifice he made to tap into creation power is tied to his spirit alone. Taking the heartwood from his possession will disable the creation power; thus, the spell he cast on the wooden soldiers will be broken."

The burden laid upon my shoulders nearly sinks me down. Stealing the heartwood and taking back my sword are monumental tasks, but I have to accept responsibility for my role in this chaos and protect my friends.

"How do I kill Markham?" I ask.

His green eyes take on a hard gleam. "Time ends lives every day. Trust us, Everley. Prince Killian will know death."

The trees around us quiver in the gales. The squalls howl so loudly I can feel more than hear the marching army.

Father Time plucks another blossom. "Time is no respecter of persons. We are the same, yesterday, today, and forever. But we have our favorites." He hands me the daisy. "We must depart now."

"Will I see you again?"

"You have everything you need. A wise friend once taught us a lesson we shall never forget." Father Time leans in and his balminess drifts over me, starting as a warm drop that ripples out. "'Miracles are forged in the heart.'"

"Everley!" Jamison calls.

I turn toward him in camp. When I revolve back, Father Time has taken himself away. I tuck the blossom into my pocket and run out to meet Jamison.

Armed soldiers and convicts assemble at the north end of the settlement. Commander Flynn shouts instructions, while nearer to the surf, Vevina and Captain Dabney load the women into a dozen longboats. Three full boats are rowing for the *Lady Regina*. I spot Quinn holding her cat next to Dr. Huxley on the second. Thank creation, they are off to safety.

Several of the men carry torches and lanterns. The storm has darkened the sky so it feels as though nightfall is ahead of time. Fire may be a good defense against the wooden soldiers unless those heavy gray clouds unburden their rain.

Jamison loads a musket with powder, shielding it from the wind with his back. He sinks the ball and patch down the muzzle of the gun with the ramrod.

"Where did you find the firearms?" I ask.

"Claret and Laverick discovered three crates of them beneath the floorboards of the governor's cabin."

The Fox and the Cat pass out more muskets down the way. The rain starts, a downpour that immediately drenches my head and shoulders. The torches suffer, their fire dimming, but the lanterns burn strong. Jamison finishes loading his musket, and not a moment too soon.

The wooden soldiers march into view, their flawless formation a dreadful sight. They don't walk like men. Their lumbering, mechanical movements are slow yet powerful. Only their joints move: knees, ankles, wrists, elbows, hip, and head. They look like gigantic, strapping marionettes, my alias given grotesque shape. In place of smiles, they wear grimaces. In place of clothes, armor. In place of stage props, battle-axes and spears. With our evacuation of the women and the ill, we are closely matched in number, yet we have not determined how our ammunition and blades will stand against their attack.

The army marches in formation toward us, about two hundred yards off. Markham and Harlow are nowhere in sight. Our troop of settlers mutter, aghast about our enemies. Proclamations of *What are they? Where did they come from? What do they want?* swell down the line. The commander loses his chain of thought, momentarily suspended in disbelief.

"Commander Flynn," says Jamison, "they're coming."

The commander retakes control. "Prime and load!"

The infantry finish arming their muskets. Every single gunman holds the line in the rain and wind. Claret and Laverick squeeze in near us with their firearms.

"Can you shoot those?" Jamison asks them. "Without experience, you could harm yourself or others."

"My brothers taught me to shoot," says Laverick.

Claret shrugs. "I can hit a tree."

Unlike them, I have no experience with muskets or pistols. Jamison quiets for further orders from the commander. I step back from the line and hold up a lantern.

"Make ready!" Commander Flynn yells, sword above his head.

The settlers bring their muskets straight up, perpendicular to the ground, with the left hand on the swell of the stock, the lock turned toward their faces, then with the right hand, they pull the lock to full cock and grasp the wrist of the gun. Laverick and Claret follow their movements a half second later.

The wooden soldiers are not deterred.

"Present!" calls the commander.

The infantry bring the butt of the musket to their right shoulder while lowering the muzzle to firing position and sighting along the barrel at their enemy. I set down the lantern and lift my sword at ready.

Seventy-five yards off, the wooden army reaches the stream and starts across, raindrops splattering the waterway.

Commander Flynn lowers his sword. "Fire!"

Gunfire goes off, sparks flaring and smoke spiraling. A full second goes by and then the smoke clears. The front line of wooden soldiers does not slow. They progress to camp with dented limbs and cracked faces.

"Prime and reload!" the commander calls.

Jamison lowers his musket into loading position, butt against his hip. All their shots fired, but at this range, the guns are less accurate and their few shots that landed did little damage.

Our gunmen ready for another volley. A trained soldier can reload in under a minute. The pesky wind and rain add to their struggle. Jamison is the first to fire again, followed by several others. I cringe at the repetitive booms but do not release my sword to cover my ears.

Laverick's shot strikes a wooden soldier square in the chest. He recoils at the impact but continues on, his torso hardly scratched.

The scene is repeated across the battlefield. Wooden soldiers pock-marked with nicks and scores, weathering our fire without a sound. Their resilience sends my ticker pounding.

The army comes within fifty yards. At this range, the gunfire is more accurate. The settlers reload again and fire. Wooden soldiers recoil. Holes blow through their arms and legs, splinters flying in a spray of shards. A lead ball blasts apart one's knee. The wooden soldier hobbles on his good leg, still coming for our line.

The men reload and prepare for another round.

A gust blows rain in my face, my sword at the ready. More long-boats have left for the *Lady Regina*. Others return to shore for the next boatload of people. Vevina and Captain Dabney are still directing the evacuation. Unarmed men and women dare the choppy waves and swim out to the ship. A longboat has capsized in the cove and its passengers are trying to flip it upright, the winds hefting them about in the water.

Markham is not among his ranks, and the *Cadeyrn of the Seas* cannot be seen along the coastline. A mist settles upon the island, driven in by the storm, and obscures my far-off view. Father Time said Markham needed to be close to his army. Did I misunderstand? Has Markham taken the heartwood and the sword of Avelyn and sailed away?

The wooden army lumbers closer, just yards off now, their battle-axes and spears ready. Commander Flynn calls for the infantry to pull back. The men without swords turn their muskets over to bludgeon with and the others draw their rapiers.

A battle-ax whizzes past us and slams into Commander Flynn's chest. He falls over dead before I can gasp. The settlers rush the front line of wooden soldiers. They whack at them with the ends of their guns and hack with swords.

A wooden soldier sweeps his arm and throws a man. The man's yell ends when he slams into a tree. A second wooden giant wades through the men, cutting with his ax, trampling over our troops like weeds.

Someone's spear goes through the man to my right. Another wooden soldier comes directly for me, ax swinging. Claret shoulders her musket and shoots. The ball goes through the soldier's shoulder, blasting a hole. He sweeps his ax at us. We roll out of the way and Jamison fires at his knee. The joint explodes and the soldier drops.

As he tries to get back up, I grab the lit lantern and throw it at him. The glass shatters, covering the wooden soldier in oil. The flame ignites in a burning hot flash.

More men toss lanterns at our enemies' front line. Fires smolder all around. One wooden soldier steps over his burning comrade. Another walks onward, his arm aflame, and hits a settler. The man falls to the ground with his clothes ablaze.

Several wooden soldiers lumber for us, some of them still on fire in places, scorched but mobile.

"Fall back!" Jamison pushes at me. "Run, Everley. Take cover!"

Claret and Laverick grab up their firearms. We dash into the deserted camp, splashing through puddles. We keep going until we are far in the middle and hide between two tents.

The three of us huddle out of the downpour. I stand guard as they reload their muskets. Laverick spills her powder horn and Claret jams down her ammunition ball with the rod. A man screams as he's thrown into the tents.

The wooden soldier who tossed him stomps closer. He swings his battle-ax and knocks down a tent, deflating it into a heap. We go still, the Fox's and the Cat's firearms halfway loaded. He turns the other way, his back to us. No one moves as the wooden soldier stalks closer. At less than two yards, he spots us.

Claret and Laverick rush to reload. I step out, maneuvering his attention away from them. The soldier lunges at me. I sink low and hit his shin with my sword. The metal carves a shallow mark in his leg. He swipes diagonally, and I roll to evade.

"Hurry!" I shout.

Laverick pulls back on the hammer and raises her musket. The soldier hits the end as she fires and the shot goes wide. She turns the weapon around and cracks him with the stock. It does not slow him. Claret presents her musket and shoots through his knee. He tilts to the side and crashes into a tent.

"Everley!" Jamison runs through the tents.

Thunderheads fill the sky, and the rain becomes a weapon for the wind to slash at us. I blink away raindrops, my head soaked.

"We're here!" I cry.

"We're retreating. Get to the boats!"

Claret and Laverick sprint for the shoreline.

I clamber up out of the mud. The soldier with the blown-out knee is trying to rise on his good leg. The wooden army is unbeatable.

I have to find Markham.

Blue peers out from the pocket of Jamison's pack. Seeing the wooden soldiers not far behind us, the pixie ducks down again. I am reluctant to leave. Where is Markham or Harlow?

"Everley, we have to go!" Jamison cries.

The prince is here somewhere—he must be close to his army—but us staying would be madness. Jamison and I run for the boats, lightning flashing overhead. The dead or dying litter the rainy beach, too many casualties to count. Fires still burn, shrinking in the downpour, as our enemy cuts apart the camp. What they leave untouched, the wind flattens or carries away.

Claret and Laverick have gone ahead, rowing to the ship in a longboat with Vevina. Captain Dabney has held the final boat for us. We splash into the sea, waves slapping and pulling at my ankles.

An ax whizzes over our heads. I heave myself out of the water and fall forward into the boat. Jamison and the captain wrestle stormy waves and push the longboat against the current.

Spears dart past us, impaling the sandy shallows. The soldiers have redirected for pursuit. At chest-deep water, Jamison pulls himself into the boat. Meanwhile, Captain Dabney loses his grip and falls prey to a large swell that tows him back toward shore. The soldiers are up to their knees in the water, casting spears. One of them grazes the boat. Another pierces the captain and he keels over.

Jamison watches as the captain is plucked up and pushed around by waves. The tide is pushing our boat back to the beach. I pick up the oars and row rapidly for the ship. Jamison takes up another set of oars and together we combat the wind and current.

The wooden soldiers try to hold their pursuit by entering the sea, but their hollow forms bob to the surface. They are too heavyset and ungainly to swim, so they float back to shore like driftwood.

Jamison rows harder, his face beading sweat. Outside the cove, through the misty rain, the back of a sea creature rises and submerges. The memory of the Terrible Dorcha's attack sets me on edge. I watch for the creature to resurface, but it doesn't reappear again in or past the cove. Dorcha would make his presence known, so the creature I saw must be something else.

A ladder and line dangle outside the hull. The other longboats have been lifted to the main deck. Jamison secures the boat to the line and then we catch the rope ladder. I leave my head down to keep raindrops from my eyes and climb out of the saltwater spray. Lightning crackles and thunder booms over us. I jump over the rail onto the deck, which is slick from the rain, and Jamison and I both come to a full halt.

At middeck, our crew, including Dr. Huxley, has been disarmed and cornered by a dozen of Markham's men from the *Cadeyrn of the Sea*. Harlow aims an armed musket at the surgeon, a rapier sheathed at her hip. Another half dozen of Markham's men stand guard over the locked hold. The other evacuated settlers must be imprisoned belowdecks.

Between us, Prince Killian holds a pistol to Quinn's head.

Chapter Twenty-Seven

My ticker stops, then restarts with a clunk. I cannot look away from Quinn's terror-filled face. I'm seven years old again, in the drawing room of our manor, standing over Mother's body. Father shouts for Markham to let me go. My heart, whole and unbroken, pummels my ribs. Every part of me knows I must break loose or I will never be free.

"Here we are again, Everley," Markham says.

The scars of the memory burn. I steel myself, funneling my concentration into my clock heart. *Be indifferent. Be a machine.*

"How did you find a portal out of my world?" he asks.

"We had help," I reply.

Lightning crisscrosses the sky. Markham's hair and clothes are drenched, the sword of Avelyn sheathed at his side. Harlow and the sailors guard the hatch to belowdecks. The crew members of the *Lady Regina* are silent. Jamison and I stand close, equal in our distance to Markham and Quinn. I draw my blade and step forward.

"Stay back." Markham digs the pistol barrel into Quinn's temple, creating a crater of flesh. The heartwood is not visible on his person, but it must be with him or his wooden army could not be swarming the settlement, demolishing it section by section.

"You have what you want," I say, calling over the wind. "Take your treasure and leave."

He scoffs at the absurdity of the suggestion. "I cannot have you pursuing me or sailing back to Wyeth. With the settlement destroyed and everyone dead, it will be months before the queen discovers my departure."

Jamison draws his sword. "Time won't prevent the inevitable. Queen Aislinn will send forces. She has probably foreseen your treasonous act. A fleet from Wyeth will already be underway."

"Her Omnipotence is a fraud," Markham says, sneering. "She hired her father's assassin and feigned the vision of his death. The king was lazy and content with his riches and lands. To colonize and explore the isle, I needed a leader ambitious about expansion. Aislinn took little persuasion. She was anxious to set herself as an idol before her people and prove her greatness to the world."

My mind reels to make sense of his claims. "But the queen made other predictions besides the king's murder, like the flood."

"Her council was losing faith in her, so she staged another prophecy. Her men dammed the river downstream, and the waters rose and flooded the city." Quinn squirms against Markham. He wrenches her head up at a painful angle and she stops. "It's finished, Everley. I'll start with the girl, then move on to your husband and crew. Once they're lying in their own blood, I'll open the hatch and execute the women one by one. You'll witness every death, and then—"

"You'll kill me too," I say, sickened by his brutality.

Markham tips his head in consideration. "You've evaded death this long, why change your luck? No, you must live, Everley Donovan. I'll abandon you here and leave you stranded on this cursed isle to ponder the deaths of your friends and loved ones."

Horror binds me, shortening my airway. His punishment is too close to how I felt all these years agonizing over the loss of my family, stranded, alone.

"Let the girl go, Killian," says Jamison.

"Lieutenant Callahan, I will miss you most. You would have remained in my ranks had Everley not corrupted your loyalty." Markham levels the pistol at Quinn's head again. "Shall we begin?"

He tightens the trigger—and an explosion rocks the ship.

Splinters fly, filling the sky. Jamison and I drop and cover our heads. The blast catches Harlow and Dr. Huxley, pitching them to the side. Markham turns away with Quinn, shielding his face.

In the clearing smoke, Laverick steps out of the hold. She takes the sword of a dead sailor killed by the blast. Vevina and Claret also climb out from belowdecks and arm themselves with more weapons from fallen crewmen. They used powder from the ammunition battery to blow the hatch.

Quinn twists from the pistol barrel against her head and bites Markham's gun hand. He shoves at her to let go, and I scramble to my feet.

Harlow sits up and aims her musket at me. Vevina kicks the firearm from Harlow's grip, snatches it up, and then knocks her in the skull with the stock. Harlow goes down near Dr. Huxley, clutching her head. The surgeon has not yet moved or gotten up.

The crews of the two ships clash, Markham's men with swords and firearms, ours with fists and any makeshift weapon they can grab.

Markham throws Quinn to the deck and takes aim at her. I rush him and push his pistol arm up. The shot travels up the mast and into the storm. He tosses the unloaded firearm aside and draws the sword of Avelyn.

I maneuver in front of Quinn. Markham taps his blade against mine to antagonize me. He has genuine training—over three centuries' worth of experience in swordplay—and wields a superior weapon. He reels back, recovering his starting position, and lunges. I parry as he advances, the rainy gusts belting me like another foe. Our blades striking, he pushes me to retreat widthwise across the deck. My back reaches the hammock netting on the portside and I go left. Markham anticipates my maneuver and feigns another lunge. I flinch and he grins.

Bloody bones, I hate him.

Panting hard, I ignore my exhaustion and keep up with him. He's not the least bit short of breath. Trying to outmatch him is folly, but my clock heart impels me on, reminding me of Father Time's charge for me to win back my sword.

Across the way, Jamison and Harlow slash at each other. She has rallied from Vevina's hit to her head. The fray spreads around us as more settlers climb out of the hold to engage in battle. Markham's men are outnumbered but better armed.

I reattack their leader in vigor. Markham blocks my onslaught of blows, his movements strictly offensive. I lunge and my blade sinks through his shoulder. He gives a pained hiss and yanks free. His next swipe is retaliatory—his blade grazes my chin.

Pain explodes there and keeps on burning as warmth spills down my jaw. Unlike his wound, my cut bleeds.

"You should join me, Everley. With time on our side, we would be unstoppable. Your shrewdness and my eloquence. All the worlds would bow to us."

I clutch my blazing chin, my blood soaking into my glove. "Your flattery may have worked on Tavis, but ingratiation holds no allure for me."

Feeling the cold of his steel under my skin has reawakened the hunger that brought me to this isle. I stab his other shoulder and wrench the blade out. As he is bent over, grimacing, I see a string necklace with a wooden heart come loose from his undershirt. He straightens, his clothes ripped from my sword, and notices the subject of my stare.

"Clever lass."

He swipes at me in earnest. I retreat and trip over a dead body. Markham drives down his sword, barely missing my side. I roll over and get up.

A few men fighting around us have halted to stare off into nowhere. If not for the raging storm, I might think someone had torn time and frozen them.

I follow their stares to the *Cadeyrn of the Seas* sailing into the cove. The massive ship speeds closer, its broadside turned toward us, gunports open and cannons presented. Markham shuffles toward the upper deck.

Across the way, Jamison disarms Harlow and holds her at sword point. They pause as the taller, wider, and longer first-rate ship flies up to our smaller vessel. Their own crewmen are aboard our ship, including the governor. They wouldn't attack their men. But as the ship comes so close that I can count each cannon on the three gun decks, it's apparent that that is precisely what they intend to do.

Jamison shouts over the din. "Prepare to receive fire!"

Men on both sides of the battle duck for cover. I run after Markham and brace against the gunwale. The cannons fire.

I count eight—no, nine—blasts in quick succession.

Gunfire pelts the deck and starboard side of the *Lady Regina*. A cannonball severs the foremast, and the top third of the mast falls toward the middle deck, where I last saw Jamison.

I cover my ears and shield my head. Markham watches calmly, unflinching as the blasts boom. His ship is firing on their own crewmen and commander. Since he cannot perish, he must have given the order at the sacrifice of his men.

Our swordplay was a game. He was toying with me, delaying for this slaughter.

A cannonball strikes the stairs to the upper deck. I shield myself from showering debris, the concussion ricocheting through the ship.

Markham's men ready the longboats for departure. He steps out into the open and tips his chin in farewell.

"Until next time, Everley."

He strides off, exposing his back to me. Arrogant blaggard.

I slice the back of his belt. He stops and clutches at his drooping trousers. I cut higher, cleaving the string around his neck. As the heartwood falls between us, blasts sound. Seconds later, the cannon fire bashes several longboats apart and the middle deck buckles under the siege.

Markham lunges for the heartwood. I drive my blade through his chest, where his heart would beat if he had one, and spear the blade into the gunwale.

He moans, his fist tight on my sword. While he's pinned, I scoop up the heartwood and fling it overboard. I look to land and see the wooden soldiers freeze. All their movements cease at once, and a few fall over, toppling like cut-down trees. Smoke plumes stream from the settlement, the camp decimated.

His wooden army has fallen.

I return for the sword of Avelyn, but Markham has pulled the blade that trapped him from his chest and tossed it out of my reach.

His wolfish eyes glow murderous, my sword in his hand. "You're a briar in my heel."

"Everley!" Quinn cries from middeck. "Help me! He's stuck!"

Without a weapon of my own, I have no hope of winning the sword of Avelyn from him. "I'll be coming for my sword," I say.

"Why wait?" Markham waves me forward, blade ready.

I back out of his range and run into the wind.

He shouts after me. "You'll never find me, Everley! You'll never see the sword again!"

I jump over the cracked and smashed deck. The dead are strewn among the fragments of planks, more casualties from gun and sword wounds than cannon fire. Everyone is wet, drenched by the unyielding storm. While the cannon fire has ceased, Laverick, Claret, and Vevina are directing survivors into the few longboats still intact.

Quinn yells for me again. I hurry around my friends and head in the direction of her calls.

Having endured the worst of the damage, the middeck is deserted. Dr. Huxley has not moved from when he was flung during the hatch explosion. I start for him, then spot Quinn. She kneels beside Jamison, who is trapped under the fallen foremast. His hair is uncovered, his hat lost to the wind. My clock heart swings wildly.

"I tried to wake Dr. Huxley, but neither of them is responding," says Quinn.

She pats Jamison's cheek and tries to shake him awake. Nearby, also pinned by the mast, Harlow fights to wriggle free.

"Everley, your chin," gasps Quinn.

I dare not ask how my face looks. Markham has probably marred me for life, this time where everyone can see.

Another volley of cannon fire sounds.

I protect Quinn's head from raining pieces. "Get to Vevina," I say.

"What about Prince? I cannot find him!"

"He'll be all right. Now *go*."

Quinn stumbles over rubble.

"My ankle," Harlow says tightly.

The mast landed on her at an angle, restraining her lower leg. She wriggles and pulls without progress. I grab the mast and lift. Harlow works her ankle free and gets up, her hair flinging around her face. She hefts her rapier and starts to limp up the deck to Markham. He's climbing into a longboat with his surviving crewmen.

"Wait," I say. "Aren't you going to help me free Jamison?"

"Everley," she says, panting, "be grateful I haven't the time to slit your throats."

Harlow limps off, her departure punctuated by a clap of thunder. I wish to the stars that she will trip and fall overboard, and then I funnel my anger into lifting the mast off Jamison. It scarcely moves, still pinning his upper half.

The ship tilts as it takes on water. I will myself not to panic, and lift harder. A section of line snaps from a sail and strikes me in the back. I fall forward against the mast in a fresh wave of pain. Across the way, Harlow reunites with Markham. He lifts her into the longboat and they lower below the rail.

"Everley?" Dr. Huxley sits up and rubs his forehead.

I totter over to him. "Are you all right? Can you stand?"

"I'm presentable," he says loudly. He must be addled from the explosion. I haul him to his feet and help him over to Jamison. The surgeon examines his condition and practically yells, "He's breathing and his pulse is strong. Help me lift this off him."

Both of us hug the mast and push so it will roll down Jamison's legs. The wooden beam hardly budges. We need more hands, but everyone else has fled to the longboats, except for . . .

"Blue!" I call. "Blue, where are you?"

Her azure light weaves through the windy downpour and she lands on Jamison's chest.

Dr. Huxley holds his head again. "I must be concussed and imagining things."

"She's real," I say. "Blue, can you free Jamison?"

She nods adamantly and then hovers above the mast and flutters her wings. Pixie dust sprinkles off her wings and lands on the mast. Almost immediately, the wooden section where the dust landed vanishes. Without the restraining weight, Jamison rouses.

I bend over him and stroke his hair. "Do you hurt?"

"I can get up."

"We'll help you," Dr. Huxley says, still talking too loudly. The explosion damaged his hearing, hopefully temporarily. "Your head is bruised, and probably your ribs. Move slowly."

Blue dives into Jamison's shirt pocket. We help him up and hobble all together to the portside. Vevina has waited there for us with a longboat.

"Where's Quinn?" I ask her.

"She's gone ahead with Laverick and Claret."

Rainy gusts wail as we climb in one at a time and start our descent toward the waves. Jamison slumps against me, clutching his sore side, and Dr. Huxley rubs his sore ears. Vevina is covered in soot from the hatch explosion, her dress torn and her curly hair fuller than ever.

The other longboats ahead of us row to shore, out of the line of fire of the ship. Markham and his men row their boat toward the *Cadeyrn of the Seas*. Someone in one of the boats below shouts above the din.

"Whale!"

A great curved back appears in the open water. The whale goes up and under repeatedly, swimming fast for the parallel ships. The harpoon scars of the Terrible Dorcha are undeniable.

"Great Creator," Vevina breathes.

Markham's men row faster across the tempest-tossed sea for their ship. The giant whale swims up to them and dives. The men pause their rowing and peer over the side as the monster passes beneath them. When it seems Dorcha has gone, he surfaces next to the watercraft and smashes it with his fluke.

The men cry out as they are thrown into the water. Dorcha wallops the boat with his tail again, destroying the chance for salvageable remains. Harlow grabs on to a floating board from the wreckage and treads water. Markham swims for his ship, slowed down by the sword of Avelyn in his fist.

Jamison and I brace against each other and watch in incredulity as Dorcha turns wide and pursues Markham at the surface. The whale shows no interest in any other swimmer. He stalks Markham, who flails for speed he does not have. Dorcha closes in and opens his mouth.

The whale overtakes Markham, swallowing him straight down his gullet, both man and sword.

I gawk as the Terrible Dorcha, having caught his prey, plunges below and out of sight.

Chapter Twenty-Eight

Three hundred and seventy dead—sailors, soldiers, and convicts—and another thirty-eight missing. We salvaged what we could off the *Lady Regina*. The trusty vessel won't set sail again. After a fortnight of preparing for departure, the enormous first-rate flagship of the queen's navy, the *Cadeyrn of the Seas*, has become our salvation for voyaging home. Despite the battle, the two crews set aside their grievances and united under the common objective of leaving the isle.

Graves litter the entirety of the settlement, the sea of headstones a warning to the next curious explorer or greedy ruler who tries to tame Dagger Island. This cursed place will only bring misery and death.

On this early morning, fourteen days after the battle, we finish the final burial. The weather has been sublime since the storm, all tempered breezes and sunshine. The island is either giving us a blessed send-off or trying to beguile us into staying.

Jamison marks the grave with a circle of stones, and Blue chews on a gnat she caught. My attention drifts to the thorny trees. We returned to the battle site to find piles of timber. Without creation magic animating the wooden soldiers, they were reduced to kindling.

And burn them we did. We lit pyres up and down the beach and their remains burned for days. Yesterday, we doused the embers and ashes with sand and buckets of seawater. My hair still smells of smoke.

Jamison lifts the headstone into position. "TAVIS DONOVAN." Though his remains weren't recovered, we honored Tavis's life and laid him to rest between Captain Dabney and Commander Flynn. May Madrona watch over all of their spirits.

Markham was given no formal resting place. Confusion still surrounds his disappearance. Most believe he's dead, while superstitious sailors and convicts think the Terrible Dorcha captured him and took him away. I have no doubt he is alive. The attack of the whale was sudden and unexpected, but if I cannot kill Markham, neither can Dorcha.

Harlow was found clinging to driftwood and was pulled from the sea. She struck a soldier for implying that Markham had become whale food. Jamison, now the highest-ranking officer and our temporary captain, ordered her chained in the hold. She will remain there our entire passage home. We embark for Wyeth as soon as Jamison and I return to the ship. I will be grateful to never again see the skyline of Dagger Island.

Jamison steps to my side by my brother's grave, his hat concealing most of the bandage around his head. Additional bandages wrap his bruised rib cage. His black-and-tan captain's uniform suits him.

"You can come back to visit him," he says.

"We both know I won't return."

"Time cannot change what's been done, but you did it, Everley. You confronted Markham and maintained your integrity."

I hear Jamison's praise, yet when I give ear to my ticking heart, I still think of my family. I don't know how I'll let them go.

Jamison slides his hand along my jawline and kisses my cheek. Dr. Huxley said the cut across my chin will heal but likely scar. Before he examined me, I had already accepted the mark won't fade. Markham leaves scars, that's what monsters do.

Jamison walks down to prep the longboat. On the way, he stops at Rafferty's grave and adjusts a stone that has slid out of place. We didn't have his remains, so Jamison buried Rafferty's snuffbox. Jamison took good care of arranging his resting place, directing his headstone toward the water in view of the sea.

Blue flies one turn about the top of Jamison's head, her radiance a cobalt halo, and then darts off into the Thornwoods. She goes there often to hunt for insects. I have stared into the woodland's shadows until my eyes crossed, yet I have not seen anything else fantastical. Not Father Time, or portals to the Otherworlds, or even a single daisy.

I shut my eyes to my brother's grave. This is farewell to him, to this isle, to the younger, naive me. The memories I make henceforth belong to the new cogs and gears of my heart. The days, hours, minutes, and seconds are mine. I will not be giving them away to liars and cads. I will not let them be corrupted, no matter where luck and time lead me.

The daisy Father Time gave me has turned brittle. I lay it in front of the headstone and cover the stem with dirt so it doesn't blow away. Beside the flower I line up the wooden figurines I made of our family. Father and Mother would be proud of the man Tavis had become. I will be forever grateful for the memories we made and the extra time we spent together.

After kissing each of my family's wooden heads, I place Tavis's figurine between our parents. "Be at peace," I say.

I tug on my mother's red gloves and tread down to the boat.

Jamison watches the tree line. "Have you seen Blue?" he asks.

"She flew into the Thornwoods. Perhaps she went home."

He frowns at the foliage. Blue spends the majority of her time in his company, hiding in his pocket and sleeping on the floor beside him at night. We have kept her companionship a secret from everyone except Dr. Huxley and Quinn. I don't imagine Blue would leave without bidding farewell to Jamison.

However, she could still be mad at us for introducing her to Prince. The cat survived the battle, albeit scragglier from his swim to shore. During his first night aboard the ship, he hunted Blue into a corner. We had to beg the pixie not to disappear him with her magical dust.

"Blue will come when she's ready," I say.

Before we get into the boat, Jamison arranges the oars for departure and I slip my regulator bell into his back pocket. Our game has become a challenge of stealth and sneakiness. I intend to outdo him.

We push the longboat into the quiet surf, get in, and row to the ship in silence. I fix my gaze on the watery horizon. I have seen enough of Dagger Island to last my lifetime. Every so often Jamison checks for Blue, but the pixie does not show.

After we are hoisted from the water to the gunwale, Jamison ties off the line and I hop over the rail onto the planking. The main deck is strangely quiet.

Vevina strides out from behind the center mast, holding her dagger and wearing a men's tricorn hat. Her cagey smile alerts me as to what is happening. Jamison deciphers her welcome differently.

"Are we under attack?" he asks. "Has Killian returned?"

Jamison has yet to state his opinion about Markham's disappearance. He must be of the same mind-set as the superstitious sailors and me, believing that Prince Killian has survived, imprisoned in the belly of the whale.

A single curl of Vevina's hair flitters in the breeze. "This, Captain Callahan, is a mutiny."

Claret and Laverick step out from behind her. They, along with a dozen or so more women and men, an even mixture of convicts and sailors, are armed with cutlasses and pistols. Quinn holds her cat and pets him, her gaze solemn.

"I have taken control of the ship," Vevina says.

"And you will captain with what experience?" Jamison counters.

"Captain Dabney, bless his soul, trained me to man the helm. The lasses have been working on their knots and riggings, and the sailors who agreed to serve under my command will be justly compensated. We are in agreeance that this ship and crew need not go to waste serving a senile queen who sent us to expire under the rule of a deceptive governor. To her, we are chattel, expendable slaves. But not anymore." The crew stamp their feet in accord. "Those who were disinclined to share our vision are locked in the hold."

Jamison glowers, visibly affronted by their knavery. This is not a matter of the women's adequate sailing proficiency but their replacing the highest-ranking officer with a con artist.

"What better use do you have for the ship?" I ask.

Vevina's smile stretches. "I've listened on the docks. Bootlegging is a rewarding trade. I suspect I'll have a flair for it."

I've no doubt she will be an effective pirate, which is not at all heartening.

"Commandeering the queen's ship is treason," Jamison says. He grips his pistol but does not draw. "Should you be caught, your crew will be sentenced to the gallows."

"We will take that risk," replies Vevina.

The crew hurrahs, including Quinn. She is too young to appreciate the ramifications of this decision, but her courage is commendable. She is not the scared little mouse I first met. I don't want her or any of us women shackled in prison, for once we return home, we will no longer be settlers. We will be convicts.

"Might you join our crusade, Captain?" Vevina inquires.

Jamison's gaze pans the masts and sails. "The sea is my home," he replies softly, "but Wyeth is my realm. I will not commit treason."

She nods sagely, as though she anticipated his answer. "What of you, Everley? Care to take back your freedom? I've a fine spot for you in the crew. Of course, I won't be sore with you for aligning with your husband."

Contrary to her light tone, she sounds nettled. She must think I will agree with Jamison only because we're married, but I have my own reasons for not rebelling. Once Vevina and her crew run from their prison sentences, they cannot return home. I want to see Uncle Holden again. As his only living relative, I cannot forsake him.

I lay down my sword. In any case, the weapon felt wrong in my grasp, the weight too heavy and the hilt too plain. All rapiers fail to compare to the sword of Avelyn.

Jamison also sets down his pistol and sword. Vevina sweeps up our weapons, and Claret and Laverick pat us down at gunpoint, the Fox more roughly than necessary.

"Where's your pixie?" Claret asks. "You know, the tiny thing with the salty temperament?"

As if we could confuse Blue with another pixie.

"She's gone home," I say. "What will you do with us, Vevina?"

"I'll think of some use for you. Claret and Laverick, lock them below." She bats us away like hovering moths and calls to her crew, "Weigh anchor!"

The sailors heed her orders, hurrying to make way, and the Fox and the Cat lead us by gunpoint down the ladder to belowdecks. A pack of fuses hangs from the waist of Laverick's skirt, and Claret's pockets are bulging with her latest pickpocketed trophies.

Down in the innards of the ship, the Fox and the Cat parade us through the cargo area, past manacled prisoners. Less than ten people have declined Vevina's offer to join her crew. Harlow is mixed in with the lot of them, the only inmate stretched out in a hammock. She stares at the ceiling, ankles crossed and mind elsewhere. Her relaxed stance drags me back to the long, cold night we spent locked in the cramped cell of Dorestand Prison. Harlow hadn't a care for what became of herself then either. She had faith in Markham's plan. Her confidence in him even now is worrisome.

We are led to an empty cabin toward the bow of the ship. Two hammocks hang opposite each other and fresh straw has been laid across the floor.

"We prepared bunks for you," says Laverick. She picks up the manacles and chains. "Bindings are better than keelhauling. Fortunately for you, Dr. Huxley opposed the ritual."

"Alick joined your crew?" I ask. Besides Jamison and me, he is the most sensible person aboard. Does he know something about Vevina's intentions that I do not?

"*He* understands our vision," Laverick replies.

"Did you know Dr. Huxley was engaged?" Claret asks. "His betrothed left him for a postman. Last night, after he'd been drinking, he told me all about it. He said the same postman his betrothed left him for still delivers his mail! Dr. Huxley would rather be lost at sea than have that man come to his door again." The Cat sighs and combs her fingers through her hair. "I suppose we all have reasons not to go back."

Laverick lifts the manacles. "Who's first?"

"May Jamison and I have a moment alone?" I ask.

The Fox side-eyes me. "I owe Vevina ten silver pieces because of you. I bet her you wouldn't choose a man over your friends."

I wince at her scorn, but more so her disappointment. Laverick and Claret *are* my friends. So are Alick, Vevina, and Quinn. I'm not trying to pick a side. I'm choosing to see my uncle again.

"Let's give the husband and wife time alone," says Claret.

Laverick stares fiercely at us. "Don't try anything clever. We'll be right outside."

Once they go, Jamison leans against the closed door, his expression dreary. The anchor chain tings stridently outside the hull as it's raised. We will soon be underway, locked in this cabin until Vevina tires of us, and then who knows what she will do.

"It'll be all right." Jamison strides to me and strokes my arms. "I saved a small amount of my inheritance. I can bribe Vevina into dropping us at the closest port. She isn't entirely unpredictable. Her favor can be bought with coin."

I pull away, stepping over the manacles. "Then what? You deliver your convict wife to jail to serve her sentence for something she didn't do?"

He balks, flabbergasted. "I would never do that. I hope to win your freedom."

"You've been through this with Rafferty. The magistrates don't issue pardons."

Jamison takes my hands in his. "Rafferty isn't my wife. We have a better chance at a life, at a future, if we go home."

What future does he expect we'll have? Besides the benefit of seeing my uncle again, I don't envision a life for me or Jamison in Dorestand. Even if he can use his nobility to ensure I am pardoned, I will always be a convict and he a disgraced earl. I will have no peace so long as Markham is out there.

Jamison may never forgive me for what I'm about to do, and I may not have another chance to do this, so I slide my arms around his waist and graze my lips across his. I finish and stare up at him, my clock heart ticking against his chest.

He stays absolutely still—and then his mouth dips closer and crushes down on mine.

His touch explores everywhere. My hair, my cheeks, my jaw, my lower back. The sensations are so overwhelming, I push him off me. We both stare at each other, winded. Unable to stand the distance between us, I leap at him and kiss him harder and longer. His nearness fills me with such happiness, I almost don't want to let him go.

While our bodies are close, I press him against the wall by a set of manacles. His palms go to my hips and my fingers to the nape of his neck. Reaching around him, I clamp the manacles on his wrist and step back.

My mouth is puffy, his own mouth red. I back up for the door.

"I'm sorry."

He wrenches at the bindings. They will not open without an anvil to bang out the peg. "You don't mean this."

"I didn't plan it. This is who I am, Jamison."

"You think I don't understand you by now? You think you can hunt Markham on your own. You need help to defeat him, Everley. The queen's navy, the army—"

"Are far away."

"He's a traitor. I didn't want to raise your hopes, so I didn't say anything, but I never planned to deliver you to prison." Jamison's sudden directness stuns me. "I intended to go directly to the queen and convince her to renounce your sentence in exchange for time served pursuing Markham with me."

"What will the queen say when you tell her we saw Markham cut his princess out of an elderwood tree and use her heartwood to animate an army of wooden soldiers? Everything we saw proves the old ways are true. She'll brand us heretics and sentence us to the pyre. Even supposing she could set aside her ideals, we don't have time to waste." I tap my clock heart to reaffirm that I am the master on this subject. "Markham could have a head start to whatever calamity he seeks to inflict next. Sailing back to Wyeth, persuading the queen, gathering a fleet—by the time we're done, he could have destroyed another world. The next one could be ours."

Jamison raises his chained arm. "You didn't need to lock me up. You could have talked to me."

"You already know what I want. So long as Markham lives, he will corrupt and destroy. We will never be safe."

Jamison crosses the cabin, stretching the chain to its end, two strides from me. "No one said you have to go after him alone."

"I wouldn't ask that of you."

"You didn't have to ask. I would have gone with you and fought by your side." Jamison turns away and plods back to where I chained him. Arms wide, he braces against the wall and his head falls forward between them.

My ticker races, pushing me to finalizing my decision. When I leave this cabin, the time that has bonded us together will end.

A hot ball flares in my throat. It takes me a moment to recover my voice. "You said our marriage would protect us from growing close. You said you didn't want to give someone else power over you, over your heart."

He scoffs bleakly. "If only I were as good as you at heeding my rules."

Tears smear my gaze. So much has changed in a short time, yet I am still the girl with the clock heart. I am still dependent on time for each breath, each day.

I flee the cabin before tears spill over my lashes. My clock heart is incapable of falling in love, but if it could, I would find no finer man in all the worlds than the one I just left behind.

✿

The officer's cabin is large and quiet. I lie on the bed and wait for the sway of the ship to ease me to sleep. We have been at sea just a few hours, yet with Jamison chained belowdecks, time feels eternal.

Claret and Laverick welcomed me to the crew and teased me about my disheveled hair and clothes. The signs of Jamison's kisses were easily readjusted and smoothed away. I did not anticipate the invisible marks he would leave, the ones no one else can see that don't appear to fade.

Before I put Quinn to bed in her cabin, she and I visited Dr. Huxley. His quarters have a window overlooking the stern. Quinn's cat sat in the windowsill and watched the wakes drift farther and farther apart until they melted into the horizon. The resilient feline is unafraid of sailing, or perhaps the cat has resigned himself to a life at sea like Alick has. When I inquired about his reasons for joining Captain Vevina's crew, Dr. Huxley's response was curt.

"Pirates need a medic too," he said.

One can hardly disagree.

I stand and pace the cabin. It is bigger than ours was on the *Lady Regina*. Jamison moved Cleon here, but most of his belongings were damaged by water and left behind. His violin rests in the corner, locked in its case, and his mother's storybook is drying on the desk. I turn my back to them and slip my hand into my pocket. Something jingles at the bottom. I pull out my regulator bell. Jamison must have snuck it onto my person at some point after we rowed from shore.

It is no use. He cannot stay locked belowdecks or guilt will devour me.

I swing open the door to look for Vevina, and Blue darts in. She dips and rises as she flies, hoisting a small scroll and velvet pouch. She drops both on my bed and lands next to them.

"Blue, you found us! Where have you been? Did anyone see you?"

The pixie shakes her head and flops back onto her wings, her little chest pumping. I open the pouch. Inside is a cache of pixie dust, about a handful's worth.

"What's this for?"

Blue makes a reading motion with her hands, flipping the pages of an imaginary book, and then she points at the scroll. I slide the ribbon off and roll it open.

The letter, written in precise, elegant handwriting, is addressed to me.

Dearest Everley,

Our fondest wishes and most heartfelt apologies for the late delivery of this letter. We would have come ourselves, but we have been summoned by the elven council. Their queens wish to discuss Prince Killian's unforgiveable destruction of the Land of Youth. We are mightily disturbed that he has been captured by the Terrible Dorcha. The monstrous whale travels freely between your world and the Land Under the Wave. Have you been there? The Land Under the Wave is a haven for outlaws. It is vast in seas and provides some of the richest resources and secrets of the natural worlds. We highly recommend you never visit, especially not anytime soon.

One minor point of business. Radella will serve as your ambassador for the Everwoods. She rather dislikes being called Blue. Radella is an apprentice, so be mindful of her dust. She has a tiresome habit of disappearing things. Please remind her we are still missing our left sock.

Your forever friend,

Father Time

I refold the letter, perplexed by the content. Father Time couldn't be accused of lightheartedness, yet this letter is practically jolly considering all that has transpired. It also explains why I did not see him again on the isle. Why did he tell me about the Land Under the Wave if he doesn't want me to go there? I would have deduced that it was dangerous based on his description.

"But of course!" I say, an idea dawning. "Radella, has Prince Killian been taken to the Land Under the Wave?"

She nods emphatically.

"Does Father Time wish for me to follow him?"

Her next nod is less enthusiastic.

I was right not to listen to Jamison. We don't need to return to the queen. We can find Markham and I can get the sword on my own.

In my excitement to exit the cabin, I drop the letter on Radella. She climbs out from under the parchment and trills a furious song at me. I apologize and hurry out.

Vevina mans the helm on the upper deck. I dash up the steps to her, arriving breathless. She takes in my flushed complexion and nightgown.

"You all right, darling?"

"Just grand. You're hunting for treasure, aren't you?"

"Always."

"What if I could promise you endless riches?"

Vevina purses her mouth. "I'd be interested if it's true."

"Will pearls as big as your head and beaches of gold sand suffice?"

She throws up a hand in irritation. "Stop asking me redundant questions and be out with it, lass."

"I know where you can find such riches, but traveling there will be dangerous. It's in a land far away, and it won't be easy to find."

Her lips split in an uneven smile. "Do you have a heading?"

I face the headwind, staring into the starry horizon. "Set sail for the nearest storm. We need to track down the Terrible Dorcha. He will lead us to your treasure."

And me to mine.

ACKNOWLEDGMENTS

A new book and another fantastic group of peers and loved ones to applaud.

First and foremost, my family. John, Joseph, Julian, Danielle, and Ryan, thanks for letting me disappear into my "book world" every day. And my parents, in-laws, and siblings for your endless cheering. Family is forever . . . That's good, right?

The Dream Team: My agent, Marlene Stringer. This story goes way back to our first months together. Thank you for your constant belief in me. Jason Kirk, it has been my pleasure to get to know you as my brilliant editor. I'm also blessed to have you as a colleague, and I consider you a friend. Thank you for all you do. You're the best editor in all the worlds. Clarence Haynes, your emails always brighten my mood. You are endlessly optimistic, intuitive, and insightful. Thanks for shining up this story and playing devil's advocate. I relish the challenge and enjoy problem-solving with you. The team at Skyscape, namely Brittany Russell, Colleen Lindsay, and Kristin King. I can't forget Kyla Pigoni and Haley Kushman. You ladies are fierce.

A huge thanks to Jessie Farr for recommending a PBS documentary you thought I would like. My fictional ship may not be the *Lady Juliana*, and Everley may not be the convict Mary Wade, but the spirit of their memory is at the heart of this story.

Hugs to Taffy Lovell for the getaway to Midway that fateful spring. I wrote the first two chapters of this manuscript at your desk. Erin Summerill, Veeda Bybee, and Julie Donaldson—wasn't that a great retreat? Kate Coursey for reading a very early draft and not telling me it was garbage (it was). You're my ride or die. Let's plan another adventure, shall we? And Caitlyn McFarland for bringing out the best in Everley and her cohorts.

Lastly, I am honored to send an enormous amount of love and respect to Camille Junca. Often there isn't justice or fairness in our world. It makes one wonder what we can do to make a difference. I wrote this story to find purpose and meaning in the chaos. I believe in monsters, but I also believe in heroes who inspire us and challenge us to do better. Camille, you're my hero. The best revenge *is* living well.

ABOUT THE AUTHOR

Photo © 2015 Erin Summerill

Emily R. King is a writer of fantasy and the author of The Hundredth Queen Series. Born in Canada and raised in the United States, she is a shark advocate, a consumer of gummy bears, and an islander at heart, but her greatest interests are her four children. Emily lives in northern Utah with her family and their cantankerous cat. Visit her at www.emilyrking.com.